The Cross Maker's Guardian

The Cross Maker's Guardian

Jack A. Taylor

Wesbrook Bay Books
Vancouver

Copyright 2016 All Rights Reserved except where otherwise noted

ISBN: 978-1-928112-53-2   The Wesbrook Bay Books Group, 3338 Wesbrook Mall, Vancouver, BC, V6S 0A6

www.wesbrookbaybooks.com

Edited by Diane Tucker; Cover Design by deniel

Interior Design by BDG Fitzgerald

This is a work of fiction. The names, characters, places, and incidents portrayed in the story are the product of the author's imagination or have been used fictitiously. Any resemblance to actual persons, living or dead, businesses or companies, events, or locales, is entirely coincidental, except as noted at the end of the book.

Contents

1

Another Mediterranean gust of wind sliced through the Galilean hills like a legionnaire's dagger cutting through the fire-kissed ribs of a wild boar. The twisting funnel of salt-soaked air whipped apart the olive branches that concealed Titius Marcus Julianus. His vulnerability to exposure lasted only a moment but the three masked figures, twirling like dervishes in the clearing of wild flowers, stopped as one and turned to stare.

Titius's brown tunic, olive skin and short black hair easily blended into the shadows of the tree but the shiver down his back betrayed the fact that he had been discovered.

The voice of Cleopas, a deceased slave teacher from Titius' boyhood, arose like a phantom and goaded his mind. *"Tee-shuss, they've seen you."*

"Shhh! If you`re going to use my name, at least get it right."

A husky chuckle echoed inside. *"Titius, wishes, sleeping with the fishes. You should have listened to me. You're a boy playing man games."*

Titius waved at the phantom like he was swatting a fly. "You wouldn't know a game if you saw one." His stomach knotted and his neck and shoulder muscles tightened. Fear, the size of a mustard seed, planted itself into his soul.

Dark-bellied clouds tumbled away over ripening fields of barley toward distant hills. The suns rays groped for the earth, just like they did at the Roman estate Titius loved so well. A single abandoned rain drop clinging to the tip of a leaf caught the rays and sparkled like a diamond. The faintest scent of roses drifted by. He smiled as the particle of fear launched away on the breeze.

"I feel you smiling," Cleopas declared. *"Abee-gail's not here, you know."*

"Neither are you," Titius responded.

Images of his family villa crystallized in his mind. Cleopas rubbing down a sword and holding it up to sparkle in the light; the raven-haired servant girls, Lydia and her sister Abigail, replenishing the incense, polishing the marble tables, plucking rose petals to float in the fountain and looking longingly across the hills, speaking of a strange people in a strange land – A land where Titius now found himself on his own.

Titius, sitting ten feet from the top of the tree, pressed his solid frame hard against the trunk of the gnarly sentinel which looked to have guarded the grotto's entrance since the first days after Noah's flood. The bitter tang of ash from the trio's ritual fire anchored itself in the back of his throat. He gurgled and spit to clear it.

The grotto was a favored haunt of doves, pigeons and ravens. Nearby fields of barley, corn, millet and wheat kept the birds well fed. As the gusts lashed the branches, hundreds of the birds sprang off their lurching perches and sailed into the winds blustering over the nearby city of Sepphoris.

A wild boar, with clods of dirt clinging to his curved tusks, stopped his rooting for tubers and sprinted off, tail high in the air like a flag pole. A small golden fox darted out of the boar's way and back into its den. A rabbit paused, sniffed, and then hopped quickly into the underbrush.

The trio of masked thespians turned away from their stare, abandoned their rituals, scooped up hidden black robes and faded into the forest coverings. One moment they stood like tree shadows and the next moment they were like wisps of smoke, vanishing without a trace. *Where did they go?*

Titius scrambled down the tree, squirrel-like, and jumped to the ground from several branches up before rolling under cover in a bush. The aroma of fresh dung was strong enough to wipe out the fragrance of damp earth and shifting flowers.

Moments later, a shadow interrupted the dappled pattern created by sunlight through leafy boughs. A second dark figure moved against the base of the olive and stared upward where Titius had been.

Cleopas hissed his ghostly whisper once again. *"They're close, Tee-shus."* The throaty Hebrew was clear. *"You waited too long. You always wait too long."*

"I don't have to listen to you," Titius muttered. "You're dead. Leave me alone."

The shadowy figures blended into the trees and vanished. Titius took the moment to crawl out from behind the bush. His elbows and knees dug into the damp earth as he moved away from where he had seen the figures. He reached a rocky outcropping and kept crawling. His knees burned as they rubbed across the choppy granite surface.

Reaching a boulder twice his height, he scrambled to his feet and sprinted around it. A sunlit meadow spread out before him with shadowed forest on either side. The tree tops continued to bend in the wind but something was missing. His neck and shoulder muscles tightened.

With the three masked phantoms around he couldn't go back and he didn't dare cross the open meadow. A patch of darkness at the base of a cliff face offered refuge. He ran into the cave and stopped, stubbing his toes hard against a surface rock hidden in the dust of the secluded enclosure. He refused to wince.

A lone figure stood an armslength away. A glistening sword flashed a finger width shy of Titius's throat and its point rested under his chin. Titus stepped back and the sword carrier followed him into the light. It was a Roman officer.

An ostrich feather crest mounted sideways above the centurion's glistening golden helmet spoke of authority. A lion's head with skin draped over his right shoulder spoke of courage. His silver breastplate, made of overlapping metal strips, featured five prominent war medals fastened in place and spoke of success. "It seems as if you are mine again," the seasoned warrior pronounced. He tucked an edge of his billowing scarlet cape into his waist belt to secure it. "Is it loyalty or fate that enslaves you to my whim?"

Titius took a step back. "Your whim would seek to enslave me?"

Piercing blue eyes measured his every movement. The aquiline nose of the soldier set above a clean shaven square jaw showed no emotion. The centurion's left hand held his sword and his right hand held the vine staff for disciplining his men. "You track the demons of death like I helped you hunt the leopards in Tripoli," he said. "You put yourself at my mercy."

Titius knelt in the dust and bowed his head. "Of what service can I be to the great centurion, Sestus Aurelius?" He raised his head and spread his arms. Dozens of ravens and a vulture circled overhead. "Surely, you have worthier dogs to pursue."

The sword bearer glared down at him. "You still wear your family ring. Since when did the lion become a dog?" Footsteps sounded nearby. "When my father marched with your grandfather into Rome after defeating the Gauls, you were there with your uncle. I saw you dressed like a miniature senator."

Titius lowered his head. "That life is gone."

Sestus continued. "Your own father perished at the hands of the Germans. You inherited his title, his estate, his honor."

"I have seen the illusion of it all."

"You give up power so easily?"

"I am a shadow. A shadow has no power."

The centurion swung the sword tip hypnotically, like a pendulum, inches from the nose of his captive. "Tell me. Why would one of Rome's potential senators be observing my thespian assassins?"

The rocks were hard on his knees. The dirt was damp to his hands. The voice was active in his head. When the sword moved back and forth inches from his throat he found his own voice. "I only wish to be one of your thespians."

Sestus stepped closer and steadied his weapon. "Help me understand. You want to leave a life of luxury so you can smash a hornet's nest of zealots in a forgotten corner of our empire? You want to live the rest of your life pretending to be who you're not?"

Titius bowed lower and spread his palms in the rain-touched dust. "I want to live in a world where I feel like a man."

"Tired of slurping pigeon tongues and pig's feet with your uncles in the Senate, are you?" Sestus sneered and lowered the sword a fraction. "Willing to give up your villa and inheritance to curl up in the dust and to beg for the trash of peasants? Ready to live invisibly, to kill quickly, to never truly be known?"

"Yes!" Titius ignored the fly buzzing around his ear.

"If anyone hears your story there will be no more mystery and no more glory," Sestus warned.

"I seek no glory for myself."

"To join us will forever erase your story from existence." Sestus sheathed his sword. "Your heritage and your pride will never let this happen."

"Let it be as if I was never born." The fly landed in Titius's beard and he tried to blow it away.

"Look up!" The three masked figures now stood behind his captor dressed in vests of mail armour with black woolen tunics. The centurion withdrew a dagger and held it at Titius' throat. "You are first and foremost a servant of the emperor, a legionnaire sworn to uphold Caesar's empire."

Titius raised an arm in oath. "I give my life again to Tiberius Caesar as my lord and protector. He above all is divine. He above all is my hope." The fly disappeared.

Sestus grabbed the hand still raised and ripped off the ring. "Without this ring you are nothing. It is yours again if the emperor dies or if I die before you." The centurion opened a small pouch at his waist and dropped the ring inside.

Titius eyed the pouch carefully and weighed his choice. "The ring is yours until you die."

The Roman centurion pressed his dagger tight against the side of the oath taker's neck and drew it slightly. "You will need this mark in the work you do," Sestus announced. A crimson line thickened quickly and blood flowed. "This is the mark of those who give their blood to Caesar. This blood will not be the last you shed."

Sestus nodded to one of the men now beside him. The masked figure flicked his wrist and magically produced a vial of clear amber liquid. He uncapped it, poured a small drizzle on his fingers, then traced the wound created by Sestus' dagger on Titius' neck.

Titius gasped at the intense sting on his neck even as he breathed in the fragrance of peaches, frankincense and myrrh. The blood flow staunched.

"I have a test," Sestus pronounced.

The three masked thespian assassins stood like statues behind Sestus. Titius knelt alone before them. The wind settled to a breeze, the trees stood straighter and a deer bounded across the far side of the meadow. The test was not obvious.

"Whatever you wish," Titius responded.

The centurion sheathed his dagger and sword. "Good." He motioned to a second masked figure behind him. The figure glided forward as if pulled by a string. With a flick of his wrist a black hood appeared.

Sestus took it and approached Titius. "From tomorrow, you will become my cross maker's guardian. If he outlives his own foolishness, you, too, will live." He pulled the hood down over Titius's head and bound his wrists with thin rope. The hood smelled of fire-smoke and incense.

"What now?"

"Stand and fight. The assassins are upon you."

Before Titius could shrug off the hood, one savage kick buckled his knees and another cracked his ribs. His attackers made no sound. He ignored another phantom whisper from Cleopas. He sensed movement in front of him and backed away. A slight shadow blocking sunlight confirmed his perception. He set his feet and raised his arms to shield himself from the assault. The attack materialized from behind.

Titius fought through the mind-numbing pain and got to his feet again. He spun, trying to sense the next point of attack. There was nothing. And then it would come again. From in front, from behind, from the side, over and over.

Pain gripped his broken ribs in a vice. Thirst parched his throat. Oxygen escaped his lungs. Panic felt for his soul.

When terror consumed him he disjointed his shoulders and performed a back flip, distorting his body and skipping over his joined wrists, so that the hands once bound behind him were now in front.

"Good!" someone said.

The kicks changed to punches, targeting his arms, his back, his chest. Titius clenched his bound hands together into a double fist and pretended to deliver a punch of his own. Instead of following through on the feigned punch he brought up a knee. He made solid contact and relished the responding grunt. Regret for fighting back was quick as a punch to his jaw staggered him and brought him to the edge of blackness.

Liquid splashed onto the side of his hood and down his arm. His senses heightened again, olive oil. The crackle of fire sounded behind him.

"Stop!" It was Sestus.

Titius spun to face the voice and waited as footsteps approached. The hood was ripped off his head and sunlight slashed into his retinas. An attacker doused a flaming torch in the dirt. Titius blinked and closed his eyes for a moment. A dribble of oil trickled down his cheek and lodged in his beard.

When Titius opened his eyes again he looked down at a dark patch growing on the thigh of his brown tunic. He slowly moved his hand toward it and a drop of crimson splashed off of his wrist. He blinked and felt a rough hand under his ear where the wound dripped freely again.

"It's enough. This test is done." Sestus turned away and waved his right hand above his head. A majestic white stallion stepped out from a small break in the cliff. The centurion mounted and gave instructions to the leader of the three assassins. "Jaennus, take this pitiful fighter to Sepphoris. Clean him. Heal him. Train him. I need him in Caesarea in one month. I need him to be a man who could be any man."

2

The training by the three assassins never seemed to end. His ribs screamed for mercy. Weeks into soul shriveling combat maneuvers, Titius finally faced off against the centurion.

Titius had discarded the galea, the metal helmet, and the scutum, the rectangular shield of wood and leather, as Sestus poked at him with a javelin. The vest of mail felt restrictive and heavy.

"Only a fool would discard his galea and scutum to escape the piercing of a pilum," the centurion snarled. "Do you think in a month that you have become invincible?"

Titius parried with his short sword, twisting and turning to avoid the targeted jabs. "My disguises will only allow for a gladius like this," he said. "I will never be able to depend on a shield or a helmet. I would be a fool now to depend on what can never be."

Sestus swung the javelin at the knees of his opponent and Titius hurdled the weapon. The centurion then swung back at waist height and Titius ducked under it. The javelin jabbed and Titius leaped back out of its reach. A swiftly approaching shadow jumped across his peripheral vision and stimulated his instincts. He dove to the ground and rolled away as a second assassin used a pilum to strike for his back.

Two horses charged at Titius from opposite sides. He could smell their lathered sweat in the breeze. Cleopas screamed in his mind: *"Fool, you play with death."* Before Titius could focus on which warhorse to avoid, Sestus leveled him with a blow to the back of his knees. The slashing hooves pounded toward him and he instinctively curled into a fetal position. *"Fool,"* Cleopas screamed. The horses stepped past him and Sestus began to beat on him.

Jaennus spoke up, "Master, we haven't faced the horses yet."

Sestus stopped the beating. "What kind of thespian assassin will he be if he can't defend himself?"

"We are first learning the secret of being a thespian before we learn all the secrets of being an assassin."

"I need him to survive before I need him to hide," Sestus growled. He poked Titius with the butt end of his javelin. "Now, get up, take that sword and fight."

When Titius sprang to his feet, waving his sword in challenge to both men, Sestus lowered his javelin and smiled. He turned to the masked warrior beside him. "What is this? A dead man pretending to live?"

Jaennus held up his hand. "He acted the coward to draw you in so that you could feel the point of his sword. It was only my instructions that kept him from severing your head."

Sestus saluted. "Jaennus, you have created a worthy guardian for my cross maker. Now, show me the thespian. Will he now be able to fool us all with his disguises?"

The masked warrior summoned his charge and disappeared into a small limestone hovel with a thatched roof. Another one of the dark clad thespian assassins stepped up beside Sestus. "We have arranged a demonstration." He pointed toward a crudely built platform near the building. "We will bring out five small groups. Each time the initiate will be among them. His success will be in your inability to know him outright."

The first group featured four distinct individuals: a paunchy Pharisee in full regalia, a gaunt blind man little more than skin and bones, an elderly woman hunched and resting on a cane, and a legionnaire in full battle dress. Sestus examined the quartet from ten strides away and finally guessed. "I would be a fool to choose any of these but for this game I choose the woman."

"Titius, stand and be recognized," said the assassin.

The gaunt, blind man rose and peeled off his goatskin hairpiece and soiled blanket. It was Titius.

"Well done!" Sestus declared. "One for you. Again."

A short time later, the second group featured five more options: a dark-skinned olive merchant, a veiled prophetess of Pan, a swarthy fisherman with his distinctive odor, a Roman of nobility, and a bushy-bearded zealot. Sestus looked long and hard. "Surely it is not the prophetess or the olive merchant. I will choose the zealot."

"Titius, stand and be recognized!" the assassin commanded.

The swarthy fisherman with his distinctive odor lowered his net filled with fish and pulled away a headpiece. It was Titius.

Three more groups paraded their looks. Each was a mixture of the first two groups. "Titius will never be who he was," hinted the assassin.

In the third group Sestus chose the legionnaire but Titius was the elderly woman. In the fourth group Sestus chose the Pharisee but Titius was the prophetess. In the fifth group Sestus chose the Roman noble but Titius was the olive merchant.

Sestus raised his gladius high. "I salute you, Jaennus." The centurion pointed at the newly revealed Titius. "A new hypocrite is born to save the empire, an actor who can wear any mask with success. A guardian for my cross maker." He turned away and called for his stallion. "Now work with him so that even his own mother won't know him."

Jaennus took Titius to a deep pool in a Roman fortress near Caesarea.

"You're a dead man," whispered the voice of Cleopas. *"You know how you hate water."*

"Still your tongue!" Titius said under his breath. "You're the one who tried to drown me."

"I was teaching you to swim," Cleopas hissed. *"I know you were trying to impress that girl."*

"I was only twelve," Titius snarled. He breathed in and out so quickly he felt faint.

"She was only fourteen," the phantom servant chuckled. *"You always did have a weakness for women."*

"You are my weakness," Titius muttered.

Jaennus, half a hand taller than Titius, seemed to tower over him when wearing his horsehair crested helmet. "You are about to face what no human being should face," the centurion's assistant said. "Some days you will want to die rather than keep your vow. Some days you will wish you had chosen the life of a gladiator. Most days you will long for your days as a senator's son in Rome."

"I only want to be a man," Titius said firmly.

"We shall see," Jaennus said. "We shall see what happens when you start remembering lounging on your couch beside your marble table, sipping your silver flagon of wine, surrounded by voluptuous servant girls, sucking on choice chunks of dolphin."

"Rome is a seething poisonous serpent. Neither my dreams nor my taste buds take me in that direction."

The rigour started at dawn each day with Jaennus physically holding Titius under water for longer and longer periods of time.

Titius was pushed to swim faster and farther. Following a quick recovery break he lifted weights, pulled himself up to eye level on horizontal wooden rods, and then ran sprints and long distances over and over.

Cleopas lectured him through the night on his foolishness. *"Tee-shus, you have the mind of a goose and the soul of a scorpion. These Romans will skewer you and leave you to rot in the sun."* Sleeplessness left him less fit for the challenges of each following day.

"Who are you?" Jaennus shouted as he stumbled in an obstacle course. "You are food for the ravens. You are slop for the swine, scraps for the dogs."

"I told you so," Cleopas echoed.

On the fifth day, under a blazing noon-day sun, the world started spinning around Titius. His knees buckled under the heavy weights he carried and he crashed to the ground. He lay still.

Jaennus prodded him in the ribs with his vine staff. "Rise, you fraud. You're more worthless than a stillborn pig, a galley slave and a bucket of slops all combined. You'll never be a man. I'd rather train a woman than a splash of dung like you."

Titius tried just to breathe.

Suddenly, the weight lifted, strong arms raised him over head and shuttled him to the pool. Like a vision in the night, he watched himself being dumped into the cool waters. He sank like a stone and called out to Neptune to release him from his trials. Somewhere he heard a phantom screech. His lungs screamed for air.

As quickly as he sank, so he was raised up out of the water. Heavy thuds pounded his back and compressed his chest until he lay coughing, spluttering water, and gasping for air.

The sun burned his skin like a fire as he lay at the edge of his grave. The spirit of death danced like an empty shadow at the edge of his consciousness. Finally, a merciful ally dragged him into the shadows of a nearby cedar tree and left him to rest.

The voices of others sounded in the distance. Cleopas's voice alone reached him. *"That insane assassin did what I couldn't do. He killed you. And still you won't come to the other side."*

"There is no other side," Titius muttered.

Gentle hands prodded him awake in the morning and fed him broth. Every muscle screamed for mercy. The hands massaged his body and left him to rest again. The faintest smell of roses kept him hanging on.

Thoughts of himself as a sixteen year old under the hands of Lydia's younger sister, Abigail, filled his mind. She was eighteen and Titius found himself making excuses to be with her. He was furious when he came home one day and found that his mother had sold the slave to another family. He had shut his heart down toward every woman since that day, even if the ghost of the Hebrew slave, Cleopas, didn't believe it.

Life had become like a dance without music, a rainbow without color, a kiss without passion. His heart was like an eagle chained to the ground.

Cleopas reached him in his fading thoughts. *"You need to quit before they kill you for good."*

Titius agreed with the slave for the first time, "You're right. I have to quit before I end up like you."

Something nudged him in the night. "Leave me alone, you stupid phantom," he whispered.

"I'm no phantom," Jaennus said. "Enough rest. Move. Meet me at the pool at first light."

Titius shook off his sleep, slipped on his gear, and satiated his thirst from a gourd of water lying at the head of his bed. The air was crisp and cool. Mars and Venus still faced off in the heavens. The moon was nowhere to be seen. The sparkle of heavenly lights fought to hold their sway as the first touches of color marked the horizon. A young maiden slipped out of the officer's quarters and disappeared into the shadows.

A trio of master assassins were preparing an obstacle course as Titius found the pathway to the pool of water which terrified him. The pungent odor of frankincense hung in the air from a recent sacrificial offering.

Titius slid away from the pathway and sheltered behind an oak tree to preview his challenge. "Did you hear about Cretius?" an assassin called.

One of the others threw a rope ladder over a wall. "Do you mean that despot assistant of Herod Antipas?"

"Guard your tongue, Marcus," his partner warned. "His spies are everywhere."

"Anyway," the first continued unabated, "I heard him bragging that he had stolen the estate of General Julianus."

The neck hairs on Titius bristled up like a cat on high alert. General Julianus had been his father, killed in the German wars. What had happened to his mother, his sister, the servants, especially Lydia? He tucked in harder behind the trunk of the tree.

"What concern is that of ours?" the assassin by the wall called out. "Those Roman senators steal each other blind while we risk our lives to help them live in luxury. I hope they choke on their pigeon tongues."

"Marcus, it'll be your tongue they choke on," the partner warned.

"The general has an heir who has disappeared. Cretius has ordered me to watch for him."

"No doubt, Octavian, he slipped you a sack of gold to watch his back," Marcus said.

"Emperor Tiberius will likely reform the senate and ensure that this shadow heir gets nowhere near power in Rome. He's probably escaped to hide in the back woods of Britannia. We just need to keep Jaennus happy."

"They're talking about you," Cleopas hissed.

Titius instinctively covered his mouth lest the trio overhear the phantom voice in his mind. Anger raced like fire through his veins. Cretius had stolen his estate in Rome.

Cleopas persisted, *"You told that centurion you didn't want it anyway. And now you're quitting. You might as well stay at the bottom of that pool next time."*

When the trio slipped into the brush on the far side of the field, Titius backed away onto the path and hurried toward the pool.

Jaennus was waiting. He was dressed in all his regalia as an Optio, chief assistant to the centurion. His raised horsehair mane above his helmet and his white-nobbed stick showed his authority to record and report all that happened among the troops. He raised his stick in greeting. "I knew you would come."

"You don't know how close I came to not coming," Titius said.

Jaennus opened his hand and held out Titius's ring. "A gift from the centurion," he said. He held it out over the water and dropped it into the pool.

Titius watched it sink.

"The pool is ten heights of a man your size," he said. "Only one man has reached the bottom. Untold treasures lie within your grasp."

"*There goes your life,*" Cleopas mocked.

"This will be your final test under the water," Jaennus said. "You will endure to the limit or you will return to Rome. You will prove you are a man worthy of being a thespian assassin or you will prove that you are no different than anyone else. Today is your day."

Titius stood at the edge of the pool waiting and stared into its depth. This dark pit would be the womb for a new life or it would be his tomb. He would not go back to Rome. Without fear, he stepped off the edge and plunged down into the icy grip of the waters.

3

Surviving the water sparked a confidence Titius had never known before. He didn't reach the bottom, and he didn't retrieve his ring, but he endured the full time that any assassin had to in order to qualify for the brotherhood. He finished the obstacle course and completed his tests of strength. He slept with a deep peace that night.

The morning sun was still a faint glimmer on the horizon when Sestus brought the butt of his javelin down on Titius' mat. Instead of the dull thud of wood on flesh or solid earth the javelin's energy was swallowed up by cushions carefully concealed under a worn blanket. Sestus lifted his torchlight higher, yanked off the blanket and reached for the rounded form of a 'head' resting under a small mass of hair. He pulled off the hair and discovered a melon. His nod and 'hmmmph' accompanied the smile on his face.

"Titius," he called. "Step out!"

A nearby mat, which appeared to be flat on the floor, moved aside and Titius rolled himself out of the hollow he had formed in the earthen floor.

Sestus stepped to the hole and examined it. "Hmmmph," he said. "It looks like your training is finished."

Titius followed the centurion without a word as the soldier exited the sleeping quarters. When his leader mounted a horse, he mounted the unclaimed one standing alongside. The short military saddle on the horse had four horns to brace legs and back but nowhere to put one's feet.

"Wait!" Cleopas whispered in his mind. Titius ignored the phantom. When the first horse moved ahead he urged his mount to follow.

The sky seemed especially active: Hawks, kites and eagles danced in the thermals and currents. A pair of cranes flapped leisurely above a forested hill while pelicans and cormorants made their way toward the sea. Partridges, spooked by some hidden predator, vaulted from cover and raced for other foliage. Warblers, starlings, and swallows darted and flitted and flapped in and out of cover. A woodpecker pounded its bill against a tree trunk in search of some hidden grub.

The sun was half way to its zenith before Sestus stopped the horse beside a small pond fed by a stream. He dismounted and motioned with his hand that Titius should do the same. A small flock of Egyptian geese paddled among the reeds along the water's edge. The birds fluttered their wings and skimmed across the surface a dozen flaps to reach the far side.

An old, black raven hopped down a branch on a nearby fig tree and focused its beady eyes to examine the intruders into its kingdom. A hummingbird hovered over a hibiscus and a swarm of gnats formed a small cloud near the horses.

"You didn't get the ring," Sestus stated. "Why didn't you fight for it?"

"I know where it is," Titius answered.

"Only one man has reached the bottom of that pool," Sestus said. "Your fate is now bound with us."

Titius nodded. "Yes, my fate is now bound with you."

Sestus picked up a rock and threw it dead center against a tree trunk on the other side of the pond. He nodded to himself and smiled.

When Titius sat and rested his back against an old cedar tree, Sestus paced before him. Finally, the soldier walked to his mount and detached a gourd tied to a saddle. He heaved it at Titius who caught it one-handed. Sestus opened his own gourd and dumped the contents on the ground. Titius did the same. Sestus knelt by the stream and refilled the gourd. Titius did the same.

"You learn quickly," Sestus affirmed. "Why a thespian?"

Titius guzzled the water quickly and then lowered the gourd to his side. "I think it was the mask of an actor that first caught my attention and pulled my heart toward the stage." Titius eyed his commander. "I was a boy, maybe ten years free of the womb. The performer moved and spoke in courageous ways before his audience. No general would dare to mock the Caesar with such impunity and live to boast. Yet, this strutting cock pulled laughter from even the Senators who lay prone on their gilded couches."

Sestus took a step toward his horse and smiled as Titius mimicked his actions precisely. "You enter theatre so you can mock the emperor? Did your father approve of your choice?"

Titius took another guzzle. "My father turned on me as if to cut out my tongue. When I first mentioned it I felt that he mocked me."

"What did he say?"

"He said, 'Theatre?'" Titius swung his arms wide and turned his shoulders as he took a few steps and acted out the scene with his father. "He paced back and forth in our courtyard by the fountain of Neptune. His scarlet tunic matched the bright red battle scar across his cheek. When he stopped pacing he drew his sword and slashed it inches from my heart." Titius staggered back as if under attack. "Titius, he said, you are the son of a Roman Legate. The heir of a warrior who has humbled the Gauls. Spit this cursed idea from your throat."

Sestus picked up a small branch and broke it. "Your uncle will curse the day of your birth when he sees you again."

Titius stepped behind a tree and spoke in a deep voice strangely like that of Cleopas. *"He will never see me again. I no longer exist. I am only your cross maker's guardian."* He stepped out into Sestus's view again.

"Don't you ever wonder what happened to your estate when you left Rome?" Sestus asked as he pulled out his javelin and sword.

Titius caught the javelin Sestus tossed to him. "Once my mother died I didn't care anymore."

Sestus circled and tested Titius' reflexes with his javelin. "You probably don't know that she died giving birth to our brother."

Titius paused a moment too long and his javelin was knocked out of his hand. He scrambled for it. Before he could pick it up Sestus had the sword at his throat. "I was told she was raped."

Sestus chuckled and stepped away. "Not at all," he declared. "My father made a business arrangement with your mother after your father died. The two estates were going to be joined." He motioned Titius to stand up again. "You would have become a senator and I would have become a general. When the babe was born we would have been brothers."

"What was your father really wanting from my mother?"

Sestus smiled. "What else? Her servant girls."

Titius surged with anger and slashed viciously at Sestus. Sestus defended every effort until Titius tired.

"Your passion will be your weakness," Sestus said. "You know that Cretius raped your mother and stole your estate. Focus your rage and filter out what you know isn't true." Sestus sheathed his sword. "Hear beyond the words that others send you like breadcrumbs. Some day you must restore your honor. Cretius must die."

"Whatever you teach me will serve my revenge."

Sestus walked to the edge of the pond and stooped to pick up a stone. He threw it non-chalantly toward the geese. A few of them fluttered and skipped further away. "I have found my cross maker. When you reap your revenge I will return your ring."

"How will you do that?" Titius asked. "It lies at the bottom of the pool and only one man has reached the bottom."

Sestus lifted his hands. "And I am that man."

Titius crouched, panting from the workout, and waited. He plucked a wildflower and cherished the pleasure of its scent. "Jaennus has planned training for tomorrow."

"We cannot wait."

The raven dropped down another branch toward Titius. The new thespian assassin drew an imaginary bow and shot his arrow at the bird. "I am ready. Take me to him."

Sestus turned and scanned the skies. Dark clouds crept over the hills fighting the sun for control. "He doesn't know yet that he is mine. He is arriving by ship from Alexandria. You will woo him to me."

Sestus walked quickly and mounted his stallion. Titius did the same.

The centurion turned to his charge. "You are my cross maker's guardian and you are every man you need to be. It is time to start your duty."

Titius groaned when Caleb walked into view. The man designated as the cross maker for Sestus was a disaster in the making. His carpenter's headpiece dangled half way off his shoulder held in place by a cross beam. He was broad shouldered, long armed, and bounced along, walking like an overgrown child up to mischief. The thong of one sandal was half-undone and the ends dragged along in his wake.

Cleopas resurrected his phantom voice to instruct Titius again. *"The centurion has bonded you to a Jewish carpenter. Galilean, no doubt. Heart of a cobra for you Romans. This is trouble."*

Titius scratched at the goat skin skull cap nestled under his head covering. "If he gives me trouble I'll feed both him and you to Neptune. He doesn't look like much of a cross maker."

The young carpenter strolled down a dirt path in the heart of a zealot community in Caesarea. Crumbling limestone huts, with chipped red clay roofing tiles, huddled in tight, almost blocked the blistering sunshine. The dirt path separating the rows of structures was packed rock hard by thousands of feet from generation after generation. It was clear from the cross maker's Roman attire and his reckless stride that he didn't belong here.

"His name is Caleb ben Samson," Sestus had told Titius.

Caleb clutched a six foot cross beam across his bulging shoulders. His dark eyebrows were furrowed and his piercing eyes focused on the shadowed archway ahead. Titius had seen a young daggerman slip into the shadows beyond the archway, but this wasn't his battle, yet. The centurion, Sestus Aurelius, had sent him to gain information on the zealots, and to keep the cross maker alive, nothing else.

Not one passerby had given a second look to Titius disguised as a pitiful old blind beggar at the side of the road. He had molded the old goat skin tight to his shaved skull and wrapped a leather thong of long white hair under his chin. A discarded blanket from the refuse pile added to the look and the odor. After three hours along the side of the road he'd gotten used to the smell of rotting fish and dung.

His random call for alms yielded nothing in this neighbourhood, but it also made it unlikely that anyone would drive him away. His walking stick rested close by in case any rambunctious youth tried to test his apparent blindness. His one mistake was pulling out the coded papyrus scroll to review the instructions from the centurion.

The passing carpenter grunted at him and fixed his eyes for a second too long on the parchment. Titius could almost sense his question. 'What's an old, blind man doing with a scroll?'

Three youths stepped into the laneway following Caleb. Each of the three carried crude daggers designed to gut a fish or slice a throat. The carpenter acted like he didn't notice them. He reached for the knife in his tool belt, caressed it like a lover, then released it. His adjusted grip on the crossbeam resting on his shoulders told Titius that the carpenter knew exactly who was behind him. His focus was ahead.

The cross maker adjusted the step of his sandaled feet and pretended to stumble. He was a poor actor but the ruse seemed to embolden the youth who increased the length and speed of their own strides. The three walked by Titius without even looking his way. The lead youth called out to the carpenter: "Caleb, carpenter of Nazareth, you betray us with your blood."

Caleb ignored the taunt behind him and wrapped his strong fingers around the beam like it was a giant club. He reached the cobblestones near the archway and swung at the shadows chest high. The fugitive Titius had seen hiding there collapsed to the ground. A dagger fell at Caleb's feet. The carpenter raised the beam and hit the fallen man again. There was no movement from the ambushed zealot.

Cleopas goaded Titius' mind: *"This one has a death wish. You'll never keep him alive."*

Titius knuckled hard against his own temple and then reached into the dust for the smallest of pebbles. All the time he faced straight ahead with his chin lowered toward his chest.

The carpenter focused his attention on the three youths brandishing daggers. Instead of dropping the beam and picking up the dagger lying on the cobblestones, instead of running, he adjusted his grip as if to throw the beam with both hands and then charged at the boys. The beam hit them at the knees and knocked them back to the ground. Before any of the youths could recover, he grabbed their hair and smashed their skulls into the cobblestones.

A bag of apricots had fallen from the coat of one of the youth. The carpenter picked it up and ate the fruit one by one. It was a dangerous play. The bag was meant to be delivered to Barabbas.

4

Two candle wicks flickered in the breeze as the door to the dockside warehouse squeaked open. Titius hunched in the shadows near a stack of bags filled with wheat kernels. A lone figure stepped into the room and closed the door. "Nabonidus!"

A bald-headed Persian in a loin cloth rolled slowly away from a reed mat and jumped to his feet. His dark-skinned body blended into the lightless alcoves but the lamp light reflected easily off of his bald head. His massive frame became apparent as he stepped forward into more light. His belly hung generously over his loin cloth but the bulging biceps proved strength and not slackness. The dull clink of chains followed him as he stepped forward. "Master?"

The newly arrived figure moved toward the Persian. Hazy smoke from the lamps wafted between the two men. "Nabonidus, did you see where they took the bodies?"

Titius recognized the voice of the carpenter, Caleb ben Samson. He shifted closer to the huddle. He couldn't hear the lengthy whispered reply of the Persian slave, but the response of the newcomer was clear.

"The blind man?" Caleb turned toward the lamp light and scratched at his beard. "If you're talking about the blind man I saw he couldn't lift an omer of barley past his knees. Are you sure he isn't working for Barabbas? There was something suspicious about him."

"Master Caleb, he says he saved your life." The Persian looked into the darkness where Titius had been hiding minutes before.

"He says he threw a stone no bigger than an olive pit to distract the zealot leader when you were chargin' him. He says when you were gone he used a donkey cart to take away the bodies."

"Where is this blind man?" Caleb backed up against the door and peered into the shadows.

Titius slipped through the darkness and stood up beside the carpenter. He stretched out his cane and tapped an unguarded shin. Caleb swung hard and only grunted when Titius ducked and put him in an arm lock with his face against the wall. "Life or death," hissed Titius. "You choose."

Caleb bent with the pressure until he was on his knees. The pitch sealing the warehouse boards blended with the aroma of spices, grain, sweat and fish. "Nabonidus, do something."

"That's not the choice I offered," said Titius firmly. "May the goddess, Belona and the god, Mars spare you from me."

"Master, just listen to the man."

"I'm listening."

Titius released the pressure and waited for Caleb to rise to his feet and turn. He back-stepped into the shadows and watched the carpenter straining to see him. "Relax and live. Are you truly the cross maker?"

"Who are you?"

"All you need to know is that the bodies are gone and you are still alive. Things are not always as they appear to be." With that Titius slipped away.

As he scurried out the back entrance of the warehouse Titius noticed four legionnaires approaching the front of the building. Time was short for Caleb and Nabonidus. Titius grabbed a handul of dates from a vendor and continued toward the place where Sestus prepared for the next phase of their journey. On the way he discarded his garb in one of the four staches he kept around the city.

Thirty minutes later he arrived without his disguise in the courtyard of the Judean Procurator, Pontius Pilate. Six Roman sentries were spaced across the entrance, hands firmly on their swords, shields resting against their legs. "Titius Marcus Julianus," he declared, "reporting to the Centurion, Sestus Aurelius."

The legionnaires might have been statues for their lack of response. Titius waited. He watched a flock of storks skim the roof tops and head for the forests inland.

A boy stepped out of the shadows. He looked up expectantly like a young bird waiting to be fed. Titius gave him what he wanted. "A message for the centurion – the man he seeks is in the home of the tanner among the Greek traders." The lad nodded, turned and walked through the sentries into the fountained gardens beyond.

Nabonidus was still struggling with the four legionnaires when Titius rounded the corner of the warehouse. The Persian slave's forehead beaded with sweat and his muscles bulged with effort. The Romans worked to buckle his knees but the tower of strength fought to maintain his balance.

When the giant fell to his knees and finally submitted to the crippling shackles that bound ankles to wrists and neck, Titius turned to watch a rat scrabble across the floor toward a basket of apricots, the fruit of Barabbas. He ignored the exit as Nabonidus was dragged protesting from the room.

One of the legionnaires stayed behind to clean up the scene. He nodded to Titius as he wiped up a small pool of blood. "Is your cross maker going to cooperate?"

Titius rose to his feet and picked out an apricot from the basket. "Depends how good your centurion is at persuading him."

The legionnaire accepted the golden orb as Titius tossed it to him. He bit off half the apricot and disemboweled the fruit of its pit. "If he favours that slave as much as you say, then he'll cooperate."

"What are the options?"

The legionnaire tossed the pit over the pile of crates and consumed the rest of the fruit. "If your man cooperates, the Persian might get off easy. If he resists, then that slave will end his life in the Ephesian Colosseum or the galleys of a warship."

Titius raised his hand as he moved to the door. "You better catch up with the others. That Persian might be too much for them."

The next two days were busy in his role as guardian. The first evening he noticed a young zealot in conference with a woman dressed like a Greek goddess. Her long blond tresses flowed over her shoulders and drew a man's eyes toward a revealing linen tunic. Money exchanged hands along with a gourd of wine. As she prepared a tray of food for Caleb, Titius told her that the man she had been talking to needed her at the door. While she was away he switched the gourd of wine for another like it. A sniff and small taste confirmed that the first wine was poisoned.

Caleb had been like a boy jabbing his javelin into a hornet's nest and having run ignored the revenge of the riled up insects. Titius intervened to save the cross maker from threats the carpenter didn't even see coming. Half way through the second morning he garroted a zealot about to ambush the carpenter with a dagger and he rode over another with a horse. Sleep was a luxury he couldn't afford as the centurion lounged in the palace of Pontius Pilate.

In the evening, sitting with his back to a wall near a flickering fire, Titius stared at the sleeping cross maker. *What would it take to break this man?*

That afternoon he had disguised himself as the old, blind man.

"Listen to this," he instructed. He had tapped his cane in different rhythms to attempt a communication system. Caleb ignored him. "Perhaps you're the blind one," he chided. In a surprise move, with his eyes closed, Titius disarmed Caleb of his carpenter's knife to prove his skills, but the cross maker was obstinate.

"Being a blind man, I hear things," he offered. "For example, I know that four more zealots are planning to ambush you when you arrive at the date vendor's cart tomorrow morning. You ignore me at your peril."

In the morning Titius followed Caleb as the cross maker took a different route and stopped by a fig vendor instead to break his fast. The guardian doubled back and noticed two young zealots loitering in the shadows near the date vendor.

Near the docks Titius tried to tap a warning when two centurions emerged from a tavern. Caleb ignored him for a moment then stepped into the shadowed archway of a warehouse.

"Why are you here?" Titius asked.

"I need to find Nabonidus," Caleb said.

Titius pushed an apricot pit down through a gap in the decking of the dock. "He's already shackled to a Roman gally as a slave. Sestus will keep him there or some place like that to ensure your loyalty. I wouldn't be surprised if they sell him as a gladiator."

Caleb snatched a large woven basket of walnuts and heaved it off the dock. Titius grabbed his wrist, bent it back and stopped him from following the walnuts with a basket of olives.

Perhaps a woman would calm the cross maker. With that in mind, Titius strolled through the local slave market and noticed a young Grecian woman chained apart from the rest. She looked similar to the woman who had attempted to poison Caleb with the gourd of wine, although now she had no linen tunic to hide her beauty. "Why is the Greek on her own?" he asked the seller who was holding a long whip.

The lusty eyes of the owner accompanied the twisted grin. "I have to break her," said the seller. "She looks like a goddess and she has the attitude of one, too. Even with nothing to hide her she acts like she is still a queen."

Titius examined the woman from her long, golden tresses to strong legs and arms. She had the form of an athlete, a perfect model for the sculptures in the garden of goddesses at his home in Rome. She had the face of youth and innocence so much like his first love, Abigail.

He called to her. The woman refused to look at him. He reached up and took hold of her chin and forced her to look his way. "I can take a goddess like you to heaven," he said, "or I can take you down to hades. The other men who will want you here will not give you that choice."

A furrow of uncertainty crossed her brow and she looked at him for a moment, blushing as she did. Titius realized suddenly that her hardness was the only covering she had to maintain a sense of modesty. "I'll take her," he said. "Thirty shekels."

The slave owner ran his hand through his long greasy beard. "Thirty might get you a chance for another look. Offer me something reasonable. I know a few zealots who would pay twice your price."

Titius saw the hope drain out of the girl. "I will pay you forty shekels now so you don't have to wait on the empty promises of zealots."

The slave owner snapped his whip near the woman's feet and chuckled when she jumped. "Perhaps I need to mark her up a little since for forty it is clear you are only wanting someone to scrub your floors and to cook your meals. Believe me, the zealots know that this one is good for something more than floors."

"I can see that this woman is hard hearted and defiant," said Titius stepping back. "Perhaps I was hasty. Name your final price or I will look elsewhere and leave you to your burden."

The slave owner looked around to see if any of the other men in the vicinity were interested in paying more. Each of them shook their heads. They were fine to stare for nothing. Finally, the owner nodded. "Forty-five and not a shekel less."

The price was higher than anything Titius had ever paid for a slave. The owner counted the coins twice and held his bag up in victory for the applauding audience. Titius left the woman with the former owner and stopped at the market to purchase a simple brown tunic and leather sandals. He returned, draped her in the garment and then removed the shackles from her ankles.

Titius walked away quickly and she shuffled along behind, with her head down, as if still bound by the chains. Titius, at first, ignored the crude and suggestive calls of the men watching them leave, but the impact on the woman was clear.

Titius slowed to let her steps keep up. "What is your name?" he asked.

"I am Taphina," she said softly. "From Sparta. This is my first time as a slave. Thank you for the tunic."

"Why are you being sold?"

"My father died of the fever and my mother couldn't pay his debts. My brother sold me to Hedicles so the family could survive."

"Are you afraid of me?"

She looked into his eyes. "Should I be?"

Titius examined the face that reminded him so much of Abigail.

"I bought you to be a comfort for another man, to be one who could tame his spirit."

"I know little about comforting men," she said. "I assume that you will train me with what is necessary."

Titius took her aside to a tavern and arranged for a meal of chicken, egg, dates, and bread. She stuffed the food into her mouth with both hands and hardly paused to swallow. The more he watched her the more his insides twisted in a mix of compassion and anger. After her third glass of wine she prepared for her fate.

"I am ready," she said. "Please be gentle while I learn."

Titius took her arm and walked her outside. He continued in the drizzling rain down to the docks. He stopped by several vendors purchasing blankets, tunics and food items. She carried his purchases without question.

As Taphina stood in the shelter of a warehouse to escape the rain Titius negotiated with a sea captain. Money was exchanged. He motioned for her to come to him and she walked slowly in obedience. Once by his side Titius reached out and held both her wrists. "I have bought your freedom. You should not learn how to comfort a man from me. This ship will take you home to your mother."

Taphina stood, her mouth open. Titius nodded and turned away. "The captain has some money he will give you when the trip is finished. Do not compromise yourself for any man."

The last Titius saw of the Grecian goddess was her wave from the deck of the merchant vessel which was loaded with sugar and spices. For the first time in years his heart felt strangely warm. Caleb would have to get along without a woman, at least that woman.

"Another woman, same weakness," Cleopas interrupted his moment

of satisfaction. *"You know she doesn't stand a chance with that brother of hers. You should have kept her and satisfied yourself."*

"Sending her home to her mother was the noble thing to do," said Titius. "I already know which woman I am looking for."

"You'll never find her," said Cleopas.

"Hush yourself," Titius responded. "I have work to do."

With the woman gone, and Caleb safe, Titius revisited the vendors to see if new information circulated in the streets. His favorite method of intelligence gathering was to loiter in the vicinity of the vendors as they engaged in discussions with their customers. Toward evening he decided to be more proactive.

Dawn would bring his departure to Sepphoris. Time was short. Titius took on the role of a drunken sailor. His Gaelic blubber and staggered gait allowed others huddled around the small alley fires to dismiss him as no one of consequence. He listened in on conspiracies to short load a grain boat, to slice the throat of a signal man who had wooed away a girl and another to mutiny against an Egyptian captain. None of it mattered to him. At the sixth fire he stumbled and fell. The speakers turned, noticed him, then dismissed him as a drunk passed out.

"I tell ya," a voice urged. "The centurion and the Procurator are plotting to silence the zealots. And now they have a cross maker. We need to bury the lot."

"What are you thinking, Alexander?" another asked.

"I know someone at the stable," the first responded. "We will never get Pilate, but the centurion and cross maker are heading to Sepphoris tomorrow. We have marked horses and an ambush set up along the way." He looked around and stood to his feet. "We need to settle for what we can get."

As the quartet of conspirators kicked apart their fire, Titius slowly rolled out of sight and then dashed toward Pilate's courtyard. On the way he visited one of his secret stashes where he picked up a pack filled with fresh clothing, some figs, dates, and bits of cheese.

A new contingent of statue-like legionnaires guarded the entrance. Flickering torches cast soft kisses of light which caressed the death soldiers. Scarlet capes fluttered in a breeze and ostrich feathers on each leather helmet bristled lightly. Glistening shields provided a formidable wall against intruders.

"Titius Marcus Julianus," the disguised drunken sailor declared, "reporting to the Centurion, Sestus Aurelius."

The sentries remained anchored in place.

"I have news of a conspiracy," Titius said. "Send a messenger to wake the Centurion." He walked to a rain barrel and wiped the soot and dirt off of his face.

"He won't want to see you," Cleopas rumbled. *"You aren't as important as you think, you know."*

"I'm not trying to be important," said Titius, as he slurped up a handful of water. "At least I was important once upon a time."

"You could have been off enjoying that woman," said Cleopas. *"Instead, you're sitting in the cold like a forgotten slave. And believe me, I know what that feels like, in case you forget."*

"I choose to be here," Titius said. "I am not forgotten. Every moment is designed for learning something."

"I'm the one who taught you that," hissed Cleopas.

"Doesn't seem that you learned what you taught," said Titius.

When no one arrived in the next hour he shrugged off his rags and exchanged them for the robe he carried in his pack.

When the new watch of legionnaires stepped into place he was quickly noticed. A stable boy stumbled out of the shelter into the early morning drizzle. Titius called out, "Simeon, for the love of Jupiter, hear me boy."

Simeon wiped his eyes and stepped tentatively toward the line of sentries. Titius called again. "Wake Sestus, son. His life depends on it."

Ten minutes later, the centurion, in full battle gear, stepped forward and breeched the line of warriors which opened a way for him. "Speak," he commanded.

Titius, now dressed as a holy man, stepped forward. "Master, it is I."

Sestus nodded.

"Plans have been made to ambush you and the cross maker on your way to Sepphoris."

Sestus reached out and turned Titius away from the line of guardians. "How?" he asked.

Titius walked ahead another ten steps as Sestus followed. "The plan is to kill the men on the bay and the black. One of the stable hands is to make sure the two of you get those horses."

Sestus glanced back toward the stables. "I will care for the alley rat." He turned back and put his hand on Titius' shoulder. "You, find a horse, dress as you must, and go to the home of Barabbas. Find out all you can." He gave the shoulder a squeeze and backed away. "When you are done, meet us in Sepphoris. I need you to train the cross maker to protect himself and to fight for me."

"I am your servant," Titius declared. "If you command it, I will make it happen. If you ask it, I will tell you."

"Today, you are my servant," acknowledged Sestus. "One day

soon you will have your revenge on Cretius and restore your honor."

"You alone know this," Titius said.

Titius turned to go but Sestus called him one more time. "Titius, you leave your soul unguarded with me. Now guard your throat with Barabbas."

5
_____

Half a day into the journey from Caesarea toward the Jordan, Titius luxuriated in the magic of silence and stillness. He chose to walk instead of ride, avoided the main roads, taking winding pathways through the countryside. The blue sky held no hint of cloud and the breeze was like the slightest caress of a lover. Flocks of sheep and goats grazed together in the open country. Five shepherd's tents huddled near a small pond.

Wildflowers dotted the hilly landscape as far as the eye could see. The rise and fall of the landscape seemed endless and he began to doubt his direction.

Cleopas didn't help his sense of uncertainty. _"You're lost, aren't you?"_ said the phantom voice. _"You never were very good at knowing where you were."_

"I know where I am," Titius argued. "It's just that I'm not sure how far I still have to go. With all these trees there are no real landmarks to help."

"What are you going to do?" Cleopas probed.

Titius looked for higher elevation. He declined the limbs of a juniper and chose instead to scale the tallest of a tightly knit cluster of oaks.

As Titius rested on the higher limbs of the oak he caught his first glimpse of Megiddo in the distance. The Kishon River snaked its way just beyond. Mt. Tabor rose north and west. Mt. Gerizim reached up to the sky far to the south with the heights of Jerusalem even further. He opened his pack, searched for some food and sucked on fresh dates as he looked back at the vast expense of the Great Sea. A fleet of Roman warships escorted a flotilla of trading vessels on their way to Alexandria or points beyond.

Below him waved ripening fields of barley. Terraced fields of wheat showed the first sprouts of green already knee high. A small wall of stones divided fields. Three large groves of pine trees and another of pistachios looked like hopeful places for shelter if necessary. A river of white winged butterflies flowed through the landscape and disappeared into a gulley.

On a plain toward the south a small herd of antelope grazed. The buck held his head high, alert. The females became skittish and moved in behind him. Two fawns folded themselves down into the grass. Two of the does dashed away leaping and bounding in zig-zagging patterns. The buck lowered his long horns and waggled his head.

The flash was almost invisible as it slashed out of the taller grasses at the perimeter of the field. A cheetah– slender, sleek, spotted and swifter than most predators– dug in its claws and positioned its tail to by-pass the buck and chase down one of the females.

In seconds the cat was closing in on the two does running side by side. The two bounced sideways and split in opposite directions. The cheetah hesitated a moment and then spun right. The fugitive antelope sprang higher and wider back and forth trying to dodge the killer.

Within a minute the predator closed tight enough to swipe at the back legs of the runner. The antelope tumbled and rolled, legs thrashing but not contacting the ground. The cheetah stiffened its front legs hard and skidded to a halt. Before the doe recovered and dashed again, the cat was at her throat.

The buck whistled and the surviving doe and fawns hustled away from the scene. *"Looks like Rome and everyone else,"* Cleopas said. *"It's just a matter of time until it's your turn to die."*

Titius looked toward the Jordan. "Speak for yourself, slave. You're the one that's already had your turn."

It took another two hours to reach the furthest grove of pines. He easily avoided the shepherds along the way. His pride at proving that he knew where he was going blinded him to surprises and he almost walked into the pathway of two young boys out hunting rabbits with their slingshots. They already had two tied by the neck to their waist belts.

The path was spotted with the scat of lion, bear and wild donkeys. Deer were numerous. An uncomfortable perch on a limb of a tree at the highest point of ground only yielded him a glimpse of an ostrich running mindlessly with its black plumage spread out as if trying to fly. He looked toward the sky and spoke out loud, "if Cleopas is right and there is a creator for this world besides Jupiter then surely this one bird is evidence of a huge mistake."

He crossed the Jordan River at nightfall, praying in desperation. There was no script for this moment. "O Jupiter, Neptune, or whatever other gods will hear me, spare me from the crocodiles who live in these waters. Grant me safe passage and spare my life." There was no conclusion, just a statement of petition. He was used to the ritualistic prayers offered to the Roman gods but this time the desire to live put a new energy into his spontaneous utterance.

He stripped down, stuffing his traveling wear into his pack, and scouted out the best place for passage. He waded in from one sheltered bank and swam under the surface as far as he could, holding his pack out of the water. He surfaced twice on his way across, arrived without incident, then took time to regulate his breathing.

Despite his efforts, his pack was wet and he wrung out his clothing before donning the simple robe of a village priest. It made the climb into the branches of an olive a little more challenging but he secured himself in the crook of his sanctuary, ravaged the deep folds of his pack and nibbled on figs, cheese, and dried bread, before forcing himself to sleep in short naps.

Sestus had assigned him to infilitrate the zealot camp and his encounter with the rebels would happen soon. The only way to survive would be to pass himself off as a zealot. Barabbas would not be easily fooled. He was restless, eager to prove himself when his life was on the line.

At dawn, he changed into the garb of a zealot. He'd taken it from one of the group who had become too suspicious of the cross maker. It fit him loosely enough so he ripped off the bottom of the robe and put on the top half underneath. This increased the look of his bulk. He squared his shoulders and made his way toward the farm of Barabbas not far from the Yarmuk River.

Jaennus had forced him to review the map over and over until he could reproduce it from memory. Others had scouted and found the family farm. The Romans had already tried an unsuccessful raid. Suspicions would be high. "Only a great thespian can make this happen," Jaennus warned.

"That's not you," Cleopas said. The two voices fought in his mind before he even reached for his knife.

In a cluster of pistachios he hid his pack. Fire smoke arose from a small shed at the edge of the farm. A few handfuls of dust on his face and clothing finished his efforts. He pulled a knife from his pack and then stood to survey the best way forward.

A burning sear along the outside of his right shoulder caught him by surprise. An arrow slashed into the brush behind him. Titius ducked behind an apricot tree stump as another arrow thudded into the wood. He squirmed out of his zealot uniform and rolled it in the remains of his priest's robe. The wound was significant. He worked to staunch the flow of blood by wrapping his shoulder with a strip of cloth cut and ripped from his tunic. Shouts in Aramaic surrounded him until he raised an arm and shouted his surrender, also in Aramaic.

He stood and waited. Blood trickled down his right arm steadily, dripping down his wrist and off his fingertips. Two young warriors, their tunics tucked up short into their belts, stepped out of the scrub brush and another stepped out from the shed. They were ready for action. "On your knees," the man standing near the shed shouted.

Titius hesitated. The men were tentative, nervous as they moved toward him. One had a bow, two had knives. He watched their approach, watched how they handled their weapons.

"You could kill them easily," Cleopas coached.

"I need them to lead me to Barabbas," Titius whispered.

He anticipated the beating. Jaennus had trained him well in pain management. *"This time they'll knock out all your teeth,"* Cleopas sneered.

"At least I have some," Titius answered in his mind.

The three sentries were in their late teens, young men set to prove themselves. He held his arms to protect his head as they punched and kicked him into submission.

To manage the pain, Titius pictured his grandfather's return from Gaul, forcing the enemy general to kneel before the angry mobs of Roman citizens. The kicks and punches drained the life out of a once proud leader and even with his death, the anger of the people was not satiated. The participants turned on each other and only the harsh intrusion of the legionnaires returned the streets to peace and celebration. Only his father's vice grip on his shoulder ensured that Titius remained impassive despite his churning anger and horror.

When the youth spent their energy and the force of their blows stalled, Titius disciplined himself to focus again on their words. "Roman dog," "Galilean pig," "African snake," the trio yelled. They didn't seem to know what he was.

"You forgot 'friend of Barabbas'," Titius said.

The kicks and words stopped immediately. "You know Barabbas?"

Titius uncoiled himself and stiffly got to his knees. "I have been imprisoned by the Romans in Sepphoris. I escaped from a work crew only three days ago. I am so hungry for the taste of apricots."

Two of the youth grabbed him by the elbows and helped him to his feet. "You never gave the secret words."

Titius reviewed Jaennus' careful instruction. "The last zealot we tortured gave us the words 'the apricots are ripe'. There are probably new words now but you can use them to show at least some connection."

Titius bowed his head before his captors. "When I was last active we used 'the apricots are ripe'. I'm sure there are new words by now but I have been kept isolated by the Romans. I need protection before I'm caught again."

That they had beaten a friend of Barabbas seemed to energize their compassion. "Let me check that wound for you," the leader said, as he cut off the hem of his own tunic and tied it tightly in place."

The shortest of the three ran to the hut and returned with a gift. "Here's a handful of apricots to help you get some strength," he said.

The youngest took a step toward another trail. "I'm Philip. I'll lead you to the camp so you can get the help you need. They'll make sure you're safe."

Titius nodded and followed.

The shrub forest was high enough to block any visible landmarks. The steep climb up to a tableland and down again revealed the continued presence of the Jordan valley as they moved south. In a forested ravine Titius followed his guide into a clearing where three small mud shelters huddled. The hills around rose up like protective parents around a sleeping child.

Titius scanned the setting. His training picked up the details. Two men knelt sharpening swords while eight women sat weaving baskets. Two other women breastfed babes and shouted instructions to three toddlers picking flowers at the edge of the clearing. Dozens of chickens pecked at the ground and ignored the newcomers. Song birds fluttered and sang like this was the first Eden. Green grasses grew knee high in the shaded areas and rich red soil formed a diamond shaped patch in the middle of the compound.

Four young women stood up and met Titius at the perimeter. A tall brunette with almond eyes took the lead. "Philip, who have you brought us?"

"A friend of Barabbas heading for the southern camp," Philip answered. "He is yearning for apricots but he needs healing."

She nodded toward a stump sitting in a patch of sunlight. "Sit there," she said. "I'm Cassandra."

Titius followed. "I'm David. Thank you for your help."

The brunette tended to his wounds with a simple herbal ointment and a strip of torn cloth. She didn't say a word before handing him over to two others for the night. By nightfall Titius was asleep on a mat in the corner of a zealot shelter.

It was a pigeon that alerted him to the arrival of a new day.

6

The pigeon's feet clicked against the stone shelf as it arrived at a feeding dish. Its call was loud in the stillness. The first trickles of morning light crept through a blanket hung over the window in the hut. A single lamp perched on a table flickered dimly. A tiny smokey spiral twisted up into the darkness.

Titius watched one of the women rise from across the room. Her long braided hair reached almost to her waist. "Miriam, the message from Barabbas has arrived," she whispered to another. "The bird is here. Watch the man."

The woman secured an outer wrap around herself and slipped out a side door. Drifting smoke from the lamp blurred the other scents in the room. The other woman left behind propped herself up on an elbow and looked in his direction. Satisfied, she lowered her head to her mat.

The room was generously equipped with weapons along the wall: spears, swords and clubs. Sets of grappling hooks rested on pegs driven into a wall stacked high with crates. The smell of strong goat cheese and apricots mixed with the musty odors arising from the orderly stash of supplies. A faint perfume like the wild roses in his mother's garden in Rome drifted on the still air.

The soft coaxing voice of the woman outside filtered into the room. "Come here, pigeon. Now hold still." She apparently succeeded in her task of relieving the bird of the message. Once back inside she came straight to Titius. She nudged him with her foot. Titius feigned awakening. The rose smell was strong. Thoughts of Abigail fought for his attention.

The woman across the room sat upright. "Sarah, what are you doing?"

"Show me your neck," Sarah demanded to Titius.

Titius slowly rose to a kneeling position. He was shirtless apart from the wrapping around his wound, spotted crimson. Sarah ran her hands needlessly across his muscular back and shoulder before tracing her finger along the faint scar made by Sestus. "Barabbas says to check your neck." She bent closer than she needed to. "You definitely have a scar."

"You should wait until Benomi returns," Miriam urged. "How do we know what Barabbas means?"

Sarah cupped Titius' chin in her hand and tilted his head up. She ran her fingers slowly through his beard and under his chin. "Look at me! Are you truly a friend of Barabbas or just another spy we have to butcher and feed to the dogs?"

Titius stared calmly straight into her eyes until she finally released him with a laugh. "Miriam, he has the eyes of a child."

Sarah backed away and moved to a small table where food was being laid out. She twisted her braid up onto the top of her head and fastened it with a headband. "Who is the woman in your life?" she asked as Titius rose to his feet.

Titius watched Sarah tie off her shawl at the shoulder. "I have no woman," he responded. "My loyalty is to one man."

Sarah scooped up a wooden bowl and filled it with pistachio nuts, apricots, and cheese. "You are a man," she cooed. "Surely you have known love." She walked slowly toward Titius eyes on him all the way. "Do you look on me then as someone who can feed your stomach or as someone who can feed your passions?" She handed him the bowl with one hand and lay the other hand on his chest.

Titius glanced at Miriam and saw the scowl in response to Sarah's flirtation. He looked straight into the dark brown eyes looking up at him. "You are no doubt the beautiful, favored wife of someone very close to Barabbas. I would be a fool to mistake your actions for any invitation that would not see me end up with the dogs."

The girl smiled coyly, removed her hand, and stepped away. "I see you know Barabbas well. Even now we are being watched. If you moved a hand toward me that scar on your neck would be removed along with the rest of your head." She waved her hand above her.

From behind a crate in the corner rose one of the two men who had been sharpening his sword earlier. This time, he held a dagger in his hand. He stepped out from his cover and moved toward Titius. He grabbed an apricot from the dish which Titius still held. "Eat quickly. We will be travelling soon."

Miriam stepped up and held out a long robe and a shepherd's staff. "Put these on," she said. "You will travel with the shepherds to our southern farm in the decapolis."

"Is there a head covering?" Titius asked.

"You should have brought your own," Miriam replied. "Do you really expect us to believe you came here without any proper clothing? Certus and Mathias will certainly find out who you are."

"I have nothing to hide," Titius said.

Miriam threw the robe at his feet. "It's obvious you have nothing to hide. You had Sarah drooling all over you. Cover up. She's promised to a cousin of Barabbas."

A pair of horses were harnessed together and a large box was laid across the blankets and boards sitting on their backs. A young boy was hoisted up to sit on the wooden crate and to guide the horses. "Did someone die?" Titius whispered to Miriam. "It looks like a coffin."

"Just make sure it isn't yours," Miriam said. "Look, the shepherds are here. Their dogs will want to test your scent. I hope you're not afraid of dogs."

Titius walked for an hour with a group of shepherds. He found himself fascinated by a herd of Oryx foraging at a small oasis. The antelope's white bodies and black leggings set them apart but the incredible feature were the two straight long horns rising like spears from their skull caps. When the animals stood sideways they appeared to match the description of the mythical one-horned flying horses which Cleopas had told him about as a child.

"Those animals are sacred to us," Hosea, one of his elderly shepherd guides, explained. "Look over there by those acacia thorn trees. There are desert deer eating the fruit and right behind them there is the addax. They appear at first like large cows with long twisted ram's horns. They are sacred, too."

Titius examined the animals who rested in the shade of the few scattered trees. "It all seems so peaceful and quiet here."

Hosea released a rumble of joy with a belly laugh. "The zealot who cuts throats for a living never finds peace anywhere," he said. "Of course, you would know that. Tell me of your sacrifices for the cause."

Titius watched a wolf skulking along the edge of a bluff as it hunted the passing sheep. The five dogs barked their warnings and rushed to stand between the predator and the flock. The shepherds ignored the side show and kept plodding.

Titius used the moment to change the subject. "Hosea, do you actually have to face down many predators out here?"

Hosea replied. "I will answer you briefly, but only so you can continue to tell me your story. It is not the animal predator you need to worry about in this area."

"What do you mean?"

"Bedouin raiders may be ahead. You will fight for us. I will not be denied the entertainment you will provide for our journey. The wolf will not care whether he feasts on sheep or shepherd. "

"What will I fight with?" Titius asked.

"That is none of my concern," the shepherd replied. Their pace quickened. "Tell me a story of your conquest." The salt and pepper beard hanging to the chest of the old shepherd seemed like a sail catching a wind. His sandaled feet stepped with confidence around each rock, over each dip, and up each incline. His weathered hand gripped his staff and probed the firmness of the footing just ahead.

Titius worked to keep up. "My stories will be stories which your great grandchildren will tell to their great grandchildren," Titius said.

Hosea stopped and Titius with him. He stared across the Jordan. "Tell me what you know about the new Messiah. We hear that he has come to take our land from the Romans and to finish our peace."

Titius stared hard. What had the man heard? Where was Cleopas when he was needed? No voice spoke so he let the words flow as they came. "By his hand or ours, we need deliverance. Many Messiahs have arisen without success. It is time which will tell us whether the claims he makes are true."

Hosea began to walk again. "So, you have met him? You have heard the words of Yeshua ben Yuseph? You have seen his magic?"

Titius fell in behind the shepherd as the trail narrowed. "I have only heard of him. I was imprisoned while the Romans tried to find charges against me."

Hosea nodded and continued. "Yes. Now tell me how you have created stories for my grandchildren and yet acted so no Roman can prove you have done anything?"

Titius racked his mind for every story Jaennus told him had been stripped from the soul of tortured zealots. He let his mouth get started as his memory caught up. "Most of my feats were accomplished in Alexandria and Libya. Perhaps you have heard of 'the desert fox'."

Hosea cleared a branch off the path with his staff. "Yes, he is well known. Barabbas says he may be the true father of the Sicarii – those of us who cut the necks of these Jews who dare to cooperate with Rome. How do you know this desert fox?"

Titius sensed the intensity in the question and eliminated the plan to pass himself off as 'the desert fox'. The old shepherd might even know the 'desert fox' personally. The noonday sun seemed hotter today. He lifted his gourd and swallowed the last of his water. "The fox was my teacher. There were four of us he trusted in his inner circle. He often sent us in his place for different attacks to make it appear that he was everywhere at once."

Hosea stopped and pointed at an outcropping of rocks near some scrub trees. "There, see? That is the true fox. That fennec fox has ears like a bat. IIe is absorbing every word you say. His golden brown fur blends in with the shadows of those stones." The shepherd used his cane to point a little further along the pile. "Near him are the rock hyrax. You can hear them chattering, warning the other life around us."

The voice of Cleopas chose this moment to reappear. *"You arrogant fool. He knows you're lying. For all you know, this is 'the desert fox' himself. They're leading you into a trap."*

7

When the sun reached its apex, the shepherds turned and scaled a small hill. "Have you been up here before?" Hosea asked.

Titius scanned the landmarks. "No."

Hosea pointed. "Toward the great sea, across the Jordan, is Beth-Shean." He pointed north. "Damascus is there, and Canatha as well." He pointed east. "On this side of the Jordan there's Gerasa, Gadara, Pella, Philadelphia, Capitolias, Raphana. Every king in his own empire despising and embracing all things Greek, Roman, and Hebrew. We live as chameleons among them."

Hosea led the way down confidently. He untied another gourd of water from his pack and handed it to Titius. "Drink a little," he said.

Titius took a sip and handed it back. The dogs rallied the sheep, bleating, barking and shouting blending together. "How long have you been with Barabbas?" Titius asked.

Hosea grabbed Titius' arm. "If you know Barabbas, as you claim, then you know: don't ask questions." He walked on.

Titius slowed his pace. A shepherd boy fell into step with him. The lad came to Titius' shoulder and wore a small striped cap. His stride was as steady as Hosea's. "I heard you question the master," he said. "I've only learned by listening to stories around the fires."

"What's your name?"

"You still ask questions?" Then he smiled. "Jonathan. I'm Jonathan."

"I'm David," Titius said. "The Hebrews have a story: a king's son named Jonathan once befriended a future king named David. It's an omen for us."

"I don't believe in omens." Jonathan pointed across the Jordan. "See the vultures circling near Beth-Shean? Some would call them omens. More likely a wolf has killed a sheep. Or a sicarii has cut someone's throat. Someone helping a Roman."

The dogs began to bark furiously. The shepherds raced toward the team of horses. The boy stepped off the box and onto the horses. Two shepherds ripped off the crate lid and began to hand out spears, swords, and daggers. There was a bow with arrows, which Hosea grabbed.

Hosea nodded at Titius. "Choose your weapon. You'll lead us. If you fought with Barabbas, now is your chance to prove it." Titius chose two long-bladed spears.

From a copse next to a river bed, six Bedouin horsemen charged, carrying curved Arab swords.

Titius rushed forward toward a small hill. "On your stomachs, side by side!" he yelled. "Plant the spear butts and point them toward the horses' hearts! Form a wedge beside me!" Several of the young shepherds threw themselves on their bellies beside him and raised their spears.

"Secure those spears in the ground," Titius said. "Like this!" He showed them how to brace a spear in a divot of earth.

Hosea began to shoot. The leading Bedouin fell from his horse. The others spread out to form a wall of thunder pounding down on the shepherds.

Cleopas' voice shrilled in terror. *"You fool, they'll trample us. Remember the Roman horses?"*

From his right hand, Titius hurled a spear into the chest of the closest horse. It reared and threw its rider. Collapsing, it drove the spear in further and rolled over, thrashing. One hoof caught its rider across the knee and he went down screaming.

The next Bedouins veered to avoid the shepherds' spears. Another one fell prey to one of Hosea's arrows. The last attackers hurtled to a stop.

The first fallen rider got to his feet and charged at Jonathan. Titius took five quick strides, lunged with his second spear and left the attacker writhing. Jonathan finished him off with a dagger to the throat.

Another shepherd felled the Bedouin who'd been shot with an arrow. Several dogs rushed in and ensured his demise. The surviving Bedouins retreated.

The shepherds closed ranks. Their attackers left to chase after the riderless horses now running off into the dry river bed.

"What do we do with the bodies?" Titius asked Hosea.

Hosea kicked the three prone Bedouins, felt for breath and stood up. "Leave them. They won't leave their own for long. Wolves or hyenas will come soon."

A bleating from behind. Titius spun toward Hosea. With one hand he grabbed the bow and with the other an arrow. He planted himself and shot toward the brush.

"What are you doing?" Jonathan demanded. He scanned the bushes. "Are they back?"

Titius started walking. "Look."

At the edge of the brush a wolf held a lamb firmly in its jaws. The lamb squirmed but the wolf was still, an arrow through its heart. Jonathan raced over and freed the bloodied lamb.

Hosea took his bow back. "Barabbas will be pleased you're back with us," he said.

Titius followed the shepherds through wadi after wadi. They traversed small stretches of desert and rested in scattered oases where sheep and shepherd alike could drink. At the third oasis Jonathan sat down next to Titius.

"I will answer your question," Jonathan said. "Hosea has known Barabbas from before he was called Barabbas. This name, meaning 'son of the Father', is because his father was honored among our people. You saw the farm, where we met you?"

Titius saw Hosea bantering with two other shepherds. "I saw the remains of a farm. Burned, and the orchard cut down."

Jonathan scooped up water with his gourd. "It's where my father died, fighting Romans. I used to eat apricots there when I was small. The Legate sent spies, disguised as harvesters, to infiltrate us."

"Did you eliminate them with a dagger stroke?"

"No." Jonathan shuddered, shaking his head. "They brought in a legion. Destroyed our families. Barabbas was a youth. He was out with the sheep and saw the smoke rising." Jonathan stood. "He found them all with their throats cut. Now he cuts the throats of all who help Rome. Rome showed no mercy so we show Rome no mercy."

8

Delayed by the Bedouin attack, they were still on the trail when the sun hid behind the horizon. A quarter moon cast a dim light. They corralled the sheep and lit small fires on their camp's outskirts. A dog and a shepherd rested by each fire.

Hosea motioned for Titius to join him. They walked slowly. As they moved past the tree line, no landmarks tracked the journey. The occasional crashing in the bush on either side sent shivers up Titius' spine. Hosea pressed on as if it were noon.

An owl's screech stopped Hosea in his tracks. "We're not alone," he said. He cupped his hands around his mouth, repeated the screech and waited. Within moments two sentries stepped onto the path and unveiled a small clay lamp. After speaking with Hosea, they lit torches for the newcomers before returning to their posts.

"The camp survives by silence," said Hosea. "When we reach the gate, don't say a word. Sleep where they tell you. We'll speak with others in the morning."

Titius followed Hosea past the sentry, through the gate and into the sleeping enclosure. Two burly men thrust torches near his face. Someone else tied his arms behind. "Roman pig!" the zealot muttered. "You look like one and you smell like one."

"I just came for the apricots," Titius said in Aramaic. The punch to his jaw made him wish he'd heeded Hosea and stayed silent.

They escorted Titius across a small courtyard to a shed. The door was open. They threw him inside, still tied. The smell of goat dung was strong; the ground seemed thick with it. He maneuvered himself into a sitting position against a wall. Hours later someone finally arrived: Jonathan.

He flung the door wide. He carried a torch. "David, they don't seem to know you here. I told them how you rescued us, so they say I can release you as long as you stay with me until morning." He backed away, covering his nose. "Can you step out? That's the dung shed!"

Titius braced himself against the wall and struggled to his feet. "I need to wash," he said.

Jonathan led him to a small barrel of water. He cut Titius' hands free and handed him a rag and a fresh tunic. "The women will be arriving soon. Wash and I'll meet you here later."

Hosea met Titius as the sun rose. Despite the wash and the new tunic, Titius still smelled of goat dung. "I see you survived the night," Hosea remarked. "You should find a better place to sleep."

Titius grit his teeth. "I'm hungry," he said.

"The women will be here soon," Hosea replied. "I'm going back for the sheep. They don't trust you. Jonathan will be responsible for you."

After a breakfast of flatbread, goat cheese, almonds, and dates, Jonathan led Titius past the gate and up a small nearby hill. Desert stretched to the southeast, the Jordan valley lay west, and to the south the low-lying scrubland toward the sea.

Titius and Jonathan sat watching the clouds play overhead. Titius saw them form a dragon.

His father had told Titius once about meeting a dragon. "During my campaign in Gaul," he'd whispered. "It was twice as tall as my tallest warrior."

Titius had been ready for bed, lamp-shadow wavering across the wall.

"My men outflanked the dragon and hurled their javelins. The weapons bounced off its hide."

"Did it eat you, Father?" Titius had asked.

His father had crouched low and moved toward him. "Only the Optio and I dared track it. We found it sleeping in a cave. I hurled my javelin into its belly and its tail almost took off my head. I dropped my lamp and there was nothing but darkness. I lay still and it disappeared into the inner darkness. It took us all day to find our way out of that cave."

"What makes you smile?" Jonathan's voice broke through the memory.

Titius glanced back at the clouds. "Memories of home," he said. The dragon cloud floated past.

Jonathan's nudge returned him to the present. He was pointing to a mount where Herod had built the Machaerus prison. "Many zealots die in that prison. Barabbas comes here often when he's home. If he lives, he'll either die in prison or rule in Jerusalem. He carries a heavy burden."

Titius looked toward Jerusalem. "I've proven myself. Let me talk with him."

Jonathan scanned the apricot orchard below. "Barabbas and the Sicarii leaders are with the Parthians trying to open a route for more weapons. No one here knows what to do with you."

Titius gazed down and tried to memorize the zealot settlement's layout. "The Romans send new reinforcements every month. Why does Barabbas keep going?"

Jonathan frowned. "If you know Barabbas, you know his

grandfather was in the battle for Sepphoris. They stole the Roman armoury. Caused great losses." Titius nodded.

"It took years, but the Romans tracked down some of the leaders and sent spies. Barabbas' father cared for his people with the money from his apricot orchard. Most people on this side of the Jordan have worked for him." Jonathan heaved a stone over a ledge. "He kept these people alive in the drought. When the Romans invaded Galilee he helped many refugees. He opened up trade routes with the Parthians for everything we wanted."

Titius pulled at a piece of grass and chewed on it. "So Barabbas' father died fighting for his people?"

Jonathan threw a rock at a chicken down the hill. He missed. "No. He taught people how to dry apricots for times of hunger. He was a man of peace."

"Then why did the Romans kill him?"

Jonathan shook his head slowly. "A Roman legion looking for Parthians stopped at his farm. They began to take bushels of apricots, more than they needed. Some people protested. The Romans killed them. They killed the witnesses and burned the buildings and chopped down the orchard. Barabbas' father was on his knees pleading when they speared him with a javelin."

"But why does Barabbas cut Galilean throats?"

"He hid in the trees and saw everything. The Romans slit his father's throat. Now Barabbas tries to do the same to anyone who helps the Romans."

"What can I do to help until Barabbas comes back?"

"The elders have decided while we were gone. Do you see the smoke rising near the well? They're calling us to come back." Jonathan started down the hill.

When they returned four old men sat at the gate. The bowl of ripe apricots in front of them contrasted with their emaciated frames. Their spokesmen looked hardly strong enough to lift the sword he held. "Kneel and bare your neck," he commanded. Titius complied.

The old man ran his finger along Titius' scar. "It is neither recent nor old," he pronounced. "We do not believe you are who you claim." He laid the edge of the sword on Titius' neck.

Titius didn't move.

The sword shifted. The cool blade angled against his throat. One quick movement would finish it all. His hands trembled until he clenched them into stillness. No prayer arose.

"No god can save you now," Cleopas whispered. *"Let them finish it quickly."*

Titius focused on the steel under his chin. The decision had already been made. He could only wait.

"We don't know who you are but you've shown yourself willing to protect us and our flocks," the elder said. He removed the sword. Titius inhaled. "We're charging you with protecting our women and children until Barabbas returns. Your betrayal is your death."

9

Titius sat by the well watching a heron overhead. He was dressed for action now, in a chiton hitched up to his knees. His belt held a razor-sharp dagger. His javelin and a sword rested against the base of the well.

A young woman stepped out of a small shelter. Her uncovered hair glistened like flax in the morning sun. Her long chiton gleamed white, draped with a thick blue cloak, a himation. She could have passed for a Roman noblewoman.

She marched toward him, eyeing him up and down. "So, you're my new guardian," she said. "I'm Phoebe, Barabbas' sister. Your life is now in my hands and mine in yours. My mother needs water." She pointed at a bucket. "Bring it and we'll talk."

"I'm David," Titius said.

"It doesn't matter who you say you are," Phoebe responded. "Bring the water." She spun on her heel and walked back through the door she'd come from.

Titius drew the water then knocked firmly on her door and waited. An elderly woman, frowning at the sun, opened the door and stood aside. She wore her himation pulled over her head and across her neck. "I'm Elizabeth, mother of Barabbas, Phoebe, and two others who are no more."

"And I'm David," Titius said. "Without father, without mother, without anyone to call family."

Elizabeth motioned him inside. "Leave the water by the door. We have porridge, bread and fruit. There are no servants here." She pointed to a basin inside the door. "Pour your own water. Wash your own feet."

Titius set down the bucket of water he had carried from the well and stood still. Elizabeth waited a moment, then picked it up, poured a little into the basin, and moved it to an inner room. Titius doffed his sandals, stepped into the basin, and scrubbed off the dirt.

Phoebe appeared without her blue himation, her hair secured by a crimson band. Titius found himself staring. Then she looked his way. His pulse quickened; he fought to control his breathing. She motioned for him to sit on a stool near a small table.

Elizabeth returned with flaxseed porridge. Phoebe retreived a platter of dried fruits and cheese. "Eat quickly. Today, the shepherds are away and we must go to the pool and bathe. You'll learn to guard without seeing or your eyes will be a delicacy for our dogs."

Not a skill he'd been taught, but clearly another test. Did they never finish testing?

Titius tested a spoonful of the porridge. It had an unfamiliar flavor. "If I'm to guard you I must guard my own life," he said. "Until I'm sure this is safe I cannot eat it."

Phoebe pointed her finger into his face. "How dare you malign my mother's hospitality? Eat what you're given."

Titius stood. "Though your brother himself offered me this porridge, I couldn't eat it without knowing it was safe."

"Suit yourself," Phoebe said. "Don't complain of hunger. Come, we must bathe quickly."

"*She should have killed you,*" Cleopas muttered. "*It seems you're charmed.*"

The pool was a large spring at the base of a hill, surrounded by trees. Titius checked a cavern near the spring and assured the women that all was clear. Seven women of various ages had come to bathe. Titius stood with his back to them several hundred paces from the pool. He tried to ignore the laughter and splashing. He especially tried to ignore the crude comments Phoebe threw in his direction. Even now she dared him to turn and die.

He occupied his mind remembering the Roman baths by his villa. Naked men and women strutted freely as they dipped in the frigidarium, tepidarium, and hot springs before enjoying a massage. The preoccupation with modesty in this land didn't make sense, but testing it was not worth his life.

"You can look now," came Phoebe's voice. "We're decent."

Fearing another test, Titius refused to turn. "Follow me home," he said.

Several hundred paces on, Phoebe grabbed his arm. "Wait! My mother can't walk this fast."

Her touch on his arm sent fire racing through him. He waited for her to walk in front of him. She wore a clingy white chiton. Her hair hung loose and dripping. Titius looked away.

"You've saved your eyes," she said. "Now keep us safe. It isn't just shepherds, Bedouins, and Romans we fear. It's snakes, lions, and wolves. If you can't look *at* me, at least look out *for* me."

Titius kept his eyes on the trail, glancing back every few minutes to track their progress. Phoebe stayed with him. "I was told to guard the women and children," he said. "I see women, but no children."

"They'll be brought once we know you're safe," she said. "Nothing is more valuable than our children."

"Too bad things weren't like that in Rome," Cleopas taunted.

A knot twisted in Titius' stomach. He'd always been surrounded by adults and slaves. The few begger children he'd seen by the market were routinely beaten. Boys and girls lived at the temples only to pleasure worshippers. No children laughed and played in the gardens.

"What happened to the children?" Titius asked.

"I told you," Phoebe said. "Don't you listen? You're like all the other men."

There were no significant incidents on the way back. Titius wandered around the compound's perimeter as the women ground grain, made bread, washed clothes, swept their homes, hauled water, and chatted and laughed together.

At noon harvesters arrived with baskets of apricots. Titius guarded the women; none of the workers gave them trouble. One behemoth who got close to Phoebe backed off quickly when Titius raised a dagger to his throat.

The women fed the crew, sent them back on their way, then processed the harvest. Some fruit was set aside for eating, some to trade, some for drying.

Phoebe stood in the courtyard, her hair braided back, managing and instructing the women. As she issued orders, not once did she stop pitting apricots. "Dorcas, put these in those baskets. Eleah, crush these apricots for supper. Lydia, bring me another load and take away these pits."

Toward late afternoon she passed him. "I think I could use another trip to the pool," she said with a smile.

Heat ran up his neck. Titius extinguished the image rising in his mind.

"Oh, you're a man," she said. "You see a woman and can think of only one thing. How did you survive guarding us at the pool?"

"I'm just a man," he said.

"You're a wise man who remains alive. For now. Next, you'll teach our young men to fight. They'll be here tomorrow." She looked over her shoulder at him. "The porridge was poisoned."

10

Three weeks into combat training, Titius had taught what skills he was willing to share with his recruits. Sestus and the assassins might soon be on the other side of the battlefield and he'd be expected back in Sepphoris soon.

Even more than the training, he enjoyed the philosophical and religious debates with the young men. They would often gather round a fire and argue until they dropped off to sleep.

Jeremiah was the tallest, with tight dark braids and an early beard. Amnon was short, muscular, and went barefoot every chance he got. Simon was the swiftest but Issachar the smartest. He could quote the Torah verbatim, recall every detail of any place he'd been, and would often be the first to find a solution to a military problem.

Timna was the best archer; Magdiel the shepherd could knock an apricot off a tree with a slingshot; Iram could track and hunt almost anything; Shaul could anticipate the weather; Ethan could outdo anyone in storytelling. All loved to debate.

Issachar pointed toward the town of Gadara. "These heathens copy Rome and Greece. They claim we're barbarians because we're circumcised. Before we cut Roman throats we should cut pagan ones."

Titius shifted uncomfortably. "We're guests in their land," he said. "When you have power you can consider your options. They live as their gods demand."

"Jupiter is the same as Yahveh is the same as Baal is the same as Molech?" Timna said to spark argument.

"Romans are descended from pigs," Shaul declared. "Their leaders are cowards. They hide behind their legions. The generals rape, steal, and destroy everything they touch. Isn't it true, David?"

"David, is it true?" Ethan said.

Titius shifted the scarf round his neck. "I can only tell you what I've heard," he said. "Romans train their legionnaires harder than we've ever trained."

"Not true," Magdiel interrupted. "I can hardly feel my body at the end of the day."

Titius waited for the laughter to finish. "A legionnaire can carry almost half his own weight in his pack: tools, weapons, food, and trowel. Every day they march twenty miles, then build a new camp before nightfall. The rule of decimation means they'll never back away from death."

"What's 'decimation'?" Issachar asked.

Titius stirred the embers. "At the end of each battle, legions are judged. If any legion hasn't done its best, the men are divided into groups of ten." He gathered sticks, then moved around the circle, letting each recruit choose one. He sat. "Each member of the group draws sticks. The one who loses is clubbed to death by the others: decimation. Every tenth man is killed. They'd rather be killed by an enemy than by their own."

"How can we fight against beasts like that?" Amnon asked.

"In a new way," said Titius.

Iram raised the bow he'd been stringing. "They'll always need archers."

"Maybe so," replied Titius. "Let's clean up and secure for the night. Set your guards."

The young men spread their blankets around the firepit and secured their weapons near their beds. A jackal barked and crickets chirped. Clouds obscured the moon. The flames died down to embers.

"David, tell us about the senators," Ethan said. "To help us sleep."

"By the will of the gods," Titius said. "Rome may destroy herself before her enemies do." He laid a log on the embers. "Generals strive for their own glory and power, the senators conspire and plot against each other, and the Emperors survive by being suspicious of those closest to them."

"It sounds," Shaul mused, "like the best way to defeat the Romans is to let them destroy themselves." They all cheered at that.

"But," Titius went on, "there's great discipline among the troops. Four thousand eight hundred troops in a legion, ten cohorts of four hundred eighty. Six centuries, each overseeing eighty soldiers, ten groups of eight."

"How do you know these things?" Magdiel asked.

"It's my job to know everything," Titius said. "Get some sleep. We'll talk tomorrow."

"Tell us about the chariot races," Ethan called. "And gladiators. Who's the greatest warrior?"

"Tomorrow, I'll tell you about the glory of Rome," Titius said. "To face your enemy, you must know your enemy better than he knows you. Until then, embrace glory in your dreams."

The next day's march passed without incident, the men begging him for details about life in Rome. Two days passed before he settled in back at the camp. His stomach rumbled as he sat with his back against the wall at Phoebe's house.

"David," she called from within. "Who impressed you the most in this group of recruits?"

"Each has his own strength," Titius responded.

Phoebe emerged holding a bowl of steaming stew out to Titius. "It's goat and it isn't poisoned," she said. "I'll taste it if you want."

"You trust me, so I trust you," Titius said.

"Barabbas will be pleased with you, David."

Cleopas whispered: "*One day you'll slip up. They'll find out who you are.*"

As Titius fulfilled his duties it seemed to him that Phoebe went out of her way to appear where he was, needing his help. In bed at night he thought: although she was self-sufficient and independent, Phoebe insisted he go with her on her morning walk. She would prolong their time away identifying songbirds as the sun climbed the heavens. She mesmerized him with her knowledge of kingfishers, bee-eaters, flycatchers, warblers.

One morning a pair of swans flew onto a pond nearby. Phoebe grabbed Titius by the arm. "This is the best day of my life," she declared.

"This day is as lovely as you are," Titius responded.

"Whether you're David or someone else," Phoebe said, "I almost don't care anymore."

"What do I still need to prove?" he asked.

"Tell me truthfully about who your parents were," she said.

"My father was a Roman soldier and a businessman. My mother was Jewish," he answered.

"Why are you here?" she asked.

"Right now I'm here because of you," he said.

Phoebe twirled in circles, her arms spread like wings. "This is the best day of my life," she said again.

"Someone knows something," Cleopas growled. *"Watch out."*

His fear of discovery grew next evening by the fire. Ethan began a story about a crazy relative of his who lived among the tombs nearby. "This man is not normal. He lives among the pig farmers." He began to act out his story, as Titius had done for Sestus months ago. "He cuts himself and screams among the tombs. My cousins have chained him and he breaks free as if the chains were string. It's rumored he's possessed by a thousand demons. We should get *him* to lead us against the Romans. He could defeat them all by himself."

Issachar and Amnon stood. "David, take us to this man. Persuade him to fight the Romans."

Inside Titius's head, Cleopas screamed: *"Don't! I won't be able to control the others."*

"What others?" Titius thought.

"David?" Shaul said, "Did you hear us? Will you take us to see the demoniac?"

"Taking you on this mission may have to be cleared by Barabbas himself," he said. "Tonight we must learn to navigate by the stars."

They were silent as Titius pointed out the star markers and marched his charges home.

Back at camp, the young men went back to their jobs as harvesters and shepherds. Titius was left to guard the women and listen to old men's stories.

Phoebe's young cousin Tamaris talked to him a little more each day. "Tell me, David," she asked one morning. "Which woman are you most likely to wed?"

Titius smiled. "Perhaps Barabbas will decide," he said.

"I see how Phoebe looks at you," said Tamaris. "Always trying to be near you. Surely you notice."

That afternoon Titius guarded the women at the pool. He stood in his usual spot and listened to the laughter behind him. He tried to think of Abigail back in Rome, but her face was fading. Phoebe's face often surfaced in her place. Once again, on the way back to camp, Phoebe walked beside him.

The next day Titius found Tamaris beside the gate sobbing alone. "What's the trouble?" he asked.

She kept sobbing until Phoebe arrived and shooed him away. "She's become a woman and doesn't understand her body," Phoebe said. "She needs to be alone."

Titius remembered a young slave girl with Abigail. He had ordered the girl: "Get me water."

The girl had knelt and whimpered. Titius went to strike her but Abigail had stepped in. "She's now a woman. Let her be. I'll get your water." It was years before Titius had understood the monthly suffering all women endured.

"David," Phoebe said, calling him back to the present, "she will find her peace. We all survive this ordeal. Come, walk with me."

Titius followed Phoebe into the orchard. "You see this fruit?" Phoebe asked. "We grow it for Barabbas. He eats it every day in memory of his father." She picked a ripe fruit and handed it to Titius. "We're all the family he has. To provide this fruit is our part in freeing our land."

"A leader like Barabbas only survives because of your loyalty."

Phoebe smiled her golden smile. The sunshine lit her hair like a halo. "Some of our best are already serving in places like Sepphoris, Ceasarea, and Jerusalem. The weaver and his daughter in Sepphoris are especially good at infiltrating the Romans and opening the silk trade."

"What more can I do?" Titius asked. *Am I being asked to be a spy for Barabbas? Is Phoebe trying to set up another test for me?*

Phoebe backed up against a tree. Looking shyly at Titius, she said, "Barabbas is the man in my family who will arrange my marriage, but he's away more than here. I need a man. I want you to talk with him."

Was she asking him to contact Barabbas so that a marriage could be arranged? There hadn't been any men around. Who was she planning to marry?

"What do you want me to say?" he asked.

Phoebe searched his face again. "David, tell him you want to be that man."

Titius' jaw dropped open. "Me?" He crushed the apricot; juice ran on to his closed fist. "How will I speak with him? You hardly know me."

Phoebe stepped toward Titius. "David, you took a Roman knife to your throat. You fought the Bedouins. You saved our sheep from the wolf. You guard us while we bathe. You train our new fighters." She reached for his hand. "I don't need to know any more than that."

Cleopas accused: *"What have you done?"*

Titius knelt, looking up at Phoebe. "You honor me more than I deserve," he said. "Where will I find your brother?"

Phoebe put her hands on Titius' shoulders. "You don't have to find him. He'll find you."

11

Titius didn't sleep that night and not just because Cleopas hounded him. What should he do about Phoebe? What would the Romans do if their thespian assassin married a zealot, and Barabbas's sister? What would it mean to have children related to Barabbas?"

If he married Phoebe and moved up in the hierarchy, he could send messages to Jaennus and limit Barabbas' effectiveness. If he married and stayed, he could bring in others to set up the network. People would trust him.

On the other hand, if he married Phoebe he'd be under Barrabas' scrutiny all the more. His disguise might not hold up to serious questioning. His death wouldn't help Sestus. It wouldn't help get his estate back. It definitely wouldn't help him stay unknown. Worst, it would mean giving up on Abigail.

He cherished the admiration "David" had earned in this community. Mentoring young warriors affirmed his sense of manhood. Phoebe's trust and compionship, and the other women's had strengthened that sense even more.

When it involved the death of passionate zealots, so much like the idealists he trained each day, he regretted being the cross maker's guardian. He loved the sense of family around him.

After his walk in the apricot orchard, Phoebe's mother had talked with him. "I don't understand why your mother called you 'David'," she said. "The men tell me you're not Jewish – you don't keep the Sabbath or the dietary laws." She put a piece of pork on a plate and he began to eat it. "You aren't Roman; you don't burn incense to Caesar. You aren't Greek; you don't worship Astarte. Are you Parthian? Armenian?" Titius remained silent. "Perhaps you're pretending to be no one. But be the man who makes my daughter happy."

Titius stared into Elizabeth's stern eyes. "I will never make a promise to your daughter I can't keep."

It took another sleepless night, but before first light he knew what he had to do: run. But had he trained the young warriors so well he wouldn't be able to escape?

He decided to test the security before dawn. He stepped into the crisp morning air and scanned the courtyard. Seven of his trainees rested outside. Two more stood fully alert with daggers, swords, and javelins. Both pulled their daggers as Titius approached. "Good," he said. "I was hoping you'd be ready. Today we cross the Jordan and prove ourselves. Go get your supplies."

They assembled by the central well. "Today, you're warriors," Titius said. "Now you know the sentries at the gates and they know you. Their replacements come before the rooster's third crow." He nodded toward the sentries. "They've been told to watch for you. First you must sneak out of the compound without anyone seeing you. If anyone sees you, make an excuse and come back." He pointed toward the far wall away from the gate. "Find places over this wall where no one will notice you. Avoid pathways: there are more sentries until you reach the first oasis." He picked up his wineskin and filled it from the well. "Don't draw attention to yourself. Meet at the second oasis, north of here, before the sun hits its zenith or you'll be left behind. If that happens, come home and say nothing."

Jeremiah examined the wall behind them, his dark braids bobbing. Amnon flexed his fingers, anxious to begin. Timna gripped his bow tighter. Migdiel swung his slingshot in nervous circles. Shaul examined the weather. Ethan stood quietly. "We're ready," said Issachar.

Titius paced around the well. The sentries watched him. He waved to them. In his peripheral vision he saw most of the recruits scale the back wall before any women emerged to make the morning meal.

Only Shaul failed to slip away unnoticed. Titius heard him tell a sentry he wanted an extra training run. Two others used the distraction to escape. The sentry refused him and Shaul returned home.

Titius tossed his pack over the wall and scaled an overhanging apricot tree where the sentries rarely walked. He looked back toward Phoebe's house before vaulting down and scampering into the brush. The compound dogs were silent. Even the song birds were quiet.

Several hundred paces from the wall he withdrew, from his pack, a chicken whose neck he'd twisted the night before. He cut it open and drizzled its blood on a robe he often wore. He cuts slashes in the robe and then tore up branches and scuffled the dirt to feign the look of a struggle. He left the robe in a bush, easily found. He stuffed the bloodless chicken back into his pack.

Titius reached the river by noon and decided to ford it north of Adam, near where the Jabbok River met the Jordan. A doe and her fawn stepped out of the tall grasses on the far side to take a drink. The usual hippos and crocodiles were out of sight. Swallows darted up and down the banks. A plover walked casually, probing a sandy patch with its beak. Women washed their clothing on the opposite riverbank. They plunged to their necks in the water when they noticed him.

Titius stayed dressed for this crossing. Wading as far as he could go, he swam as slowly as he dared until his feet found the ground again. The women watched him until he emerged and hid himself among the scrub trees. He wrung out his robe as best he could and belted it knee height.

Once the zealots missed him they'd send out a search party. He couldn't leave any trace of his journey.

He skirted up into the Samaritan hills and by evening had reached Mount Gilboa overlooking Scythopolis. His stomach growled but he refused to approach anyone to ask for food. Discovery was one poor choice away.

He drank from a creek and took shelter for the night in an oak tree. In the dark Cleopas plagued him: *"Don't go back to those Romans. Octavian and Marcus will be watching for you. By now they know you're the heir of the estate Cretius stole. They'll kill you and say they mistook you for a deserter."*

"I suppose you think I should go back and marry Phoebe. How did I learn anything from you?"

"How did you learn anything at all?" Cleopas retorted.

Titius pressed both sides of his head, "Certainly not from you."

"Don't tell me it was Abee-gail."

"Why do you think I came to this cursed land in the first place?"

"You'll never find her."

Titius picked up a stone and threw it as far as he could.

When the sun crested the Galilean hills he was already rushing toward Sepphoris. The time away from Jaennus had softened him; he was panting when he rounded the last corner and saw the resurrected city on the hilltop.

The legionnaires on duty were playing knucklebones; they had wagers of salt on the outcome. When he passed they didn't question him. He went to the newly-built soldiers' quarters and left a message for Jaennus: "the apricots are ripe for picking."

Then Titius slipped away and wandered among the market vendors. He examined different materials and weighed their use for new disguises. He filled his belly with the freshest breads, the finest leeks, onions, and olives.

Near the back of the market he noticed a bright canopy fluttering in the breeze. Under it sat pyramids of orange balls. Around them a dozen men stood in animated discussion. He sauntered to the vendor and picked up one of the balls — a fruit. He bit into it. It was sweet, juicy, tangy, with a flavour he'd never tasted. He washed it down with a small gourd of wine.

Then he curled up in the market's back corner, behind crates of pistachios, and waited.

12

Sleeping behind the crates, disguised as the blind man, Titius dreamed: he and Abigail plucked petals from the villa's rose garden. Her laughter bubbled like a brook as she threw petals into the breeze. Her chiton clung tightly to her. She fit perfectly with the garden's marble statues.

She was every goddess: Diana, huntress; Pomona, gardens and fruit trees; Aurora, the dawn; Venus, love; Ceres, mother love and Vesta, home and family. She was the divine essence in all living things, what Romans called "numina."

Nearing wakefulness, he remembered seeing his father in the garden stroking Abigail's hair. Jealousy and anger churned his insides like a dust devil. He saw his mother crouching behind a hedge, watching. How could his mother allow this?

He'd determined too woo Abigail, but she'd disappeared before his father returned from his next campaign. When Titius asked Abigail's sister, Lydia, where Abigail had gone, she'd replied, "Ask your mother. Abigail needed to go home."

Home for Abigail was somewhere in Galilee and he was here to find her. Two things stood in his way: getting his estate back from Cretius and finishing his term for Sestus as the cross maker's guardian.

Overhearing Octavian, the thespian assassin, forced Titius to really wake up. "Marcus," Octavian said. "Titius is back. We have to find him before Jaennus. Cretius is getting impatient."

Marcus shot back, "Not my problem. You're the one he paid."

"I can't believe the cross maker didn't get his throat slashed," Octavian said. "We should send someone else down to Nazareth to finish the job. These Sicarii are incompetent."

Titius huddled under his blanket. He heard a merchant's voice: "Ah, some of Rome's finest here for some of the homeland's best fruits and nuts. I'm back to serve you. It seems you know what you like."

"We've eaten what we wanted," Octavian said. "If you wanted to sell this trash you should've stayed on your watch. You never know what kinds of thieves and no-goods are likely to take it."

Marcus laughed as the pair wandered away.

As the merchant cursed gods and Romans, Titius rolled out from under his blanket. "You stupid beggar," cried the merchant. "What are you doing here?" He kicked at Titius' ribs but Titius blocked the kick with his shoulder.

"Alms for the blind, kind sir?" he chanted. "Alms for the blind?"

"I'm sorry, old man," said the merchant apologetically. "I didn't know. Are you hungry?"

After eating his fill of fruit and nuts, Titius tapped with his cane back toward the secret passage leading to the centurion's quarters. He took off the goat skin cap and white beard. He discarded the dirty, smelly rags and put on his assassin's mask.

The entrance was hidden behind a blanket near the bakery and was just wide enough for a man moving sideways. He inhaled the heavenly scent of fresh loaves before entering the passage.

The tunnel twisted and turned. After several sharp curves the light disappeared. The stone walls dripped with moisture and mud mucked up Titius' sandals. He counted two hundred paces, then felt for the blanket that marked the hidden entrance to the assassins' den.

He stepped through and slid into the shadows. A young woman was lighting a fire. When the wood crackled loudly, she turned and began to dust a bust of Tiberius Caesar.

Titius emerged. "Peace. Do not fear," he said.

She bowed; her shawl covered her face. The feather duster quivered in her hand.

"You're new," Titius said softly. "This mask is no cause for alarm. I'm a messenger with news for the centurion."

She shook her head.

"A message for the centurion," he said in Latin. "The guardian has come back to finish his duty."

She bowed, still trembling.

"Repeat the message," Titius said. She mangled the words. He repeated it in Aramaic, Hebrew, Greek. At last she said in Greek, "The guardian will do his duty."

He slipped back up the passageway.

Nazareth was less than an hour's walk by road, but Titius slipped through the forest to ensure that he wasn't seen. He changed into a carpenter's garb before emerging on to the road to the village's main gate.

Two young men were dragging a large branch out of an olive grove. "Let me help you," Titius called. "My name is Bartholomew."

The taller lad nodded. "I'm Simon. This is Judas. We're sons of Yuseph and Miriam from Nazareth. Many thanks for the help."

"Is this Caleb ben Samson's house?" Titius asked.

Judas pointed toward the gate, a hundred paces away. "He lives with our family near the synagogue. My brother Yeshi was here yesterday helping him with his wound."

Simon said, "The Sicarii cut his neck and beat him badly."

"Then wild dogs attacked him," said Judas. "It's a miracle he made it home."

"We're going to be carpenters in Sepphoris with our father," Simon said. "He's making special sticks to help Caleb walk. We need to get him this wood."

Titius walked the length of the branch and nodded sagely. "He'll be pleased with your choice."

The two young men lifted one end of the branch and Titius hoisted the other onto his shoulder. The weight threatened to buckle his knees. Within a dozen steps Judas called for rest. They concluded it was best if all three of them dragged their treasure.

At the gate they stopped. "Wait here," James said to Titius. "We need to find out where to put this."

Titius couldn't wait. The gatekeeper was preoccupied with two children and a goat. Titius slipped by him and made his way into the settlement's heart. Near the synagogue he found the rabbi perched on a rock, bowing over an opened Torah scroll.

He stepped up and waited until he was acknowledged. "Yes, my son?" the rabbi said.

"Rabbi," he replied. "I wish to know where Caleb ben Samson is resting. I'm a friend and want to pray for his recovery."

The rabbi stared at him with piercing, dark eyes. "Friends don't often come hidden, not knowing where friends live." The rabbi pointed toward a home not far away. "Your friend is there, at the house of Yuseph and Miriam. A miracle has happened. Perhaps he will tell you how he was healed."

13

Titius hid behind a thorn hedge where he could spy into the yard. Caleb the cross maker was sitting on a bench eating some bread. A young woman was wiping his brow. They'd shaved his beard. There was a scar on his neck up toward his right ear. A middle-aged woman swept as chickens raced around her feet.

"He could have been killed while you were off with that zealot woman," Cleopas whispered. *"Your weakness with women will get you killed, and kill those you're responsible for."*

The older woman set down her broom and went indoors. Titius listened.

"Why did you have to come back now?" the young woman asked.

"Rebekah, I know you're betrothed," Caleb answered. "I really was coming to see Yeshi."

"Those men almost killed you," she responded.

Caleb ran his hand over his scar. "I can't thank you enough for your care."

"What else am I supposed to do?" Rebekah said as she dipped the cloth back into a bucket and wrung it out. "You're like a brother to me. Maybe more."

"When will Yeshi return?"

"He's gone back to Capernaum," she said. "We hardly see him anymore, not since the rabbi and the others tried to throw him off the cliff."

"I wish I'd been here," Caleb said. "I still can't imagine them doing that. Yeshi grew up in this synagogue."

Rebekah sat and rested her forehead on her fists. "He's always been good, but things have changed since the Baptizer immersed him."

Caleb rested a hand on her shoulder. "He's been doing amazing things like that wine he brought out at your sister's wedding."

Rebekah stood, brushing off his hand. "I still don't know what to believe. The servants say one thing, the master of the feast another."

Caleb stood and stretched. As he looked round, Titius ducked. "Your cousin says Yeshua used deep magic to stop a crisis."

Rebekah glared. "Stop a crisis? After that he went to Jerusalem and threw the money changers out of the Court of the Gentiles." She picked up the broom and swept up a dust cloud. "People started talking like he was the Messiah."

Caleb put a hand on her broom. "Rebekah, we know him. These are crazy times. People want our land back. They want peace in Jerusalem."

Rebekah left the broom in Caleb's hand. "It's not just Jerusalem," she said. "I heard that the Samaritans think he's the Messiah, too, because of something he said to a woman there."

Caleb leaned the broom up against the house. "Things will settle down. Give it time."

"Time? The rabbi tried to *kill* him. He doesn't have time."

"What will you do?"

"We're leaving," Rebekah said. "I'm going to Cana, Dad to Sepphoris to work, and the rest of the family are going to

Capernaum. Someone has to talk sense into Yeshi." The two went in the house and shut the door.

Titius saw the rabbi crane his neck and step in his direction, so he took off a sandal and played with the straps. After fumbling enough, he put it back on and walked around the hedge as if going to the house.

Titius wouldn't be able to stop long enough to visit Caleb: Sestus needed this information. As he slipped out of the village, Titius looked back: the frowning rabbi was still watching him.

Once Titius had jogged to the first section of forest he slipped out of his carpenter's disguise and rolled the items up in a brown woolen wrap. He hid them in the hollow of some tree roots, covering them with dirt and leaves.

Titius then donned a disguise new to him: barefoot and covered with a short, dirt-stained farmer's tunic. Near Nazareth he stepped onto a side path and started east. Soon some of the villagers from Nazareth were rushing by him.

A short, stocky man in a blood-spattered apron huffed to a stop. He smelled of blood and carried a large knife. His free hand tugged on his beard. "Did you see a carpenter running this way?" he asked between gasps. "Someone about your height and build."

Titius responded to the Hebrew question in Aramaic: "No."

The butcher went back toward Nazareth. Soon the rest of the group rushed back past Titius and took a trail heading toward Sepphoris. Titius took the next trail heading north.

Ten minutes later he heard wings overhead. A flock of quail dropped around him and Titius picked up several stunned birds, wrung their necks, and put them in his pack. The detour doubled his travel time back, but he arrived before nightfall. He headed toward the secret passage beside the bakery.

In his thespian assassin gear, he paused at the blanket door. On the other side, Octavian was speaking with Sestus. "Marcus and I followed him to the edge of the Jordan. Our spies confirm: he's training young zealots to attack us. He'll expose us and destroy our operations."

"What does Jaennus think?" the centurion asked.

"Jaennus suggests more time," Octavian said. "Perhaps Titius is a better actor than we thought."

"Are you questioning my judgment in choosing him?" Sestus barked.

"Not at all," Octavian said. "Perhaps the zealots have turned him. You know the story they tell about how we treated Barrabas' father."

"Send Jaennus to me," Sestus said. "Go back to Capernaum and see if Titius is hiding with the new Messiah. I hear there are zealots joining his ranks. Perhaps you and Marcus will become disciples of Yeshua ben Yuseph." A door shut.

Titius stepped into the room and once again faced the centurion's sword point. Sestus lowered it immediately. "For the love of Jupiter, where have you been?"

Titius knelt on one knee and offered up his dagger. "Octavian has given you his report. My neck is yours."

Sestus walked to the door and checked the hallway. He then looked through the curtain into the passageway. Satisfied, he turned to Titius, still kneeling. "Rise," he said. "Sit! If you survived two months with Barabbas and his ilk, who am I to sever your neck? Especially before you've given your report."

Titius sat and reported on Caleb the cross maker and his miraculous recovery.

Sestus paced, rubbing his chin. "Impossible," he muttered. "I saw him after they cut his neck. He cannot be healed already. What kind of magic does this Messiah have?"

A gentle banging on the door. Sestus opened it slowly and welcomed Jaennus in. The Optio took off his helmet, nodded to Titius, and took his position guarding the door.

The centurion asked for a report on the zealots. Jaennus wrote as Titius recounted the journey, not mentioning the women. He said nothing about Sarah, the sentry duty at the washing pool, Phoebe's proposal, or Esther's demands. He neither added to nor diminished his role with the Bedouins, the wolf, the shepherds, the young zealots or the escape home.

"Did they tell you of Barabbas's father?" Sestus asked sarcastically. "How we slashed his throat and burned his precious trees?"

"The evidence I saw supports the story," Titius answered. "True or not, they believe it and they use it to motivate their fighters."

Sestus grabbed the report Jaennus was writing. "Go over the story again, from the beginning. When you're done we will go over it one more time with questions. Jaennus, I want every word."

The night was half done when Sestus dismissed himself. "You two sort this out," he commanded. "I want a plan for what we do next."

14

Sestus returned hours later with a servant carrying a tray of food and a flagon of wine. Jaennus held up the report, but Sestus waved it off and went back to pacing.

"The Sicarii killed five Nazarene carpenters last night," he said. "Throats slit like pigs. This changes everything."

"Do we *know* it was the Sicarri?" Titius asked.

Sestus stopped and stared. "Only the Sicarri butcher innocent people like this. Perhaps they found out who you were and sought revenge. Perhaps they heard about the cross maker being healed and wanted to send a stronger message." He grabbed the report from Jaennus, tore it to pieces, and threw the pieces in the fire.

"Sir?" Titius said.

"Thirty thousand people are moving into this city and we won't put their necks at risk because of a few zealots!" Sestus shouted. "No more compromises. I want that cross maker covering this land with his work. We will bring peace through the power of the cross."

"This is the monster you have given your life to?" whispered Cleopas. *"You risk your soul and he pronounces everything you do worthy of the flames."*

Titius ignored the jab and watched the pacing centurion. *"Only he can get my ring from the pool of death,"* he thought.

The centurion chewed on a handful of almonds. Finally he

turned to Jaennus. "I don't trust Marcus and Octavian to give me an accurate report on that Messiah. Something is up with those two." He reached for more almonds.

Titius raised his hand. Sestus glared. "I may know something about Marcus and Octavian but I've taken the code," Titius said.

"The code is for troops with each other. You know if you speak falsehood about another assassin that I myself will club you to death. Quickly, speak the truth."

Titius told him he'd heard the two talk about the stealing of General Julianus' estate, and the bag of gold that was offered. He also mentioned overhearing in the agora the pair implicate themselves in the attack on the cross maker.

Sestus threw another log on the fire. "I'll send someone to recall them," he said. "Titius, you'll go to Capernaum and be with this Messiah for a fortnight. Bring me a report of all you see. After that, you'll go back to guarding the cross maker. By that time he should be back with me."

The centurion marched to the door and turned back. "Good report, Titius. What you've given us is too valuable for others to see. Only the flames and our minds will guard the truth."

"You might as well jump into the flames," Cleopas urged. *"You've betrayed both the zealots who worshipped you and the comrades who hate you."*

"He's my commander."

"Now he sends you to waste your time following that pseudo-Messiah," Cleopas mocked. *"He's finished with you. Go back to Rome."*

"How dare you tell me I should run like a dog with my tail between my legs! Cretius is here and the battle for my estate must still be won."

Titius gathered a generous pack of supplies and slipped out of the city. A cloudless sky spread over mountains and valleys. Thousands of slaves were busy tending the vines in Antipas' vineyards. The blistering sun had ensured a perfect crop.

Cleopus kept taunting: *"Not only will you betray the zealots and the assassins, now you'll also betray the Messiah so this Roman can crucify him. Have you learned nothing from your family?"*

"I have learned everything from my family," Titius growled. "From you I've learned nothing."

"Your great grandfather was with Crassus in Rome," Cleopas went on, *"when they crucified the six thousand slaves from Spartacus' revolt along the Appian Way. Your grandfather told Crassus that my father was a secret rebel. They crucified him for nothing."*

"That's nothing to do with me," Titius said.

"Then why repeat history?" Cleopas said. *"When they brought the Gauls into Rome and crucified them along the Appian way, you pointed to me as their secret informant! Weren't there enough crosses? For no reason, you had me crucified!"*

Titius removed his pack as if it were a burning coal and tossed it away. "Not for nothing!" he yelled.

"Then for what?"

Titius pounded his temples. "You hounded me to forget about Abigail. You mocked me as a child who knew nothing about love. You wouldn't stop."

"You had me crucified to shut me up?" Cleopas laughed faintly. *"Now you get to listen to me until you're with me on this side forever."*

Titius kicked a boulder and cried out at the pain.

Cleopas laughed again. *"I told you your weakness was women."*

Titius retrieved his pack and marched through the high bushes until he found a stream. He put his foot in the water. His toes still ached. After taking a long drink, he curled up under a mulberry tree and took a nap. Thankfully, Cleopas was silent.

The cross maker's guardian woke refreshed. His toes ached less. He heard birdsong and a fox bark. He nibbled on dates and figs.

Titius laid out his disguises, trying to decide who to become next. "I don't think I'll meet the Messiah until I'm sure Marcus and Octavian are back in Sepphoris," he said, holding up the wig for his blindman's costume. "There's no use risking my neck unnecessarily."

"Too late to worry about your neck," Cleopas replied as Titius resumed his journey. *"Worry about mine. That Messiah isn't who you think he is."*

By mid-afternoon Titius came to a point overlooking the new town of Tiberius. He sat and watched fishing boats along the edge of the Sea of Kinnereth in Gallilee. The arid basalt tableland across the lake reminded him of the zealot encampments.

What had the zealots done when they realized he was gone? Who'd found his bloodied robe? Would Phoebe grieve for him? Would they still believe David was someone they could trust? Would he ever meet Barabbas' forces again?

By nightfall a breathtaking sunset touched the skies with slashes of pink, orange, red, yellow, and purple. A young woman on the lakeshore raised her arms toward the heavens. Titius remembered Abigail doing the same thing during one sunset. She'd danced and sung one of her favorite Hebrew songs. She hadn't seen him watching her from an upper balcony. She seemed as free as the hawk with whom she longed to fly.

Abigail's home was Bethsaida, near Capernaum where the Messiah was building his following. A stop in her village first would ensure that Marcus and Octavian were out of the way.

It wouldn't hurt to know something about this Messiah before meeting him. His stomach churned at the thought that she might actually be there.

Cleopas whispered, *"She won't be there."*

"She'll be where she's supposed to be," Titius said.

15

From his hiding place Titius felt the vibrations: two Roman legions thundered by on their march toward Tiberius. Twenty cohorts and twelve centurions pounded their studded sandals in unison. They beat their shields with their swords in time to the marching.

He watched the oak trees empty of birds toward the lake. A rabbit raced by. The legionnaires wore full battle gear: tunics covered with metal breastplates. Brass helmets. Full packs. The standard bearer's helmets were covered with open-mouthed bear heads and they wore grotesque metal masks.

Titius understood now the young zealot's question. How could poorly-equipped young followers of Barabbas accomplish anything at all under Rome's thundering feet?

Two hours after the soldiers had settled into their quarters below, Titius skirted the town. He later jogged by Magdala, Gennesaret, Chorazin, and Capernaum. By sunset he was descending into Bethsaida. The last of the fishermen were storing their nets for the night.

"Bethsaida" meant place of fishing. Many boats were moored there, right at the river mouth as it opened into the sea. Titius, dressed as a Greek tradesman, sat on a log near where three fishermen bantered animatedly by the water. As they were saying their farewells, Titius rose and walked in their direction.

"Peace to you," he said.

"Peace to you," one of the fishermen responded. "You're new here. What's your name? Where are you from?"

"I'm Alexander. I come from Sparta."

"You don't sound Spartan," the tallest of the three declared.

"I've spent a long time in Rome," Titius answered without hesitating.

"I'm Philip," the fisherman said, "and this is Simon and Andrew."

"Did you have a big catch this evening?" Titius said.

"Someone should give you a torch," Simon said. His broad shoulders and dark skin told of many hours pulling up nets under the sun. "There's not a fish in the boat. If you overheard us talking, it's because of what the Messiah did." He pointed to a house up the beach. "Galilean hospitality won't let us abandon a stranger. Come and eat with us. If you have nowhere else to stay we have room."

"I would be grateful. I've only just arrived and I missed news of the Messiah." The cool water lapped against their sandals as they walked. The fires in the nearby village guided them home.

Simon continued. "The Messiah is Yeshua ben Yuseph of Nazareth. He's preached all over Galilee, the Decapolis, the Jordan, even Jerusalem. We can't count the numbers who are following his every word."

A feeling like ants running up his spine made Titius shudder. *"Leave these men."* Cleopas hissed. *"They're deceived."*

"Today in Capernaum," Andrew added, "he healed a leper with a touch, and a centurion's servant with a word from a distance. He even cured Simon's mother-in-law of her fever! That's why we're so amazed."

"He is like no other man," Philip said, laughing and raising his hands. "He casts out demons, he raises the paralyzed, and he calls us to leave all to follow him."

"*Run!*" Cleopas shouted.

"Do the Romans know about this healer? Do they understand the magic and power he has over the people?"

Simon doubled over with a belly laugh. "You think Yeshua is a magician?"

"Yeshua is a prophet from God," Andrew declared. "He works under God's power."

Philip continued, "Yeshua has spoken to all the people about God's kingdom. He's called us to be peacemakers, to forgive, to live pure lives."

"But what do the Romans think of him?" Titius asked.

Andrew grunted. "You should have seen them earlier, marching into Tiberius like they owned the world. When Yeshua heals the servant of the region's leading centurion, what can they say?"

"He tells us that when the Romans demand we carry their pack for one mile, we should carry it for two, so what can *we* say?" said Philip. "He preaches peace and love to all."

They reached a house near the beach. "This is our family home, where Andrew stays. Philip lives up the hill. I live with my wife's family in Capernaum right now, but the door is always open here."

"We can see that you're a trader," Philip said, "but where are you going from here?"

Titius looked east. "I've heard the Parthians are opening up the road for Chinese silk. I'm sure some of our delicacies and sculpture will fetch something worthwhile."

Philip pointed out the road where several traders were pulling into an inn for the night. Their torches flickered in the breeze. "This is the crossroads of some major trading routes so if they buy our fish they may buy your delicacies as well. Come in and rest."

Once inside, Andrew threw a log onto the fire. "North of here is Caesarea-Philippi, south is Gadara, east is Aram and west Capernaum and Magdala."

"I've been on the western roads a long time," Titius said and sighed. "Perhaps I'll rest a while and see what Galilee has to offer. Tell me more about this Messiah."

The fish-and-lentil soup and bread satisfied Titius. The family sat around the fire and talked on and on about the Messiah.

Simon exclaimed, "We saw him produce wine out of water and heal a nobleman's son in Cana. He's been casting demons out of people and making fevers, leprosy and disabilities disappear."

"His teaching makes the religious leaders angry," Andrew said, "and that makes the people happy. He's a defender of the weak. He fears nothing."

"Should the Romans fear him?" Titius asked.

Simon laughed. "Fear someone who preaches love and peace? Who heals and teaches people to be good followers of God and the authorities? Why?"

16

Titius sensed the strong presence of the man stopped next to him. He squeezed his eyelids tighter, held out his rag-clad arms and called out, "Alms for the poor."

Gentle laughter reached his ears. Yeshua bent closer. "My friend, pretending to be poor and blind doesn't mean you're not *really* poor and blind. You're more than you seem. So am I."

The torrent of human voices rolled over Titius as the crowd moved, many calling for the Messiah's mercy. Titius had given his farewells to the fishermen the morning after the fireside. He'd slipped into Capernaum in his blind man's disguise. For three days he'd moved unnoticed among the houses, until Yeshua walked by.

Titius recognized Simon, Andrew, and Philip, among those lingering close to Yeshua. They sorted out those needing healing or a compassionate word. They passed an arm's-length from Titius without recognizing him.

Yeshua was like a benevolent king spreading riches to the masses. He was like a confident conquering general. But this man had time for children, women, and beggars.

Titius remembered his grandfather. The great general, after routing a tribe in Britannia, rode his golden chariot through Rome, sun glistening off his golden armour. The crowds cheered more loudly then they did for winning gladiators.

Titius had been six years of age, standing on a dais beside his mother, lost in the pageantry. But when his grandfather's chariot passed, it stopped. He walked over to where Titius stood in his little toga. Grandfather had lifted him up high, causing another tsunami of shouting. For years, that's all Titius had longed for: to be like his grandfather. To hear the people's cheers.

Titius shook his head and squinted around. The crowd had moved on. A few shekels lay at his feet.

"He knows who you are and he knows we're here," Cleopas murmured.

Titius moved away toward an alley behind the synagogue. He'd hidden his pack in a bush. Within moments he changed from a blind man to a Roman noble in a purple-edged toga. Changing clothes took only minutes, but donning a new persona inside took longer.

Cleopas pestered. *"Do you really think you'll be someone important just because of a toga? Maybe in Rome, but not here, with him. Do you know who this is?"*

He pondered Yeshua's words: "…pretending to be poor and blind doesn't mean you're not *really* poor and blind." What did that mean? "You're more than you seem. So am I." What did he mean?

As Titius walked he noticed a tax collector counting money. Middle-aged, with thick, curly hair, wearing an opulent striped robe. The man counted, recorded, and locked the money in a box.

Titius sauntered to the booth and threw two shekels on the table. The man looked up and examined him. "Peace to the nobleman from Rome. I'm Levi, at your service. What do you declare for taxation?"

"I am Portius Festus," he said. "From Alexandria." A few tradesmen were nearing so Titius spoke quickly. "No declaration; I seek only information."

"No declaration, then no taxation," he said. "I take only what's required."

Titius had never met a tax collector who didn't take any money he could get. "I see," he said. "Does that mean there's also no information?"

"What do you want to know?" Levi asked.

Titius leaned closer to Levi. "The Messiah: what do you know of him?"

Levi chuckled. "Surely you just saw him pass. He brings me good business. He pays his taxes. He comes for a week, he leaves for a month, then returns for a week. What else do you need to know?"

"Where is he from?" Titius asked. "Who is he, really?"

The traders waited patiently now. "I've never heard anyone accuse him of deception," Levi answered. "Anyone like him deserves a following."

Titius nodded politely and backed away.

Over the next five days he used seven disguises, to gain as much information as possible from different sources. Every time he got close to the Messiah he attracted a look, a smile, and a nod. It unnerved him. Was this the only man who could see through his charade?

As the Roman nobleman, he asked the inn keeper if he'd heard of a slave named Abigail who'd worked in Rome. As the Greek trader, he asked a local fig merchant about Abigail. As the fisherman, he asked a rabbi. The answer was always "no."

There wasn't going to be much to report to Sestus. The Messiah's message was always the same: "Repent, for the kingdom of heaven is near." He told parables and stories that seemed little more than entertainment for the crowd. Sometimes he stood in a boat and spoke; sometimes on a small hill. He never seemed to be too rushed for anyone who needed him, especially children. Nothing Rome needed to worry about.

Cleopas was strangely silent during reconnaissance missions but was relentless at night, urging Titius to leave as soon as possible.

On the sixth day Titius determined to confront Yeshua with what he meant by his words and his looks.

He got up at the second rooster crow, ate and went out. But Yeshua was gone. And so were the crowds.

Sepphoris was racing to become a Roman jewel in Galilee. The year after Titius was born, rebels had seized the armoury of the hill fortress. The Syrian legate had ordered his legions to crush the town. It was burned to the ground, the inhabitants sold into slavery. Herod Antipas, fresh from his education in Rome, arrived as its new king and focused his energies on building a Roman masterpiece on the ashes. Every carpenter in the area was recruited for the work.

Herod secured vineyards and tracts of wheat and barley to feed his population. Soldiers, artisans, slaves, traders, and many visitors had to be satisfied day after day to ensure happiness and peace.

Titius approached Sepphoris dressed as a carpenter, tunic hitched to the knee, apron belted firmly, shawl over his head. He kept his eye on the legionnaires posted along the city wall.

To hide his approach, Titius walked beside an oxcart pulling a single massive limestone ashlar from the nearby quarry. It glistened white under the mid-afternoon sun. Titius walked with one hand on the stone as if steadying it. The craftsman on the other side never even lifted his eyes.

"They're waiting for you," Cleopas whispered. *"They know you have to report back to Sestus. They've seen all your disguises."*

"Shhhh."

The moment Titius prepared to step away from the cart's protective cover, he heard Octavian shout at one of the workman. Titius saw a burly foreman keeping watch over every slave and passerby. A large oaken crane prepared to lift another load over the walls. Its pulley system provided the leverage to draw up the heavy stones.

Titius watched a craftsman stand on the load and use his weight to keep it balanced as it rose up. Titius stepped into line and when the next ashlar was secured on the crane, he jumped atop it, as had the craftsman before him. As he swung up over the walls, he saw Octavian examining the next cart pulling into line.

After ensuring his stone's safe landing, Titius melted into the general population. By evening, he'd filled his belly, quenched his thirst, and changed into his assassin's attire. The baker, assigned to cover the secret entrance, slipped him a fresh loaf as he stepped behind the blanket.

No one was there; the fireplace was cold. He left an apricot pit on the table by the door and stepped back into the passageway. As he waited, he dozed.

Between snatches of sleep Cleopas baited him: *"How do you know they haven't turned the centurion against you? You know this game. Your uncles played it to get into the Senate."*

"My uncles were worthy men."

"Ha!" Cleopas mocked. *"The Emperor has eroded most of the Senate's power. You're no different from the others, prancing around in purple so the poor can slander you behind your back."*

"My grandfather earned his way with Julius Caesar. My father survived Augustus' reforms. I qualify for my role under Tiberius."

"By the skin of your teeth," Cleopas hissed. *"You're thirty and only now do you have enough military and administrative experience. You must still become a quaestor."*

"I could still qualify if I wanted to."

"*Except,*" Cleopas said. "*Cretius took your estate. Without it your senate title is useless.*"

"Hush!"

"*Or what?*" Cleopas said. "*You can't kill me again. You sealed your fate when you gave your heart to that woman.*"

After supper Titius watched the thespians flaunt their skills. The theatre seats were cushioned and inviting. Spectators babbled in Latin, Greek, Aramaic, Persian, Egyptian, Hebrew.

Unlike in Rome, in Sepphoris the actors used make-up instead of masks. They could portray emotion and thought with just a change of expression. He loved how the play could mock, empower, or give voice to reality. Perhaps there was still time to evade his oath with Sestus and take up a simple actor's life. He would first talk to Jaennus.

18

Jaennus was offering incense to a bust of Caesar when Titius slipped past the blanket into the meeting room. Without turning, Jaennus said: "I hope you wanted me to find that apricot pit."

Titius warmed his hands at the fireplace. "I leave my fate in the gods' hands."

Jaennus rose to his feet. "As do I."

Titius accepted the tray of dates and figs Jaennus offered. "I need wisdom."

"Wisdom is experience's reward."

Titius nodded. "I'll have to depend on your experience then." Putting himself in the role of student to master, Titius sat on a nearby stool. "I'm listening," he said.

Jaennus tossed a log into the dwindling fire, then returned to his stool. "You're pulled by fear, doubt or love. Which is it?"

"Perhaps all three." Titius clutched his temples between his hands. "I fear my mind. I doubt the loyalty of the brotherhood. I want to love."

Jaennus picked up a date. He chewed it and spit the pit into the fire. "Wanting to love, you must control," he said. "Doubting the brotherhood's loyalty will preserve your life. Fearing your mind... that will take more discipline."

"Before I submitted to Sestus, I was preparing to be a senator in

Rome. But Antipas' assistant has stolen my estate. I fear for my family. The woman I cherished is somewhere in Galilee."

Jaennus stroked his clean-shaven chin. "What is your desire?"

"I want to leave my vow, or take time away from it to reclaim my estate, to restore my family's honor."

"You've given all to Caesar and Sestus," Jaennus said. "To the emperor and to your centurion; to the brotherhood of thespian assassins."

"So I'm bound then?"

"Until death – yours, the emperor's or the centurion's."

Titius rose and bowed. "I know my duty. The cross maker waits for me."

"You may sleep here until morning," Jaennus said. "I'll send you some food and wine."

As Titius slipped out in the morning and worked his way down the muddy passageway, Cleopas spoke up. *"Why didn't you tell him you don't want to guard a cross maker?"*

"Why don't I want to guard a cross maker?" Titius responded aloud.

"You had me crucified! Your guilt consumes you!" Cleopas said. *"Every time you see a cross or see that cross maker you think of what you did."*

"And now I'm cursed with your hounding, because of a fit of childhood anger?" He emerged from the passageway and exchanged his sandals for a clean pair. He slipped into his shepherd's disguise and stepped into the bakery.

The bakery was in front of a large purni oven that burned wood, not just the charcoal used in village kilns. It was lined with stones instead of clay. The loaves, thicker than the unleavened loaves used in homes, baked on a sheet over an opening above the fire. The baker made many varieties with different flours, many flavored with fruit and vegetable juices. Titius bought a loaf flavored with orange juice.

"Who were you talking to?" the baker asked.

"No questions," Titius responded.

"Should I expect another brother?"

"No, no one's coming," Titius said. He bowed his head and disappeared into the crowded agora.

He descended the acropolis on the western side, away from the road to Nazareth, where the last grapes were being gleaned and made into wine. Clouds announced the coming fall rains. He took a hidden trail that circled back to a valley extending westward to the Great Sea. He caught up with a small trading caravan travelling toward the Via Maris and walked close behind it to protect himself from bandits and to confuse any of Octavian's spies.

As he neared Nazareth he remembered the rabbi who was suspicious of him disguised as Caleb's carpenter friend. He took out the goatskin cap and white beard for his life as a blind man again. When would he be able to go without a disguise? Would he ever feel that normal human freedom?

Caleb hadn't seen him like this since Caesarea. He tapped with his cane and moved along the road toward the main gate.

Old Samuel was on duty at the gate but slept under an olive tree. Titius moved quietly around him and made his way to Yuseph and Miriam's house. He tapped by a butcher shop. A skinned goat hung from a hook while a living one nibbled grass beside the shop.

"That's you," Cleopas said in his mind. *"Nibbling away by death's door."*

Titius could smell the bread made earlier in the day. He squinted: the baker lay with his head on his arm. A colorfully-dressed woman sat fanning herself under an awning outside her shop of cloth, spices, and fruits.

"I smell something good," Titius said as he tapped toward the shop. The woman stood. He deliberately tapped himself toward a post sticking out of the ground.

"Watch out, old man," she cautioned. "There's a post three steps in front of you. Go right. Come to my voice. Come! Come!"

She took his hand and rested it on her chair. "Sit. I'm Hannah and this is Nazareth."

"Ah," he said. "I've been looking for Nazareth. Hannah, may the Almighty bless you with all you can dream."

She smiled, touched his shoulder. "Be careful, old man. I can dream a lot."

"I am Benjamin ben Jonas, born blind in Bethlehem."

"So far from home," she said. "You really lost your way."

Titius lowered himself into her chair. "My feet," he said. "Some days it's a blessing not to see them."

"I'll bring you water and bread. Stay. The bakery and well are close by."

He saw two children playing with a floppy puppy in their small home's doorway, happily oblivious to the heat and dust. An old woman waddled toward the synagogue down the road. The rabbi was nowhere to be seen.

The merchant returned with a flask of well water and a barely warm loaf. She set them down on a table by Titius, then gave him a few dates and figs from her own stock.

"May the Almighty bless all that he's given through his servant," Titius said. "May the land's bounty be hers as long as she lives."

"Amain! Amain! Amain!" the woman said. "Now Benjamin ben Jonas, eat and tell me how you came to Nazareth. Almost everyone here is chasing after that 'Messiah' because he was throwing things around in the Jerusalem Temple." She swatted at clouds of flies and rotated some overripe apricots. "You know, we almost killed him here."

19

Hannah proclaimed that the next generation was losing its way. The Sicarri were terrorizing the villages! They murdered five carpenters, Caleb almost the sixth. And the theatre being built at Sepphoris would, she swore, warp the workers' values. By mid-afternoon Titius had taken in as much as he could.

Cleopas laughed in Titius' head. *"You think listening to* me *is bad."*

Titius broke into the verbal stream when Hannah paused for a sip of water. "I actually came to see Caleb ben Samson at Miriam and Yuseph's," he said.

Hannah stood, wiped her sweaty hands on her chiton, and grabbed another tray of dates. He pretended not to notice.

"There are more dates by your left hand," she said. "Eat! It's a mercy you were born without sight." She sat and wagged her finger. "If you'd seen what we've seen. Such scandal! Not that this isn't known outside heaven, but... Miriam and Yusuph had their first child before their betrothal ended. The child was never schooled by anyone with a name, but now he's abandoned his carpenter's trade and passes himself off as a rabbi."

"Is the family at home, then?" Titius asked. He groped for his cane and made as if to rise.

Hannah stood and swatted at flies. "Praise the Almighty! It looks like they're moving on. Not really from around here, you know." She took a few steps. "Their things are still there if you want to go. I'm sure, since you're a family friend..."

"Is Caleb ben Samson still here?"

Hannah took Titius' hand. "Benjamin ben Jonas," she said, "let me take you. The man you want left for Cana yesterday to see his sister. She's newly married, you know." She tugged Titius to his feet and took his arm. "People claim Yeshua turned water into wine, that he healed lepers, made blind men see. Even that he healed Caleb after his throat was slashed. Our rabbi told us to use our minds, not our eyes. We know there's darkness in this land."

At Yuseph and Miriam's house Titius settled on a stool. The home was simple, plastered with limestone, floors and furniture all immaculate. Through an open shed door light fell on carpenter's tools arranged neatly: squares, chisels, plumb lines, levels, saws, mallets, planes, adzes, bow drills, dowels. Two axes leaned against the shed. Under an overhang lay untouched lengths of walnut, cedar, olive, cypress, pine and oak.

Hannah picked up a small carved flute. "Caleb makes these things. Can't imagine how, but the Almighty has blessed him that way."

Titius tapped in the wrong direction toward a wall.

"Whoa," Hannah grabbed his arm. "Wrong way! There's no one here and nothing to see even if you could, so let's go. Where to next?"

"What did they make here?" Titius said. "I smell wood."

Hannah looked around. "Nothing special," she said. "They're carpenters, just like a dozen other families hereabouts."

"May I touch something they made?" Titius asked.

Hannah led him to a table. "This table is oak, very heavy. Yuseph carves, and makes chairs and stools on his lathe." She ran her fingers over a carved village scene. "They make lamps, beds, bowls, plows, yokes, carts, wagons, threshing boards, houses. I guess we wouldn't do too well without them."

Titius took her arm and they went out the door. "It's too bad they had to leave. I guess I'll go see if I can find Caleb in Cana."

"You can't walk blind all the way to Cana, old man. I think the rabbi is taking his cart over that way tomorrow. Let me see if he can give you a ride. You can stay in my shop tonight."

"Hannah, I've walked here from Sepphoris. Cana isn't much further. I can travel at night. I won't be troubling the rabbi on this trip, thank you."

Hannah shrugged and led him to the front gate. "Go in peace," she said as she walked back to her shop.

Samuel sat carving a small whistle.

"Hello, Samuel," Titius said. "I see you're on duty again."

The old man blew his new whistle but no sound came out. "Nothing gets by me," he said. "Have I seen you before?"

Titius tapped his cane. "Nothing gets past you? Then of course you've seen me before. Peace to you and yours."

"Watch out for the wild dogs," Samuel said. "You'd be easy prey for them. Go in peace."

Titius tapped his way toward the bluff overlooking Sepphoris, a cliff three hundred paces high. This was where Nazareth's people had tried to kill the Messiah. Yeshua had grown up in a tough neighbourhood.

Titius noticed shadows growing larger on either side of him. The sun hadn't quite reached the hills. He lowered his head and turned. Three broad-shouldered, full-bearded, scowling young men stood five paces away.

Their leader rushed at Titius. As he reached out, the old man stumbled and brought his cane up under the attacker's jaw. The young man crumpled to the ground, motionless.

"Hello, is someone there?" Titius called. He pretended to stumble over the prone figure and crawled back to it. "Hello? Hello, are you well?"

"Get your hands off of him, you beggar!" the second man shouted. As he reached for the blind man, the cane came hard across his knees. He staggered and hardly felt the cane catch him on the back of the neck. Two bodies now lay on the bluff. The third man stood open-mouthed.

"Hello?" Titius said. "What's happening? Is all well?"

"You ask too many questions," the third man snarled. "The rabbi sent us to bring you back."

"Who are you?" Titius asked. "Where am I?"

The third man stepped sideways and pulled a dagger. Titius angled his head toward where the young man had been. "Hello? Who are you?"

When the man lunged, Titius sidestepped, grabbed the wrist above the knife and snapped it across his knee. The knife fell to the ground and Titius flicked it over the cliff with his cane. The young man grabbed his broken arm, screaming, and charged again. Titius swung his cane against the young man's head and left him, unmoving, with the other two.

20

Once down the road toward Cana, Titius stepped into the forest and walked through the brush to find his hidden pack. The sun was already halfway below the horizon when he'd finished changing into more comfortable traveling gear.

City gates would be closed by the time he got anywhere. This meant another night in a tree. Better a night in a tree than another moment listening to Hannah. As the sun gave its last light he headed back toward the Cana road, where he found a sturdy cedar to sleep in.

He heard baying – wild dogs, moving quickly toward him. Before he could settle himself as well as he wanted in the tree, they arrived at its base, barking and growling. Fighting off a leopard was terrifying enough. A pack of wild dogs was certain death.

"Welcome to the end," Cleopas said.

Sometime before dawn one of the dogs picked up the scent of easier prey and they left, still baying.

Long ago Cleopas had told Titius stories about wild dogs, how intelligent and ruthless they were. "One pack was so smart," Cleopas had said, "they used the shepherd's own dogs against them. They used their wild females to lure away the domestic males. The shepherds set fires, traps and guards around the flock, but in the morning there would always be one sheep missing."

Titius remembered his teacher crouching in the gardens as he talked. "The shepherds figured out how to keep their dogs near them, but each time one sheep would still be dead. They couldn't eat something dead, so they left it for the wild dogs to eat."

Cleopas had acted out the scene. "They tried poisoning the dead sheep, but the dogs would never touch that meat. One night they tied up all their own dogs and nothing happened. They did this for several nights until the wild dogs got hungry and attacked. They killed two of them and the rest never came back. Never underestimate a wild dog."

Cleopas had been urging him to forget the distractions of women and focus on his studies, but tonight it seemed the gods were calling him to see the story in a different way.

Titius prepared to descend at first light. He always waited until a rabbit or deer or similar animal passed the base of the tree to show there were no predators near.

This day, nothing passed his tree. The hair on his neck stood up. The sun rose above the hills and still things didn't look safe. He rubbed the blind man's chiton with anchovies and wrapped it round his pack.

Near a tree stump he noticed some bushes that looked different than they had the day before. He heaved the pack into the bushes.

Three dogs sprang on the intruder, shredding the pack with their fangs. Then they gathered at the base of the cedar tree and glared up, their heads cocked.

Titius had already concealed himself in the branches of an adjacent walnut tree, and he waited. The trio got too hungry, so they raced off after their pack.

"Cleopas, I am in your debt," Titius whispered. "I did learn from you."

"That's not what I was trying to teach you," Cleopas said.

"I know," Titius whispered, and smirked.

"*I can feel you smiling again,*" Cleopas said.

"I know." Titius kept smiling.

Late that afternoon, he neared Cana and knew he must get into town before the gates closed. Without his pack he must find a disguise. He "borrowed" some clothes drying on a fence behind an inn at the edge of town and changed in the bushes.

Beside the inn he noticed a donkey cart filled with wine casks. The owner seemed to be enjoying the fruit of his labor inside. He'd only need this prop to get in, dressed as a wine merchant. Once past the sentries at the gate, he left the donkey and cart near a fountain.

Once evening shadowed the settlement he began to wander the streets purposefully. Thieves and vagrants slunk through the shadows – he saw five muggings within a block of the market. As he passed an alley he noticed a shadow moving along the rooftop above him. He braced himself as a club-wielding villain jumped on him. Titius leapt aside and kicked the assailant's jaw. The man slumped. Titius left him behind an inn like a sleeping drunk.

Titius was passing near a small house in the center of the village, keeping in the shadows, when, several strides away, a giant of a man, stepped out of a doorway nearby and called out, "Thief!"

Caleb, the cross maker, appeared from the back of a building and ran into an alley. Soon, half a dozen men were in pursuit. "*What had Caleb done now?*"

Titius joined the chase. The last man in line glanced back briefly before Titius' cane cracked the back of his skull. The man crumpled like a rag doll. "*Not exactly how Jaennus mentored.*"

Titius took out one man at a time until only two were left. Caleb hurdled a low section of the perimeter wall and tumbled downhill toward an olive grove. Titius melted into the shadows as the last two stopped to catch their breath. He left them retracing their steps.

Titius slowed his own heartbeat and breathing. The strap on one sandal had broken and he adjusted the leather. He followed Caleb back to Sepphoris and reported to Sestus.

Titius waited for Caleb in the bakery. He sampled the bread and counted palm trees that had appeared in greater numbers around every villa.

Finally the cross maker emerged from his debriefing with the centurion.

"So you were there for me," Caleb affirmed. "You're like the guardian angel my grandmother told me about."

Titius smiled. "An angel I'm not." He broke off a chunk of raisin bread and handed the rest to Caleb. "For some reason Sestus wants us to survive this ordeal and I have another job to do."

"Anything I can help you with?" Caleb asked.

"Only if you can learn everything I'm supposed to teach you," Titius responded. "Tomorrow we begin."

Titius would be Latin teacher and combat instructor, performing for Caleb the role Jaennus had performed for him. It was brutal exposing another man to his weaknesses before he'd taken care of his own, but Titius knew his role and performed it well.

Time passed: workmen plowed the fields. Faithful Jews celebrated the Feast of Trumpets, the Day of Atonement, the Feast of Tabernacles.

He was right next to Caleb two months into their training when five hundred and fifty troops marched through Galilee in their hob-nailed boots. The signal bearers wore grim metal masks under helmets fitted with lion and bear heads. They wore breastplates of tightknit metal rings over blue tunics, veterans and centurions also wearing battle medals. The cohort moved shoulder to shoulder, in perfect step.

The fourth day after that march, Caleb and the other new recruits were fully armed, pushed to the front with javelins, supported by veterans and cavalry and chariots. They crested the hill pounding their shields, giving full battle cry, to face a few hundred poorly-armed rioters.

A light snow had fallen overnight. The peasants huddled together from fear and cold. A waterfall of arrows began to fall, people collapsing even before the infantry engaged. The cavalry thundered down on the edges of the mob, forcing them to stay together and face the army's full wrath.

Titius coached Caleb to keep his javelin low and when the command was sounded they were the first to pierce the feeble human shield. The battle was over in minutes as the veterans finished their mercy kills of the wounded.

The cross maker looked for his weapon soberly as he stepped around the mutilated dead. He looked from body to body. Pools of red stained the snow. In the leg of a young boy who'd been given a mercy cut to the neck, Caleb found his javelin. He fell to his knees and vomited. Titius stood and waited. This is going to be harder than I thought, Titius realized. What kind of man is this? He makes crosses but can't handle death.

A centurion watching the scene kicked Caleb. He grabbed the retching soldier, forced him to his feet and dragged him to Sestus.

The centurion demonstrated his disappointment with a rod across Caleb's shoulders. He applied the rod across Titius' back as well. "I expect better from my soldiers! Take him back to

Sepphoris and train him as a thespian!" The centurion turned his stallion and joined the other centurions analyzing the battle.

The two removed their battle gear, left it with a charioteer, and began the long walk back to Sepphoris.

The debriefing with Sestus two days later was humiliating but expected. They had to stand in a cool underground room in their loin cloths for several hours, waiting. When Sestus arrived he spent the first hour pacing and muttering. Without provocation he would hit one or the other of them across their legs or back. After the hour he called for a chair and sat staring at them. Finally he asked them to review their battle experience, moment by moment.

Titius just let it all happen. The centurion had to keep up his reputation and respect. When it was over, Sestus met with him in the thespian assassins' private room and told him Octavian and Marcus had been sent undercover to the Decapolis to infiltrate the zealots.

"I'm off to Ephesus," Sestus confided to Titius. "My cross maker's Persian slave is making a name for himself in the arena." He rubbed his chin and paced back and forth. "After Ephesus I'll be going to Rome and Alexandria. I need you to take care of my cross maker. I need him to be strong when I get back."

Titius shuddered. Whatever Sestus' plan for Caleb, it probably meant more direct exposure to death. How could he prepare a carpenter for such a fate?

For the first week, Titius taught Caleb basic fighting skills. Caleb was motivated by something deep and learned quickly. "That's good for now," Titius thought, "but how will he be in a real battle?"

As the pair went on longer and longer training runs, Titius thought often about his revenge on Cretius, and about Abigail. He wasn't sure which he wanted more. At the end of the second week he decided to pursue Abigail. Regaining his estate as a bridal gift might not even be worthwhile.

Titius began to schedule the training to gain some freedom. As his reprieve got closer he found himself often distracted. Caleb almost pierced him on several occasions when he daydreamed during practice duels.

"Titius!" Caleb said. "Either I'm getting too good for you or you are living somewhere else."

Titius agreed. "There's something I need to do."

"I can help," Caleb said.

"Not this time."

During the week that Jaennus taught Caleb horsemanship, Titius rode to Bethsaida and inquired after Abigail. He had five days. For three days no one he asked knew a former slave of that name.

Cleopas asked, *"Would she announce she was a Roman slave? Would she come back to her home town when she's probably lost her family?"* Titius tried to ignore him. *"They were probably Parthian sympathizers in conflict with Rome."*

Walking, Titius was nearly run down by a horse-drawn cart. He jumped aside with a handwidth to spare. "Watch it!" the tile merchant yelled. "I could have killed you!"

"Too bad," Cleopas said. *"We'll have to improve our timing next time."*

"What did you say about Parthians?" Titius asked.

"Parthians?" Cleopas responded. *"I was talking about the tile merchant."*

"You said Abigail's family were probably Parthian sympathizers. It makes sense. That's why they ended up as slaves."

"Forget the girl," Cleopas said. *"What about that tile merchant?"*

"I need a new disguise," Titius said. "Someone has to know something about her family."

Titius dressed as an olive merchant. He walked into a tavern and asked for the owner. A large-bellied man at a table waved his hand. "What are you selling?" he asked.

"Nothing," Titius said. "I'm looking for family of mine who used to live here. Parthian sympathizers," he said. "They were taken away to Rome."

"No one I know," he said.

An old fisherman in the back said. "I might know them."

Titius was near him in three strides. "What do you know?"

"Sounds like old Judah ben Jonas," he said. "Used to put up Parthian scouts at his place. He had four little ones, two little girls and two boys. Romans took them all away in chains."

His heart beat quickly; he worked to control his breathing. "Would you show me where they lived?' Titius asked.

"The Romans burned it," the fisherman said. "Then piled rocks and dirt on it. No one's dared to build there."

"You don't know if any of the little ones ever came back?" he asked.

"Can't see why they would. Might still be a relative over in Capernaum."

Titius thanked the old man and walked out into the brisk night air. It was his first hope, only one day before he had to leave.

His last day yielded no more information. He headed sadly back to Sepphoris.

All year, news of the Messiah was like fire on people's tongues. The Messiah brought the synagogue ruler's daughter back to life in Capernaum; the Messiah calmed a storm with a single word; the Messiah gave his powers to twelve men who were casting out demons and healing all who came to them.

Cleopas increased his chatter, reciting Titius's weaknesses. Caleb chopped down trees, made crosses, and took several covert trips to Cana. Titius kept training and watching the cross maker. All was stable except for Titius's raging desire to be released and pursue Abigail.

Sestus returned from Alexandria and sent Titius to monitor the Messiah's mood. Apart from increased prayer vigils, Titius noticed only a small change of pace in the healings and exorcisms. The Messiah was always expanding his efforts, sending the followers to lead while the master worked with those who came his way.

Then, disguised as the olive merchant, he overheard a group of Pharisees speaking Hebrew. They were talking about the Messiah. One voice finally declared: "We have to kill him."

21

Titius dismissed the threat he'd overheard. It couldn't be serious. He busied himself gathering the rumblings and praises about Yeshua floating through the community.

One day he was able to nudge closer to Yeshua and his followers eating lunch together.

Yeshua turned to Titius and spoke gently, with no judgment: "The Almighty looks behind the mask to the actor's heart. Nothing is hidden from his eyes."

Titius looked into Yeshua's eyes. No matter what disguise he wore, the Messiah knew him. Could this man help him find Abigail? He bowed and backed away.

He followed them at a distance. What else did this Messiah know? While Titius was in Sepphoris, the Hebrew workers claimed that the Messiah had made wine out of water. A man who was deaf and mute had been healed with a special touch and prayer. Old rumours carried long life.

Later, in Bethsaida, Titius stood watching the so-called Messiah at work.　　Caleb was away on another assignment, so Titius was free to take up his quest. Like a shadow he followed Yeshua from Capernaum, even mingling with his close disciples. Outside Andrew's house, the crowd pressed in on their teacher. The master massaged his temples. He rotated his tense shoulers, bowed his head, and sighed. He shared a half-smile with Simon and turned to face the people behind him.

A blind man was pushing through, calling "Make way, make way!"

"Yeshua, son of David, touch his eyes," a woman called.

"Yeshua, make him see," a young man pleaded.

Yeshua rose and took the blind man's hand. The group parted like the Red Sea and the Messiah led them outside the town. Titius stayed close. He stopped only steps from Yeshua.

Yeshua spit in the blind man's face, on his eyes, then rubbed the spit on his eyelids. No one seemed offended by this vulgarity. "Do you see anything?" the healer asked.

The blind man looked right at Titius and blinked. He looked harder and blinked. "I see people looking like trees," he said.

Yeshua rubbed the man's eyes again. He stepped away. The man opened his eyes... he grinned broadly. His eyebrows lifted. He touched the Messiah's face. He looked at Simon standing next to Yeshua. He turned and saw Titius. He looked into face after face and began to scream with joy.

"Don't go back into Bethsaida," Yeshua ordered.

"But his family needs to see this," Titius thought. What kind of Messiah was this? Spitting in people's faces, making them see, ordering them away from their families?

The crowd pressed in on the man as he walked away toward Capernaum. Titius was caught up in the crush. He pushed hard against the press of bodies, but by the time he got clear, Yeshua was nowhere to be seen.

"*Good riddance,*" Cleopas spoke up. "*You know he sees us, don't you?*"

Titius squeezed his skull between his hands, "Who is 'us'?" he asked.

"*Me, you, us,*" Cleopas said. "*How do you think you play so many parts so well? We help you.*"

"I'm good at what I do because I'm trained." Titius said. He walked toward the beach, waving his hand as if lecturing. "I've practiced the magic arts. *I* have learned the secrets of disguise. *I* have learned to speak without accent. Not '*we*'."

"*Speak for yourself,*" Cleopas said. "*You have no time to keep searching for that woman. You feed your weakness with false hope.*"

Titius shook his head and rubbed his ears hard. He couldn't stop the tremors that ran up and down his spine. He headed for the water's edge. "I don't need your help to be who I am," he said.

Cleopas was quiet.

The sea was little more than rippling glass. He looked up and down the shore at the stream of humanity moving slowly toward Capernaum. Some stood, like him, along the shore, thinking about what they'd seen.

One such man, a Pharisee, joined him. He still wore his phylacteries, the long tassels hanging from his robe. His face was lifted toward the sun as if God's favour smiled on him, a son of the law. His deep-set eyes were confident under grey bushy brows.

Titius looked toward the smoke on the far shore and wondered how Octavian and Marcus were integrating into the zealot camp. Would Phoebe marry one of them and be heart-broken when she was betrayed? Would one fall for Sarah's flirtations and be killed? Perhaps one would gain the trust of Jonathan or Hosea and find their way into the core. One day they'd still have to deal with Barabbas.

"How blind people can be!" the Pharisee exclaimed.

"How much one can see if he only looks!" Titius replied.

The Pharisee turned and nodded. "I am Zedekiah ben Saulus, from Jerusalem."

"I am Jonah ben Gad, of Sepphoris," Titius said.

"You seem perceptive," Zedekiah said. "What do you think about this charlatan of a Messiah?"

"I'm a follower of the theatre," he said. "He plays a hero to bring hope to his people."

Zedekiah grunted. "He plays with fire like a child. He doesn't see... soon the Romans will squeeze the life out of our land and temple."

"They make roads, stop bandits, secure trade." Titius replied. "What life are they stopping?"

"This Messiah caters to tax collectors, harlots, foreigners. Everything that's good will be sent to Rome."

Titius picked up a smooth stone and skipped it on the lake. "I do see the forces of fear and love preparing to collide," he said.

"I know that no prophet comes out of Galilee, or I may think you present a forecast of doom." The Pharisee turned away.

"If you know about the Baptizer then you know the authorities don't deal well with those who oppose them," Titius said. "They've killed almost every prophet who claims some judgment from God."

The Pharisee stopped and pointed up the hill to Sepphoris. "You couldn't find two more different men: Antipas, surrounded by opulent finery and sucking on pig's feet, and the Baptizer, living in the wilderness gnawing on locusts." He spread his arms like a great bird. "Rumour has it that now Antipas is after this new pretender."

Titius turned toward Capernaum. "It doesn't take a prophet to see. The leaders with a heart, jealous for the people's adoration, won't stay quiet long when those people love another."

"Do you speak of Antipas?" Zedekiah queried.

"Perhaps I speak of you."

Titius walked away. The Pharisee called after him, "You should go back to Sepphoris before you're led astray. One day even the blind will see."

Why did everyone keep talking about the blind seeing? The memory of the healed blind man rejoicing rushed into his mind. Yeshua's words echoed in him: "You don't have to pretend to be blind, to be blind."

"*Quit thinking that,*" Cleopas demanded.

As he walked, a deep conviction settled in Titius: "I'm not just playing the part of a blind man – I *am* a blind man." He looked toward Bethsaida where the blind man had been healed. "Cleopas, how did Yeshua know?"

"What?"

Titius rubbed his eyes. "How did Yeshua know I'm not really blind?"

"Ignore him."

"How can you ignore someone who sees through your disguise?"

22

On the morning he left, Titius woke refreshed. Something had changed. The fishermen returning with their catch were jovial. The bird song was clearer. The flowers at the market were brighter. His lentil soup and bread surged with new energy in him.

He packed his gear and headed for the hills. Sestus would be waiting. He wondered what he would say. He took a last look at the lake and took a shortcut between some oak trees. He was smiling.

The undergrowth was thicker than he remembered. He headed for the main road. As he emerged from the forest he noticed five fishermen cresting the hill on their way to Sepphoris. He was about to hail them when he noticed Caleb among them.

What was Caleb doing with the Messiah's followers in Capernaum? Titius slipped back into the forest and shadowed the group.

"There's your cross maker," Cleopas sneered. *"You've done well watching him."*

"Curse that son of Hades," muttered Titius. He sorted through his disguises. Caleb was too familiar with Titius for the usual. No Greek trader, Roman nobleman, blind beggar, or legionnaire.

"You can't even be yourself anymore! Do you even know who you are?"

Titius mumbled, "I've never had the chance, thanks to you. Whoever I was supposed to be was not good enough."

He belted on a rougher, thicker tunic. He rubbed dark red powder mixed with dust and cream into his face and neck, and put on a long grey beard and a silvery wig. A shepherd's prayer shawl completed the outfit. Then he jogged through the forest to catch up. His full pack caught on some low branches and he fell.

"Curse that carpenter," he growled as he got up and examined his scraped shin. He set his wig and shawl back in place.

"Still glad you took this assignment?" Cleopas mocked.

"Curse you, too," Titius muttered.

He heard shouts ahead and ducked behind a mulberry tree. He abandoned his pack and crept through the shrubbery. The beard kept snagging on undergrowth. A swarm of bees hovered over him when he crouched.

More shouts reverberated through the trees. Latin. He scooted behind a pistachio tree's spreading roots. The fishermen cowered on the other side of the road. A Roman cavalry scout, his javelin drawn, trapped them. Other scouts on horseback joined him, surrounded the men, and forced them down. They fell to the ground, begging for mercy.

Five scouts with javelins. The cross maker had put himself at risk again. Perhaps a diversion would work, so he could eliminate the five and send Caleb on his way.

"Will you take out the whole Roman army for one man?" Cleopas asked. *"Sestus will understand. There are others who can make crosses."*

"Shhh," Titius said.

The thespian assassin climbed an oak and made his way along a large overhanging branch. He would knock off a scout, steal his horse, and lead the others away. He moved slowly. The shepherd's garb was a nuisance now.

The scout leader's shouted questions were drowned out by hundreds of hobnailed boots pounding: a legion of soldiers paraded by, drumming their shields. Titius hung on the branch, hoping no one would look up. He almost choked on the dust.

After the cohort passed, the scouts moved their horses away from the fishermen. They galloped off through the dust raised by the soldiers.

"Obviously afraid of a good fight," Titius muttered. "Run along, little horses."

"Someday," Cleopas said, *"Your luck is going to run out."*

"Not until I kill Cretius or Caleb."

Titius waited long enough to make sure the fishermen were safe, then scurried down the tree and rushed back for his pack. He cut through the grove of oaks and crossed the road ahead of the travelers.

He tried to run along the trails, but the shepherd's garb snagged over and over. Finally he took off the headpiece, tucked the tunic into the belt, and changed his sandals. After another hour he stopped to rest by a stream, cooling his face and neck in the rushing water. A small sip was all he permitted himself before heading off again at a brisk walk.

He kept going until he reached the city's familiar aqueducts. Neither Octavian nor Marcus were on duty at the gate he approached so, undetected, he slipped by the sentries. He found a secluded perch on the wall near the market entrance. Goats bleated; cattle lowed. Vendors and customers haggled. Two doves settled under the bakery awning. Still Titius watched to see if Caleb might arrive there with the fishermen.

His stomach grumbled at the smell of bread, but he stayed at his post. The sun slid toward the Great Sea. He watched the golden glow of red-bellied clouds.

The last of the returning merchants came through the gates as the guards yelled warnings. One of the sentries beat a beggar. In the falling shadows Titius almost missed Caleb hiding behind an ox cart as its owner protested against a legionnaire who'd struck his donkey.

Titius slipped down off the wall and began to follow. The cross maker wove his way past the agora and stepped around a pile of slops under a window. The rains had been poor and the sewage ditches running down each street were clogged.

Caleb stopped at a weaver's house and knocked in what was obviously code. Nothing happened for several minutes. Then the door opened a few inches.

"The stench of death is great," a female voice said.

"The hope of life is greater still," Caleb answered.

She let him in.

Titius had warned Caleb about this weaver's daughter, Deborah, and her ways with men: her loose hair, her silk robes, her wooing ways. She was the spider and men the flies. He'd warned Caleb weeks before: "Beware the spider and the fly. Test all before you taste. The rebel heart can beat under the most beautiful face."

Well, the fly was on his own now. Titius walked away, but feared for Caleb. The man was a cross maker for the Romans. What other excuse did zealots need to assassinate him? Deborah, Eustace and unknown zealots often met secretly around the city. They were planning something.

Deborah's cruelty would spew like lava and a moment later soften to a purr. Men seemed helpless around her. Caleb was as a fallen leaf before the wind.

Titius scrambled back to the bakery entrance and into the secret room. Jaennus was offering incense. Titius waited a few moments, then told Jaennus about the cross maker's destination.

"It's foolish," Jaennus confirmed. "I'll alert Sestus. Your charge needs a lesson he won't forget. Perhaps in our dungeon. Leave it to us."

"One more thing," Titius said. "The religious leaders are planning to eliminate the new Messiah. That may unsettle things. If they don't, they hope Antipas will kill him."

"I'm not sure how much political capital Antipas has to work with. His list of betrayals is long."

"What do you mean?" Titius asked.

"Do you remember what happened after Herod died? The zealots captured the city, ransacked the armory, and took control. Who helped the Romans regain the city and burn it to the ground?"

"The Arabs under King Aretas."

Jaennus picked up an orange and threw it to Titius. "And what political arrangement did they make afterward?"

"Antipas married the king's daughter and secured a treaty between his kingdom and the Arabs at Petra. He built the new palace for her on the spot where her father claimed his victory for Rome."

"Yes!" Jaennus peeled his orange. "Antipas planned to eliminate his Arab princess so he could marry his brother's wife. He meant it to happen while he was in Rome. She found out and snuck away before he could do it." He broke his orange in half. "The treaty is broken. Aretas is looking for revenge."

Titius finished his fruit. "So... Antipas betrayed his wife, his brother, and the Arabs all at once by taking his brother's wife."

"The Baptizer lived along that border by the Jordan," Jaennus said. "He knew the stakes. The Arabs control the trade routes and they're proud warriors. Betraying them could strangle this land."

"Then why would Antipas risk an uprising?"

"It's Herodias, his wife," Jaennus said. "She manipulated things so he had no choice. Antipas wants this new Messiah out of the way as he wanted the Baptizer out of the way. He needs to keep the emperor happy."

"I remember how upset the emperor was last time there was trouble here."

Jaennus looked hard at Titius. "Antipas wants someone else to take care of things before he has to. He must keep the religious rulers, the people, and the emperor happy. His forces are searching for a way to take the Messiah quietly."

"What must I do?" Titius asked.

"Go back to Capernaum and track the Messiah. And keep your eye open for Antipas's spies and zealot infiltrators." Jaennus knelt before the altar and added a pinch of incense to the flame. "Don't betray me and don't betray your gods. Your cross maker will be out of commission for a while."

23

On the way to Capernaum, Titius counted twenty-three different species of birds and imagined birdwatching with Abigail. He hurled small rocks at tree trunks and felt an inner satisfaction when each missle struck its target.

And he worked to fend off Cleopas.

"Which of your gods made that bird?" Cleopas mocked as a pelican flew past. *"Why are you aiming for big trees you can't possibly miss? If you keep letting that woman distract you, you'll be useless."*

A few paces later, three bandits attacked him. He used his shepherd's staff to knock the closest two unconscious with whacks to the jaw. The third he rammed in the belly and then smacked on the back of the head. He dragged them into the bushes and left them.

"I should have slit their throats," he announced aloud. "Why didn't I?"

"Losing the thirst for blood?" Cleopas questioned.

The smell of the pigsties he passed was unmistakeable, pigs raised by Roman proxies for banquets and altars. Horses for Herod's cavalry grazed in an irrigated pasture. Legionnaires guarded a herd of imported cattle for some wealthy land owner. As he left the main road he noticed a camel caravan under huge loads, their drivers plodding as if asleep.

Titius felt the welcoming arms of the forest over the road and breathed in an inner peace. It seemed all of creation was settling in for the coming rains. Dust scattered with each step. Withered grasses lay stretched out on the hard earth.

Abigail had been the one who identified the birds in the garden. Here there were different birds. Ducks, geese, herons, cranes and spoonbills filled the waterways along the road. He saw bee-eaters, starlings, larks, swallows, ravens. Occasionally a partridge would race across the road to distract him from a nest. A pair of storks flew through the cloudless sky.

In the afternoon he took time to trap a rabbit, which he roasted over a fire for his supper. The meat and bread, almonds, and dried apricots filled him up nicely. He drank from a stream. He stored the leftover meat between two pieces of flatbread and stuffed it into his pack.

His peace changed to weariness and he looked toward the forest. An ancient olive tree looked perfect as a bed for the night and he hung up his pack. He tied himself into the crook of two branches and settled in. As he closed his eyes, he heard a snarl.

He forced himself to lie still. He could hear the bushes rustle as a leopard's silky hide slunk toward him. It circled, waiting.

"It smells the rabbit meat," said Cleopas.

"It also smells me."

Once before he'd encountered a wild leopard, in Libya while hunting with Sestus. A small contingent of Roman noblemen and soldiers were capturing the black cats for the empire's zoos, circuses and arenas. Sestus wasn't yet a centurion and Titius was hardly grown. His father had sent him for an adventure. The group had captured six beasts in netted traps and secured them in cages.

On the hunt's final evening, they lit the torches. Five of the cats had been fed and were tearing into the meat. The sixth lay sleeping in its cage, seemingly uninterested in the food Titius offered. He moved closer, swinging the meat, calling, insulting, wooing. He wondered if the cat were dead, but he'd seen it pacing and snarling earlier in the day.

It proved unresponsive to his javelin pokes, so he moved in closer. The laughter and drunken talk of everyone else covered up any other noise.

With one hand Titius unlatched the cage door. He stretched to put down the meat and the cat launched itself at the door, which knocked Titius onto his back. When it swung open again, the black leopard sprang at him. He planted the butt of the javelin in the ground and swung the point into his attacker's throat.

One claw had raked across his arm and he still bore the scars. Sestus had been first to his aid and had speared the beast before it could recover its footing.

When his father had heard of the encounter he'd only said, "Waste of a good cat."

The leopard snarled at the base of his oak tree in Galilee. Titius readied his javelin and dagger and waited. The cat paced below. Time dragged by.

"Throw down the meat," Cleopas urged.

"I've got other ideas," Titius said. "It wants me to show fear. Any sudden moves and it'll stop waiting." He reached for his pack and began to empty it slowly.

Hours passed. Finally the leopard made several feigned charges up the tree. Titius didn't move.

The cat sprang onto a lower limb and started toward him. It had been devious, snarling a short distance near Titius, then slithering to the far side to reach the branch. It had scouted well.

But Titius had also scouted well. While the cat was pacing, Titius had draped ropes from one branch to another, webbing himself in. When the cat began to climb, the ropes blocked it. The moon finally crested the hills and its light penetrated the forest. The leopard's glistening eyes and flashing fangs sent a shiver down his spine.

At first, Titius hoped the black demon would give up and leave. When it didn't, he set his javelin and thrust for its heart. The high scream that pierced the night sent a thousand arrows of fear into Titius. What was this creature? The impaled beast lost its footing and fell to the ground. It thrashed and snarled and whimpered as it died.

In the morning he skinned the carcass, wrapped the pelt in his shepherd's cape and kept on toward Capernaum. All sense of peace was gone. Every tree became an enemy's hiding place. He walked quickly and purposefully.

"I don't think that was just a leopard last night," said Cleopas.

"I skinned it," Titius said. "It was a leopard."

"I've heard that scream before," Cleopas continued. *"It's not something you could handle."*

"I handled it just fine," Titius said.

"You're fortunate there was only one."

When he reached the hill above Tiberius, he looked down on the palace where Herodias lived with her daughter, Salome, and Antipas. Carpenters scurried over the palace roof like ants. Ox carts lined up as craftsmen unloaded Persian carpets, Grecian tiles, Roman statues, Cretian pottery, and basket after basket of fruits, nuts and local delicacies. There seemed no luxury this king of the Jews would deny himself or his queen.

When he reached Capernaum, Titius moved easily into the

streets. He'd salted the leopard hide to secure it against any predators who might smell it.

Dressed as the nobleman, he stopped near one of the gates to look for Levi, the tax collector. He needed an update on the Messiah. But now a red-bearded, squinty-eyed, round man sat in the booth with a guard on either side. A new tax collector.

"Peace to you," Titius said.

"Peace to you as well," the tax collector responded. "What can I do to serve a nobleman of Rome?"

"I am Portius Festus, formerly of Alexandria," Titius said. "There used to be another man here, Levi. Curly hair, russet robe."

The squinty accountant knit his eyebrows together. "If you owe him something, forget it. He's gone off with that new Messiah."

"What do you mean?"

"Strangest thing," said the tax collector. "I'm here talking with Matthew Levi about expanding our booth. This Yeshua ben Yuseph from Nazareth walks up to us with his fishermen and says, 'Come, follow me'."

"So...?" This didn't sound right.

"Levi goes. Leaves everything!"

Titius scratched behind his ear. "Is this Messiah against paying taxes?"

"Not at all. Even the voluntary ones he pays. When some of the religious leaders and tax collectors came up from Jerusalem asking about the Temple tax, Yeshua sent Simon out fishing, with a hook and line if you can imagine! Simon comes back with a fish. And in its mouth – a shekel! Yeshua told him to pay their tax with it."

"Where do I find this Messiah?"

"Walk into town and follow the crowd," Red-beard said. "You can't miss him."

Titius turned to leave. "One warning," the tax collector called.

"What's that?"

"Watch your neck." He slashed his throat with his finger. "With the zealots around here there aren't too many Romans walking the streets. You might be safer in Tiberias."

24

Titius heeded the warning about zealot desire for Roman blood, went back to the forest and changed into his Grecian olive merchant clothes. He descended the hill and, after reeentering the town, saw a familiar fruit merchant. He knew this man was fluent in Greek.

"May the peace of Aphrodite rest on you," said Titius. "I am Stephanus from Corinth."

"Shalom," answered the vendor. "I am Zechariah from Damascus."

"I seek sustenance and information."

"The price for either will please you," Zechariah said.

"A shekel's worth of dates to begin," Titius said.

The merchant scooped several handfuls of dates into a bag and laid it on his cart. "What would you like to know?"

"Who in this town knows everyone and everything?"

The man pointed toward the inn. "Hiram, the innkeeper."

Titius paid his shekel and made his farewell.

Men lounged outside the inn drinking, laughing, and making ribald comments at passersby. Two men mocked his short white tunic and joked in Hebrew that he had a woman's knees. He brushed past them into the building.

He found Hiram sharing his knowledge with three others at a table. Titius ordered fish soup and waited until the three men left. Then he asked Hiram for information.

An hour into the innkeeper's dissertation, Titius already regretted disguising himself as an olive merchant. He'd heard everything about Galilee anyone would want to know: how the land could be travelled north to south in one day or east to west in one day and every step was fertile land for olives. Hiram told him the whole history of the immoral Samaritans to the south, the Phoenicians, north and west, plus the people of Gaulanitis and the Decapolis across the Jordan River to the east.

There were over two hundred villages in Galilee and every one of them produced olive oil. There was no end of possibilities for a wise merchant. And this innkeeper just happened to have a cousin who knew the man who could make the whole deal for just the right price.

Titius knew a con when he heard one. He paid for his meal and left.

He went to the beach where he skipped a few stones. A fisherman appeared beside him. He had strong shoulders in his rich red tunic; he worked hard. His blue-banded head covering showed high status. His face was Hebrew but his beard cropped short.

"Peace be upon you," the fisherman said. He had the same accent and vocal inflection that Cleopas had had.

"And to you," Titius replied. He bent down and selected three more smooth stones.

"I am Isaac of Magdala."

"I am Porpherus of Corinth," Titius said, unsure exactly which name he was using. He skipped another stone.

"Are you here for the Messiah?" Isaac said.

"Isn't everyone?"

"He's in that fishing boat," Isaac said, pointing at a vessel several lengths from shore. It was large enough for twelve men or a few hundred fish. "Walk with me."

Titius kept pace with Isaac as the man increased his pace over the rocky shore. Titius' ankle turned at one point but he ignored it and pushed on. "Are we going to hear the Messiah?"

"Two hundred boats on this lake and the Messiah chooses Simon's," Isaac said. He pointed toward the dozens of low-sided craft bobbing just off shore. Men cast their nets then pulled them back in, over and over.

One boat was crowded with men but no one cast nets. Yeshua stood in its bow facing the beach. The shore was crowded with people straining to hear.

"You have a boat?" Titius asked.

"Of course," Isaac said, "I'm a fisherman. Even my cousin Mary is there, with the crowd, listening to Yeshua's every word. He cast seven demons out of her."

Cleopas screeched in his head; Titius put his hands against his ears.

"I assure you," Isaac said. "She is well."

"How is your cousin now, without the demons, I mean?"

"It's a whole new world for her," said Isaac. "But I can't get her to help me pickle fish anymore. She's enamoured with the Messiah and wants to spend all she's earned on him."

"It must make you mad at this Messiah," said Titius.

"No, praise the Almighty," said Isaac. "I found a new girl, Abigail.

Says she learned to pickle fish in Rome. Finding her was a miracle."

"Abigail?" Titius asked.

"Yes," Isaac replied. "She says her family used to live here when she was young. She doesn't want to talk about what happened but she seems happy to be back."

"Is she married?" asked Titius.

Isaac squinted at Titius. "None of my business," said Isaac. "I haven't heard her speak of a husband. All I care is that she does the work."

"Maybe I'll come see what kind of pickled fish you have," said Titius.

"Good, Porpherus," said Isaac. "I need to hear this Messiah for myself."

Titius tried to listen, but Cleopas talked louder and louder. He moved away from the crowd to deal with the pain in his head. "What are you saying?" he said to Cleopas.

"Did you hear?" Cleopas said. *"This Messiah bewitches women! Steals them from their homes!"*

"What?" Titius asked. "Isaac has found Abigail. We need to get to her."

"This woman is not who you thought she was when she was young," Cleopas said. *"She's been gone for years. She may be married, or ruined by other men. Let her go."*

Titius looked back. Simon's boat moved slowly to shore. "I have to know!" Titius said.

People began to go back toward the town. They walked around

him so closely that Titius couldn't walk forward. He sat on a log and waited for things to clear. When there was enough space, he noticed Simon's boat had actually moved away from shore again.

"Forget about him," Cleopas said. *"You're not really looking for him, are you?"*

"I do need to find Abigail," Titius agreed. He decided that by mid-afternoon he'd change and go to Magdala. First he needed to find out where Isaac prepared his fish.

He couldn't find Isaac in the crowd. As he rose to go, a great yelling sounded from the fishing boat on the lake. "James, John. Bring your boat. There's too many! Hurry, we're sinking. Hurry." Titius recognized Simon's voice. Silver flashes glittered around the boat.

Titius moved to the edge of the lake. A similar vessel set out. When the two boats were side by side the nets were pulled up and up and up, load after load after load of fish. The filled boats settled so low in the water it looked like they might sink. Dozens of men, shouting their amazement, waded out to help the boats in the last few lengths.

Yeshua stepped off and waded ashore, laughing with the others. He looked to heaven. "Praise be to the Almighty who gives us the bounty of the sea."

Titius stepped toward him but Cleopas screamed, *"Run!"*

25

A woman, her smile radiating like sunshine, twirled and danced, surefooted and carefree, along the beach toward Titius. Her cream-colored robe fluttered in the breeze like butterfly wings. Her midnight-dark hair floated across her shoulders.

Five other women walked serenely in her wake, chatting. They stopped to look back at the fishermen hauling the last of their netted fish ashore. "Yeshua is Lord," sang the dancing woman. "Yeshua is Mighty, Yeshua is Messiah, our hope and our life."

"Mary," called another woman. "Your cousin Isaac was looking for you."

She stopped dancing. "I hope he doesn't expect me back in Magdala. I'm done with pickled fish. I follow the fisher of men." They all laughed.

Titius stepped in her direction. "Mary?"

"Do I know you? Do you follow Yeshua?"

"I spoke to your cousin Isaac about your business in Magdala. I think I know the woman working for him, Abigail."

Mary smiled. "I haven't met her. I've been with Yeshua since he freed me."

"Freed you?"

"Yes! The voices are gone, my mind is clear. My spirit sees the Almighty as he is."

Cleopas whispered, *"Leave! Run! Don't listen to her."*

Titius's stomach churned. His mind fought to think as a blind man gropes in a maze. A claustrophobic darkness surrounded his soul. His heart raced. His knees weakened. "Does the Messiah help everyone?" he asked.

"No," she said. "But he helped me and I'm free." She stared into his eyes and he looked away. "This peace is worth everything you have," she said, before dancing away, the other women following.

Titius looked back to where he'd last seen Yeshua. There were only fishermen filling basket after basket with fish.

Over the next two days Titius walked the shoreline, skipped stones, argued with Cleopas and

made discreet inquiries about the Messiah around Capernaum. Titius recorded them for Sestus: "His magic breaks my boredom." "The place is much quieter when he's away." "He's good for business." "I wish he'd get on with ousting the Romans."

Some people loved him: "He healed my friend." "He raised my daughter." "He touched me." "He held my baby." "He speaks peace to my soul."

Magdala was close by. Titius would stop at the fish shop on his way back to Sepphoris. If Abigail were there, Sestus could wait another day.

He kept playing the olive merchant in case he met Isaac. He worked his way south around the lake, keeping to the lake road. Hundreds of others were on the move after the events at Capernaum. Titius fell into step with a group of peasants. "Peace to you," he said.

"Peace to you as well," one of them responded, sweat pouring down his fleshy cheeks.

"I am Porpherus of Corinth."

"You look as Greek as my grandmother," said the spokesman. "For you, today, I'm Assander of Magdala. These are my brothers and uncles."

"I hear Magdala is a great city."

Assander grunted. "It was greater before Antipas decided to steal all our fish processing. Now the best workers go to him."

Titius saw the earthen towers near Magdala, by the lake. "I'm going to Sepphoris. The main road goes right through your town, doesn't it?"

"Yes," said a young man. "At the towers you turn inland."

"Do you know a fisherman named Isaac?"

"Is he helping you start an olive business?" asked the young man. "We can do better."

Titius shrugged. "I'm here to see Magdala. Especially the pickled fish."

"There are many Isaacs in this land," said Assander.

"This Isaac had a cousin, Mary, who used to work for him. She follows the Messiah."

Assander laughed. "The Messiah? You mean Yeshua, the carpenter from Nazareth?" They all joined his mocking laughter. "Everyone begs him for bread and freedom. I say get back to work. Earn your own bread."

"I'm more interested in Isaac and his business."

"Yes, we know this man. He has a business near ours. He also has a beautiful new helper. Elkanah, my brother, wants to marry her." He pointed at a thick nosed man with a generous belly.

"Is this woman's name Abigail?" Titius asked.

"Who cares?" Elkanah said. "She'll give me beautiful children!" More laughter. Elkanah's belly bounced even more.

"Rumour is she's a Roman whore," a tall boney man said.

"You just want her for yourself," Assander declared.

"I know a zealot who'll slit your throat if you touch her before I do." Elkanah said without laughter.

Titius restrained himself and stayed silent.

A group of older boys on a log hurled stones at the peasants' donkeys. One donkey brayed in protest and skittered sideways, almost dumping its load.

Elkanah reached under a blanket on the donkey and pulled out an Arab scimitar. "I will cut off your heads and serve them to your mothers!" he yelled. When he stepped toward them, waving his sword, the boys turned and fled, screaming.

They continued without further incident. Elkanah describing to everyone what he'd do to boys who disrespected men such as himself.

Assander turned to Titius as they neared the Arbel cliffs by the town. "Porpherus of Corinth!" He grabbed Titius and pointed at a large establishment. "There, where the Arbel stream empties into the lake, is the Isaac you seek. On behalf of my brother, Elkanah, keep your mind on fish and olives and forget the Roman beauty doing the work." The men laughed as they walked off down the road.

Titius sauntered along the stream and found a shallow crossing. The community was busy; he was greeted but not asked his business. He set himself on a tree stump near Isaac's shop and watched as, on the lake side, fishermen prepared for night work with torches and nets. On the other side of the buildings, ox carts were filled with crates of pickled, dried, and preserved fish for transport.

"Forget this woman," Cleopas whispered."You heard the men. She's probably been a Roman whore. Let someone else have her."

"She's not an old carpet I can give away," Titius replied. "Love has its price."

"You know nothing about love," Cleopas responded.

Titius marched to the main entrance and pushed his way in. His costume gave him rights and he intended to use them. Smoky olive oil lamps hung from the ceiling, casting a flickering light over a crowded room. Many voices yelled over each other. Two men keeping accounts and two weighing fish stood behind a table. Others raced to retrieve the orders.

One of the accountants nodded to him. "I need to see Isaac and Abigail!" Titius shouted. "Zeus, Hermes, whatever gods there might be..." he prayed silently, "bring her to me."

26

"Isaac is on his way to Jerusalem!" the accountant shouted. "Abigail is in Sepphoris."

Titius's heart pounded at both her closeness and with disappointment at having missed her. Was this the gods' cruel game?

At least she was exactly where he was going. If he started now and rested along the way he could enter the market gates at first light.

As he passed out of the shadows sheltering the town, the sun slid down out of sight. At first he welcomed the fresh sounds of the night, crickets, frogs, bush babies. Then a leopard's snarl unsettled him. With one hand he felt for the newly cured skin in his pack and with the other he grabbed his dagger.

Carrying only small weapons was a hazard of some of his disguises. A human might be outwitted by a quick mind and a sharp tongue but a beast of prey rarely stopped to consider.

Cleopas fed off any whisper of fear. *"You hear them, don't you?"* he mocked. *"They know you killed their brother. Now they'll get you."*

"If I took out one, I can take out another," Titius said. He turned in the road, looking for movement. "No fear."

"You were safe in a tree last time," Cleopas noted. *"Now, you're in his territory."*

"If he gets me he gets you," Titius said, "Don't distract me. I need my senses."

"If you had your senses you'd have stopped chasing this woman," Cleopas declared. *"I told you your weakness with women would destroy you."*

The stillness alerted him more than any sound. There was no snarl, no footfall, no breathing.

The hairs on his neck stood like a cat's. He felt it in his flesh: something, somewhere, hunting him.

"You know it's here," Cleopas whispered.

It was closing in on his left, tracking him, waiting. He moved to the far side of the road. The moon slid up, a mere sliver in the night. Clouds covered most of the stars. At a bend in the road the presence seemed to fade briefly, then it reappeared on his right. He crossed the road again.

Titius reached an oak tree. He flung a rope from his pack over a low branch. He wrapped the rope around his wrist and pulled himself up. A demonic snarl pierced the darkness and fire pierced the calf muscles of his trailing leg.

The cat was up the trunk in a moment but Titius kicked it away with both feet. It landed on its paws and circled the tree. Blood flowed down his leg; he knew the cat could smell it. Would it wait for him to bleed out or attempt another attack? How had this happened again?

He tied off the wounded leg to stanch the blood. He wrapped the sliced calf as best he could and waited. The cat circled and snarled.

Titius took his leopard skin and hung it from the branch. He braced himself, set his dagger, and began to yell as loudly as he could. The yelling angered the cat and it made several jumps up the trunk. Twice, Titius was sure his dagger cut a paw flashing in his direction.

An hour into his standoff, he heard human voices and saw torches coming down the road. "Help!" he called. "Help!" In Greek, then Latin, then Hebrew, then Aramaic, then Arab.

"Where are you?" responded an Aramaic voice. "What's wrong?"

"I'm in a tree," Titius yelled. "There's a leopard here."

The torches moved quickly toward him and the leopard ran into the darkness. Six bearded faces looked up. "The cat seems to be gone."

"There is a lot of blood here," one observed.

"It's mostly mine," Titius said, "but I think I got him a couple of times with my dagger."

"Please, let us help you down," an Idumean said. "Drop your pack and your dagger."

Titius lowered his pack and they caught it. Their leader started laughing. "What's this? A leopard skin? You have one and now you're using yourself as bait to get another?" The others laughed.

"I needed to get to Sepphoris," Titius declared, lowering himself and preparing to jump down.

"You're out of your mind to be walking alone at night," the spokesman said. "You're not even dressed for hunting." He pulled a wig and tunic from the pack. "Look!" he cried, dropping the pack and holding up a bag of coins. "Thank you for contributing to our cause!"

The men began to walk away with the coins, his pack, and the leopard skin. "Wait! Those are mine!" Titius yelled.

"The gods left you a choice," the leader replied. "Stay here and face the leopard alone or express your appreciation by rewarding those who rescued you. Our hope was to capture a caravan and relieve them of their treasures but you're the only fly that's come to the spider."

"There is nothing valuable in my pack," Titius pleaded. "You'll only increase Rome's wrath if you rob its citizens."

The leader held his torch up toward Titius. "Are you a Roman citizen?" They broke into laughter. "Hung in a tree like a side of venison? We'll see what Rome does to protect its citizen from the leopard."

And the men left him.

Titius cursed himself. Cleopas added to his humiliation as the cross maker's guardian felt himself getting weaker and weaker. He lowered himself to the ground.

27

Delirious, suffering from blood loss and stumbling around a forest in the dark, he forgot about the leopard. Titius saw himself back in Rome, sitting with Cleopas as they discussed his future in the Roman senate. Cleopas led the lesson. *"You need military and administrative experience."*

"How can I get that without getting killed?" asked Titius.

"Focus on the swordplay," growled Cleopas, *"instead of that girl."*

"She's more interesting," Titius said. "What'll I do? Beat down Gauls or Germans? Rome has the fittest fighting force in the world. Who'll stop us?"

"Many would love to try."

"I can't be a quaestor for ten more years," Titius moaned. "After that, I have to get my aedileship, then praetorship, then consulship. It could take half my life!"

Cleopas pointed to his chart. *"As soon as you become even the lowest magistrate you'll be gaining political and judicial powers. Your word will carry life and death. And you and your class alone can choose and advise the emperor."* Cleopas rolled up the chart. *"When people see your purple-fringed toga you'll get privilege, position and recognition at the games."*

"How gullible are people?" Titius asked. "Is one man better than another because of what he wears?"

Cleopas said, *"Do you think one woman is better than another because of what she wears? Look beyond what you see."*

"One woman is definitely better," Titius said.

He felt the wind knocked out of him. He was sure he was in the pool, submerged, darkness gripping his mind. *"You're almost here,"* Cleopas said.

"No!" Titius said. "No! I want Abigail!"

He forced himself to open his eyes. He heard early birdsong. He crawled toward the road… and then all faded.

When Titius next sensed light it felt like an earthquake had seized him. He reached out to steady himself and heard a woman say: "He lives, he moves."

A cool cloth left his forehead. A woman's hand caressed his cheek. "Peace, my friend. Peace."

Warm sun stroked his body. He had no strength to move. Trees blocked the sunlight for a moment and he saw a raven-haired princess smiling at him, upside down. A ruby nose ring matched the ruby studs in her ears.

"We found you by the road," she said, her voice like a dove.

"Ahhh," Titius groaned.

"Micah says a leopard got you," she continued. "We're taking you to Cana. There's a healer there."

"Ahhh," Titius groaned. All went black again.

A flickering torch broke up the night. A more calloused hand touched his forehead and placed a cool cloth. Fire raced through his body. He plunged back into darkness.

Titius dreamt memories. His mother, in Rome, stood beside a sobbing woman, a neighbour. The neighbour's husband slapped her in the face. She stood tall and quiet but shook. She watched her newborn son given to a white-clad priest. Drums and horns drowned out the boy's cries.

The priest walked up to a large stone statue of the god Chemosh. A fire burned in its hollow belly. Its extended arms glowed red hot. The priest held up the child. He incanted something then lay the babe on the glowing arms. The arms fed the child into the god's fiery mouth.

Titius' mother shielded herself from the terror with her own son, crushing his arms. Moments later they fled, but his mother's mind was never the same again. "We have no god but Caesar," she said. "Caesar takes my father and husband but leaves my son."

Abigail and her sister had tried to calm his mother with incense, jasmine, rose petals. Nothing helped. Mother just paced the garden, mumbling. Father never spoke of the matter and stayed away from home for longer periods of time.

Cleopas worked hard to distract Titius from what was happening to his mother. He lengthened his class hours and planned more trips to the pool and the countryside. He pointed out the delicate designs of an intelligent mind shown in flowers and insects.

Despite all Cleopas taught him about a Creator, Titius vowed to never trust another god. He'd seen many gods worshipped in temples and at arenas. Now their faces haunted him as they reached for his soul.

In the midst of his family's confusion, Cleopas had taunted Titius about his weakness with women, Abigail in particular. Titius became more beligerent, even throwing his slate at his teacher. As the days passed he refused to leave the house. He skipped lessons, feigning illness.

Father was distant and paid more attention to slave girls than to his wife. To get his father's attention, Titius had reported his slave as an informant. He had watched, unflinching, as Cleopas was crucified.

Now Cleopas' gasping face on the cross forced itself into his dreams.

28

The day things came back into focus, the raven-haired beauty was wiping his brow.

"Hello, stranger," she said. "I'm Rachel. My brother is Micah. You're with my family in Cana."

"May the gods bless you," Titius whispered.

"Oh no. We follow Yahweh, the Almighty, the true God, the only God."

"My allegiance is to Caesar," Titius said.

The girl dipped the cloth into a bowl. "Today is the Sabbath," she said. "Micah went to the synagogue. He says that Yeshua ben Yuseph of Nazareth read the Torah scroll today. He spoke of deep things that made the rabbi and the landowners angry. The Pharisees got even angrier when he healed an old woman in the service."

"I know this Yeshua," Titius said.

"I wish Micah had brought him here to heal you," Rachel said. "Six days is a long time to have a fever."

As soon as he tried to move, Titius felt the stiffness in his legs. He found all his scabs and wounds not only on his leg but across his arm and stomach. He'd been severely wounded.

Rachel spooned broth into his mouth and brought him water. His parched throat protested. "Chicken broth is what my mother used to make for us when we were sick," she said. "My mother died of a fever like yours. I didn't want you to die like she did. It was very painful."

Titius drank in her dark eyes' light. "Thank you for stopping."

"We had to," she said. "Yeshua told a story about a Samaritan stopping to help someone who was beaten by robbers. Micah said helping a Greek hurt by a leopard was the same thing. How did you keep the leopard from killing you?"

"Bandits," Titius said.

"Bandits?" She spooned more broth into him.

Titius swallowed. "Bandits came while the leopard was attacking. It ran away."

"Did they help you?" Rachel tipped the water to his mouth.

"No. They stole my things and left me."

"What?" She stood up and paced the floor.

"They left me nothing."

"Well praise the Almighty we found you," she said. "The leopard could have killed you. The bandits could have killed you! You could have bled to death! God is so good."

"That's not exactly the way I'd put it."

Rachel knelt beside him and put the cloth back on his forehead. "I don't know your name."

Titius attempted to raise himself on his elbows. "I'm only a man who thinks you're an angel," he said.

She smiled and pushed him back down. "You're more delirious than I thought."

An hour later Micah arrived and that was the last Titius saw Rachel. "She's gone to my cousin in Capernaum," Micah said. "She needs to know more about the Messiah and less about you. Where can I take you? Your family?"

"I've no family," Titius said. "If you will, you can take me to Sepphoris. There are people who will care for me there. I thank you for what you've done."

They went to Sepphoris two days later. The city's noise seemed greater than he'd ever heard it before. Just after noon the donkey pulled up to the gates. "Ask for the Optio named Jaennus," Titius urged.

After some argument a legionnaire peered over the edge of the cart.

"Titius Marcus Julianus, servant to the centurion Sestus Aurelius. Jaennus is my Optio."

"Wait!"

An hour later Jaennus peered into the cart. "So, the prodigal has returned. You let a leopard get you? What was the point of all that training?"

Several legionnaires dragged Titius out. They carried him wordlessly into the soldier's quarters and left him on a blanket near the entrance.

Soon after, Sestus walked in. "What kind of guardian are you?" he asked. "Your cross maker is out of the dungeon and finishing the crosses for the zealots we captured. You can watch. After we're done I expect your report on the Messiah."

Titius had no intention of watching crucifixions, but two legionnaires gave him a new robe and walked him to a site overlooking the scene, where thousands had gathered. Vultures circled overhead.

Six zealots were being led to the crosses. He recognized three of the young men he'd trained across the Jordan. Jeremiah's dark braids had been chopped off; he stumbled forward, bent and broken. Magdiel looked more like a boy than a man. Ethan hobbled silently. The other three were equally subdued.

Sestus presented the six to a magistrate. A legionnaire stepped up behind each captive and forced him to his knees, a dagger to his throat.

The youngest openly whimpered when sentenced. His companions turned away, ashamed of his betrayal. Other legionnaires approached carrying crossbeams and tied them to the zealots' outstretched arms.

When the beams were secured, the soldiers forced the prisoners to their feet and prodded them on their death march. When his former trainees were nailed in place Titius looked away. Their screams joined the memories he tried to bury.

As the screams continued he used a wall to get to his feet and inched away along the cobblestone path. Cleopas mocked him at every step: *"You could stay and watch* me *be crucified but you can't watch these children?"*

For a day after that, no one came to see him. For three days no one brought him food or water; his hunger and thirst raged. Finally, two legionnaires picked him up and walked him through corridor after corridor. When they finally put him down, Titius recognized the fireplace, the place of incense, the cushions, in the room where he usually met Jaennus and Sestus.

Two flagons of wine sat alongside some bread, fruit, and goat cheese. He ate without hesitation and lay down on a cushion to rest. The blanket covering the passageway shifted and Marcus stepped in. He opened the door and Octavian followed him in. They smiled at him like grinning hyenas.

29

Marcus set two javelins against the wall near the tunnel exit. "We almost got our necks cut because of you!" he said. "We made it through two camps of those rebels but I couldn't get close to Barabbas' sister. Because she thought she was in love with you and that someone must have killed you!"

"That Hosea!" Octavian snarled, drawing out his dagger. "He wouldn't let us out of his sight!" He hurled it into the wall above Titius's head.

"They interrogated us. We insisted we knew you and that you were a great threat to Rome." He drained the flagon of wine. "How did we not know you'd been imprisoned and cut? How did we not know about your exploits with 'the desert fox' in Libya?"

Titius struggled to sit upright and moved back against the wall.

Marcus picked up a handful of dates. "Those zealots praised you as a great friend of Barabbas. They vowed revenge on the Romans. Those young zealots were crucified because you made them believe in themselves."

Octavian finished off the other flagon of wine. He wiped his mouth and sighed contentedly. "For that we thank you. I liked looking into their faces and telling them who you really were. Hearing them scream. It's time to get the rest of those naïve zealots."

"However," Marcus said, "We can't thank you for breaking our code." Marcus pulled out his dagger and got down on one knee by Titius. "Somehow Jaennus found out that Octavian had another job with Antipas' assistant Cretius. He found out we were working to keep you from your inheritance. He tried to ship us back to Rome. But here we are."

"And here *you* are," Octavian said. He retrieved his dagger from the wall above Titius and handed it to Marcus, who swung it back and forth inches from Titius's nose.

Titius watched it for a moment, but it was the eyes you had to watch. Marcus' eyes were intense, on fire.

"Yes, here we are," Titius said. He stood and went to the fireplace.

"You know we can't finish this here," Marcus warned. He pushed a table in front of the hallway exit.

"Finish what?" Titius asked, kneeling before the fire, his back to them.

"Our honor is at stake," Octavian said. "The zealots know who you are, we know who you are, and soon Cretius will know who you are. You won't see it coming, but by next full moon I'll have my sack of gold and you'll meet your father."

Titius stood and walked to the marble bust of Caesar near the doorway. The emperor's head would be a useless weapon against two professional assassins. He caressed the carved laurel wreath. "What do you know of my father?"

Marcus put on his hungry hyena smile. "It wasn't the Germans who got your father. He was too smart to die in battle. Lord Cretius wanted your estate. Your father was in the way."

The realization hit Titius like an avalanche. "Lies! My father died a hero. Cretius is a worthless thief."

Octavian picked up one of the javelins and pointed it at Titius. "Let's hope he never hears you say that in one of his torture chambers." Octavian snuffed a nearby lamp wick between his fingers.

They picked up the two remaining lamps, stepped into the passageway, and were gone. The embers in the fireplace hardly penetrated the deep shadows.

Exhausted, Titius rested against the wall and slept.

Early next morning a servant girl opened the door and relit the lamp. She rekindled the fireplace and then turned to straighten the cushions. She screamed and stepped back.

"Peace," Titius said. "Peace. I mean no harm."

She slipped out the door in a hurry. Two legionnaires arrived minutes later with their gladius' drawn. Titius hadn't moved.

"Peace," he said again. "Peace. I wait for the Optio to hear my report."

"Come," the senior soldier said. "The centurion wants you."

Titius tried his best to keep up as each soldier held an elbow and forced him to walk quickly. Just inside Sestus's quarters he was thrown to the floor and left. Four legionnaires, swords drawn, stood along the wall.

"This is not good," Cleopas whispered.

Titius struggled to his feet and surveyed the room. The floor-to-ceiling Persian carpets belonged in a palace, not a soldier's room. There were marble statues, the best of Rome. Golden incense bowls, silver wine flagons, jade sculptures… Sestus had exquisite taste. A chair covered in a lion skin sat at one end of the room.

"What's this about?" Titius asked.

No legionnaire moved a muscle. Titius stepped toward the chair; every eye moved with him.

Someone knocked on the door softly, twice. The legionnaires drew their swords and hemmed him in. Titius'shoulder and neck muscles tightened with anticipation.

Sestus opened the door and walked purposefully toward the chair. He sat straight-backed and extended his centurion's stick. "Kneel."

Titius knelt, as did the others. Sestus had never ordered him to kneel before.

"It's your choice: die slowly or quickly," Sestus said. "By the sword or by strangulation."

Titius' heartbeat quickened. His palms moistened. His shoulder pain moved to his back. "What are the charges?"

Sestus lowered his stick. "Abandoning your assignment. Defecting to the zealots. Refusing to report to your superior. Murdering a Roman officer."

"Who are the witnesses?" Titius asked. *What is this about?*

Sestus waved at a legionnaire, who opened the door. Marcus stood there, dressed in his full black assassin's attire.

A shiver raced up Titius' spine. He rested his knuckles against the cool floor.

Marcus slithered across the floor to Sestus and knelt, his head bowed.

"Speak truth or forfeit your tongue," the centurion commanded. "Roman justice is swift."

"From my time with the zealots," Marcus said, "I learned that this man, Titius Marcus Julianus, taught zealot fighters how to beat Roman armies. He sought to marry the sister of Barabbas, the zealots' leader. He didn't return from his assignment in Capernaum but followed his own pleasure. Now, his bloodied robe has been discovered by the body of Jaennus, the Optio who crucified the zealots Titius trained."

Titius could not believe what he heard. Everything was technically true, but the way Marcus described made its implications deadly.

"The record is clear," Sestus said to a legionnaire who had taken up a stylus and wax tablet. "Is there another witness?"

"Yes," Marcus said. He left and Octavian came in and knelt.

"Speak!" Sestus ordered. "Speak truth or forfeit your tongue."

"From my years training as a thespian assassin with this man, Titius Marcus Julianus, I know he has broken the brotherhood's code. He betrayed those he swore to protect. He has not guarded this garrison's cross maker. Because of this, the cross maker was attacked and nearly killed by zealots. When commanded to stay and watch the executions, he left."

"The record is clear," Sestus announced. "The witness may go. We will read the charges."

The legionnaire stepped forward and read: "Let it be known and let it be clear that Titius Marcus Julianus is charged with the following requiring his death: he joined forces with the zealots. He abandoned his post. He murdered a Roman officer. He broke the code of brotherhood. He was delinquent in his responsibility. He refused an order."

Sestus turned to Titius, still kneeling. "What do you answer to these charges deserving your death?"

Titius bowed low, as he'd done in the cave when he first

submitted to the centurion. "Thank you for letting me speak. I know that such charges usually result in immediate death without defense. First, I know nothing about the death of my dear friend Jaennus. Until this moment I hadn't heard of it. I am willing, before this judgment seat, to give a moment-by-moment account of my whereabouts to prove I am blameless."

"So you shall," Sestus said. The recording officer readied himself to wite down Titius' words. "Regarding the code of brotherhood, I was instructed by my Optio that truth spoken to officers did not qualify as breaking the code. I have spoken to no one other than my Optio. I will tell you what I told him before this judgment seat as long as there are no non-officers in the room."

"This too will be," Sestus said, furrowing his brow. The recorder finished writing and Sestus nodded for Titius to continue.

"Regarding the charge of abandoning my responsibility for the cross maker, I was re-assigned to find out more about the one called Messiah. I was doing my duty when this event happened. I am willing to give a full account, before this judgment seat, of where I was and what I learned."

"It will be arranged," Sestus said, nodding again.

"Regarding the charge of training zealots to defeat Romans and betraying my command by seeking to marry Barabbas' sister, I have already reported to my Optio and my centurion. I can give a fuller report before this judgment seat if that is required. I deny any act outside my duty: to infiltrate and gain wisdom on the strengths and plans of the zealots. I am willing to speak more on this."

"So you shall," Sestus said. "Next charge."

"Regarding leaving the execution, I was dragged to the event without knowledge. I was recovering from a leopard attack and a fever. I have only my ignorance to blame for disregarding a command. This I admit, but I am also willing to give a full account of what happened when I left the event."

"My judgment will be just," Sestus pronounced.

"Regarding my failure to return directly to this city but following another path, which led to being attacked by the leopard, I say that coming from Capernaum through Magdala is still a somewhat direct route to Sepphoris. I was following up on new information. I am willing to give a fuller report before this judgment seat."

"So you shall," Sestus said. "Legionnaires, you've protected me well. Send three officers who can take your place, all of whom can record. We'll be here awhile."

Titius still bowed low as soldiers were exchanged. When Sestus dismissed himself Titius was left alone, except for Cleopas in his thoughts: *"I would choose the sword. You deserve the cross but you're a Roman so they can't do that. Strangulation is too clean. Beheading gives them a mess to clean up."*

Titius put his hands on his own throat. "Hush, spawn of the evil one."

"What did you call me?" Cleopas asked.

Titius looked around. Dozens of oil lamps burned overhead, giving off their olive oil scent. The polished marble floor still shone. A strange presence lurked at the edges of the room, something that smelled like peace. Inside him, Cleopas whimpered.

The door opened and Sestus returned, followed by three other Optios. The three took their places behind tables. Each held a stylus and a long parchment on which they wrote. The interrogation for Titius' life began in earnest.

After an hour, Titius's knees and back cried for mercy. After two hours his mind begged for relief from having to recall so many details. After three hours his soul craved release. After four hours of questioning and repeating and rephrasing, he prepared his spirit for a quick end.

At last it was over. Sestus rose, called for the Optios to bring the parchments, and left.

30

Titius' bladder ached. An hour passed. He stared at the door and willed Sestus to return. He shifted from knee to knee. He was preparing to disgrace himself when an elderly slave stepped in and put a chamber pot in the corner. Titius used it quickly and knelt again in the center of the room.

He heard legionnaires changing shifts as they finished their half-day watch. This happened twice and still there was no word from anyone. Titius slept on his knees, his forehead to the ground, waiting. His body ached, but he dared not add another crime to his list.

When a third shift of sentries came on duty he began to wonder.

"He's arranging your execution," Cleopas said. *"It won't be long until you're with us."*

"Who is 'us'?" Titius asked.

The door opened. The same slave replaced the champer pot with another. A young girl stepped in and left a tray of food. Titius ate the dates, figs, bread, cheese, yogurt, apricots, not waiting to make sure it was his. If he was to die, at least he'd die satisfied.

"That's your last meal," Cleopas hissed.

"Sestus wouldn't waste food on a condemned man, especially one who murdered his Optio. I rest my soul on Roman justice. This centurion will not come to judgment quickly."

"They'll still get you because of the girl," said Cleopas. *"If you'd run*

and come back instead of going to Magdala, this judgment may never have happened."

"I had to find Abigail," said Titius. He thought of her twirling happily in the Roman rose garden.

"Now you never will," Cleopas said. *"Women were always your weakness."*

A legionnaire came in and pulled Titius to his feet. His legs felt like rubber. He forced himself to move alongside the soldier.

"It's time," Cleopas growled. *"They'll pronounce your death."*

He led Titius through a series of tunnels into a spacious room in the fortress dungeon near the palace. A tray of food sat on a small table and a fresh chamber pot rested in the corner. Titius estimated that two days had passed since his confrontation with Marcus and Octavian.

A fortnight of sunrises and sunsets passed without any human interaction but the slave who changed his chamber pot and the girl who brought him food. Although they never exchanged a word, near the end of the second week the girl looked him in the eye. He nodded. She blushed and hurried out.

Titius paced. "Next time I will speak," he said. "I will appeal to the great gods. No subject should feel the cruelty of isolation for so long."

Sitting unwashed day after day started to make his skin itch. He wanted to ask the girl for a little water to wash with. His beard itched, his back itched, his head, his legs, his feet itched. Pacing became his daily exercise. The arguments with Cleopas changed from silent ones in his mind into loud, passionate verbal exchanges.

One morning, as a rooster crowed, the door opened and another legionnaire led him back to Sestus' room. He knelt and waited. Sestus marched in with his guardians and sat.

"Titius Marcus Julianus, stand!" he commanded.

Titius stood, his head bowed.

"Titius Marcus Julianus, I have considered all the evidence given." Sestus took out a scroll and examined it. "Yet, there is more to be considered. For now, I sentence you to forty lashes less one for putting yourself in unnecessary danger so you could not guard the cross maker. This sentence will be carried out immediately, after which you will be returned to your quarters until further decisions are made. So it is decided, so let it be done."

Two legionnaires pulled Titius from the room. He didn't know whether to be happy or terrified. The leather lash, with its embedded bits of bone and stone, would rip the skin and flesh from his back. It would be like the leopard attack all over again. But at least he'd be alive.

His legs felt heavy as his mind tried to fend off images of other floggings he'd witnessed. The soldiers dragged him across a small courtyard, through a tunnel, and into the main courtyard.

In the inner courtyard, he walked numbly to the post. They stripped off his robe. Witnesses surrounded him, watching as his wrists were bound.

The lashes began. He screamed loud enough to drown out Cleopas' laughter.

At lash twenty, the fire across his back and sides paralyzed his senses. He forced himself to remember a picnic he'd had with Abigail and her sister. The girls had chased butterflies and birds and splashed in a small waterfall. White clouds had tumbled into different shapes and they all imagined what they saw in the sky. All was peace. Cleopas wasn't there.

A searing pain ripped at his chest. Titius gasped for air. Another bone-tipped strip of leather bit into his rib. On that picnic with Abigail and Lydia, he'd fallen asleep in the sun. Now under the lash he longed for the lotion Abigail had applied to him for days after his skin had burned.

He awoke to a young girl bathing him and singing. He was stripped down to a loin cloth and a coat of bloody wounds. He tried to pretend she was Abigail, but the girl's voice was wrong, her touch was wrong, her smell was wrong.

Titius forced himself to dwell on childhood adventures, hunting expeditions, his awe at the victory parades through Rome. When he was alone again he rolled onto his side and clenched his teeth. Pain was his friend. He was *alive*.

Abigail's face sustained him, but another face began to surface in his thoughts. Yeshua ben Yuseph, the people's Messiah, had clearly seen through Titius's disguises, yet had never exposed or humiliated him. Titius knew he was a master of disguise. How had Yeshua done it?

Titius recalled the healer's words in Capernaum, when he'd been dressed as the blind man: "My friend, pretending to be poor and blind doesn't mean you're not actually poor and blind. You're more than you seem, as am I."

While Titius had been playing an olive merchant, Yeshua had said: "The Almighty looks behind the mask to the actor's heart. Nothing is hidden from his eyes." Each time they'd seen each other after that, Yeshua had nodded knowingly, acknowledging who Titius really was.

The healings, the miracles, the acts of compassion, moved like puzzle pieces in his mind. But the picture had to be wrong. Some miracles could be explained away as fortunate coincidences. But the face of the blind man at Bethsaida, joyful after his healing, had burned itself into Titius's thoughts. What did Yeshua see that he didn't see?

Titius opened his eyes to nothing but the dirt-smeared limestone walls.

"Who is he?" Titius thought. "Who am I?"

31

As Titius lost track of days, he lost hope. His wounds healed. The girl stopped coming with her life-giving songs. Life's only constant was the changing chamber pot. Eventually he stopped pacing his room. For two days he lay curled in a corner.

The next day a legionnaire opened the door. He dropped a clean robe on the floor for Titius to put on. Titius forced himself to his feet, pulled it over his scabbed and scarred torso, and wobbled down the hall after the quick-stepping soldier.

After many corridors they climbed some stairs and emerged at the edge of the agora. Titius blinked in the unfiltered sunshine.

"Resume your duties," the legionnaire said. And he left.

Titius crumbled against a wall, but his wounded back recoiled from it. Through blinking eyes he surveyed the scene. Everything looked normal. The almond trees were blooming. Piles of oranges and lemons dotted the marketplace. Several tables had taken down their canopies and stood open to the sun.

Titius shuffled toward the bakery. There was someone working there he didn't know. He continued past it toward the fish vendor.

"*No,*" said Cleopas. "*Don't go there.*"

Titius stopped and looked at the pickled fish, none longer than his fingers. "Are these from Magdala?" he asked.

The vendor smiled. "The man knows fish. Yes, the best pickled fish in Galilee come from Magdala."

"Are these from Isaac?"

"You know Isaac?" The vendor grabbed a small bag from under his table. "His are the best, but they don't come cheap, my friend. How many would you like? Perhaps, since you're his friend, we can make a deal."

Titius's pulse quickened. "Did his helper Abigail come by?"

"Ah, you know fish and women." The vendor began to scoop fish onto a scale. "She has a face to dazzle a man's heart. But I warn you, many men would kill to have her for their own."

"Do you know when she'll be back?"

The vendor leaned across his table. "My friend, my fish smells better than you. A wild dog is better groomed than you. The beggars look healthier than you. Don't chase what you can't catch."

"I just need to know when she'll be here," said Titius, surveying the other stalls. He grabbed the vendor by the wrist. "Where did she go?"

The vendor wrenched his arm away. "I believe I overheard her tell her partner they'd enjoy their new place in Caesarea."

"Her partner? Not Isaac?"

"A young wealthy businessman. She seemed quite happy with him, if I know women. Now, do you want the fish or not?"

"Typical woman," Cleopas snickered. *"Puts a hook in your heart and then rips it out."*

Titius turned away in a daze and made his way to a nearby fountain. He sat, ignoring the water slowly soaking his robe.

As he waited, Caleb and Deborah strolled by arm in arm, lost in love. The spider had caught the fly. Could he do his job when his heart was no longer in it?

He forced himself to shadow the pair and watch them. It soon became apparent the walk was an act. Caleb was enduring her chatter and attention; Deborah watched what was happening around her. So Sestus had created another team to learn the city's hidden activities. Who was watching him as he watched others?

He followed Caleb and Deborah until they stopped near a legionnaire. When the two sat down to eat, he slunk back toward the bakery. He needed more information.

Through the baker, Titius received instructions to take over at the baker's table every morning and then shadow the cross maker. He used the time to perfect a few new disguises and replace what he'd lost to the bandits. His appetite increased and his strength slowly returned. His scabs fell off and his step was sure again.

"Is this what you gave up your estate and senate seat for?" Cleopas mocked. *"Is this the life to bring pride to your father and grandfather? What kind of man are you?*

"I'm more of a man than you'll ever be again."

A month after his release, a trumpet sounded near the main gate and a cohort of legionnaires in full regalia marched into the square. Sestus stood atop a staircase and read a proclamation: "Our Roman legion is proud to announce that Emperor Tiberius himself asked two of our best to represent him in the 'Best of the Gladiator Games' in Rome. Marcus Flavius made it to the second round. Octavian Juventus made it to the fourth. Their memories will be honored. They died honoring their Emperor. Long live the Emperor!"

The crowd's cheers seemed out of place to Titius. Two thespian assassins had given their lives for the emperor. Two "heroes" who'd betrayed Titius and tried to destroy him were now destroyed. While Titius had been in the dungeon, feeling the sting of injustice and death, Marcus and Octavian had faced the real strength of Roman honor and justice.

Sestus stood, fist on chest, chin square, back straight. There was neither pleasure nor sadness in his face. Titius knew that if he himself had been the one chosen to die by the centurion, this same look would have greeted any observer. He shuddered, then stood like a statue at attention.

When the commander and honor guard disappeared into their quarters Titius returned to his post at the bakery. Titius realized that Sestus believed him. It didn't take away his body's scars, but it healed something inside.

On the Sabbath he stopped by the synagogue to see if any of Yeshua's followers were there. Dressed as a Jewish carpenter, few paid him any attention.

The attendant took a large scroll from a cabinet and handed it to a visiting rabbi, the rabbi from Nazareth. The rabbi read a passage Titius didn't understand, then spent an hour warning people about false prophets, seditious leaders, presumptious and prideful men. Clearly he was referring to Yeshua ben Yuseph. If the talk in the service wasn't obvious enough, the talk among people afterward certainly was.

A burly butcher shook his finger in a scribe's face. "He speaks of Yeshua, doesn't he?"

Titius shouldered his way through the tight crowd of men. A weaver said to a tailor: "That Nazarene has made enemies. There've been too many Messiahs. Rome will crush him as it did the others."

A young Pharisee raised his fist. "It's true," he cried. "I heard it from Rabbi Gamaliel in Jerusalem. All false Messiahs will fail."

Something was changing. Messianic fever in this land had been strong for years. Everyone knew Rome had destroyed the last three "Messiahs", back in the time of Yeshua's birth. In the year Antipas's father, Herod the Great, had died, Simon of Perea had led a rebellion that Rome crushed. A few years later Athronges, a shepherd, raised a rebellion against Herod's son, Archelaus. They too were defeated. About the same time, Judas of Gamala had founded the zealots in this area and faced his own destruction.

An old man, bent and frail, raised his cane over his head. "If Yeshua isn't the Messiah, how can he open the eyes of the blind, or heal lepers? How did he change water to wine?"

Bodies swirled around the man, every one screaming his viewpoint. Titius pushed his way out of the room.

After freeing himself from the synagogue madness, Titius changed and walked through the city, taking in all he could observe. As a blind man he'd gained much information because people let their guard down around him. His new guise, a beggar, involved a cane, a significant limp, and a well-bandaged head.

Day after day he waited near the fish vendor. He hardly noticed the smell anymore. There was still no sign of Abigail and no contact with Sestus or the Optio who'd replaced Jaennus. To break routine, he followed Caleb out to the forest and watched him cutting down trees and shaping them into crosses. Several times he noticed Sestus riding out, apparently into zealot territory. Rumours among the legionnaires claimed these trips meant significant zealot losses.

One day Titius followed Caleb into an olive orchard. He loved the cool air and the fresh scents of earth and foliage.

Caleb met there the same raven-haired beauty who'd calmed Titius's fever with cool cloths after the leopard attack. To Titius it appeared a chance meeting. Caleb applied his charm and walked with her back to Cana, where he met her father, a rabbi.

"Another good man falls for a woman," Cleopas said. *"You've taught him much. His weakness is also women."*

Hours later Caleb left the synagogue where he'd been talking with the rabbi. His brow was furrowed and he walked slowly – apparently the talk went badly. Titius followed Caleb back to Sepphoris.

Titius took up his post at the bakery. Caleb fed him information while stopping for bread. Then Titius passed on intelligence to the cross maker. He urged him to be cautious with Deborah. Others in the secret network stopped by: a mason, a tiler, a legionnaire, an actor, a vendor, a beggar. This became Titius' routine.

Titius discovered that Deborah was part of a conspiracy to open a new route for the Chinese Silk trade. One day Titius followed her to Tiberius and got his first actual look at Barabbas.

Sestus ordered Titius to begin more intensive training with Caleb. Hours each day the two would fight with wooden swords and javelins. They'd swim and ride. They'd concoct new disguises, as beggars or slaves. They listened in on conversations all over the city.

Caleb had instinctive survival talents, strong mental abilities, and increasing physical strength. Titius urged Sestus to consider including Caleb more in the intelligence gathering. Sestus embraced the idea, so Caleb disappeared from Sepphoris.

A week later a legionnaire came to the bakery and reported that Caleb had been manipulated into crucifying Deborah. She'd been pregnant with Barrabas' child. They beheaded her father. Sestus had ordered many crucifixions around Sepphoris.

Caleb was no longer just a cross maker. Barabbas and Phoebe wouldn't take these losses lightly. Titius went for a long walk around the city. He dunked his head in a fountain and shook it like a dog. What had he done?

Titius, playing the blind man, delivered three loaves and a scroll to Caleb's quarters, trying to contact him. The scroll read: "The spider has been squashed. Your time for training has risen like an eagle on the wind. The apricot feeder is within your grasp."

Things were changing too fast.

32

Titius, wrapped in two blankets and an extra tunic, was hiding beside the fish-vendor's stall when he heard the first ear-piercing wails. He jumped to his feet. The orange vendor and the olive vendor embraced and wailed.

The date vendor hurried between the fluttering canopies. "The Baptist!" he cried. "The Baptist is dead!"

A shudder shook Titius to the core. He grabbed the herald. "How? Why? Where?"

"That Jezebel, Herodias, tricked Antipas at Macheraus," said the date vendor. "Herod was drunk during his birthday party. Herodias' sleazy daughter seduced him into agreeing to behead the Baptizer. They put his head on a silver platter."

The fish-vendor turned to Titius. "What do you think the Messiah will do?" He glanced over his shoulder. "The Baptizer is his cousin. Maybe he'll join Barabbas and help us finally get rid of these Romans."

Until that moment the Messiah had seemed unstoppable. It was rumored he'd fed five thousand men plus their families with only five loaves and two fish and stilled a storm with a single word. Another blind man could see. He was healing people everywhere.

The market legionnaires on duty were tense. "Patronius, what do you think this Messiah will do?"

"Festus, if he tries anything we'll call in the legions and crush him.

For now, he's just a distraction. Keeps the people's minds off of their troubles."

But the days went by without rioting or revolt. The soldiers began to relax.

Three months after Titius' trial, Sestus called for him. This time Caleb was there too in the assassins' secret room. None of them said a word about the trial and its aftermath.

Sestus paced as usual. "Titius, you will mentor Caleb. He remains my cross maker but will be more. You must ensure this."

Sestus left, leaving Titius and Caleb alone.

"Sestus wants you to take another step," Titius began. "You will perfect your language skills." With a flick of his wrist, Titius produced an orange and tossed it to Caleb. "People use language to communicate *and* to conceal," he said. "They hide secrets in language they think others won't understand."

"I already know Hebrew, Greek, Aramaic, and Latin," Caleb retorted. He tossed the orange back to Titius.

"Your Hebrew and Aramaic are fine," Titius responded. "Your Latin needs help. It sounds like pigs rooting for acorns. Greek should sound like an eagle on the thermals. You make it sound like a fox flushing a partridge."

"Most people understand me."

"You must do more than get by." Titius reached behind Caleb's back and produced a gladius. With a quick movement, it disappeared. "You must understand accurately, and speak so that it sounds natural to any passerby."

Caleb flopped down on a cushion. "The only reason I'm doing

this is to avoid the dungeon, to protect my family and to get my slave Nabonidus back. Why do you put up with these insane demands?"

"I wanted to become a man," he said.

"And how has this helped you become a man? Apart from helping you do magic tricks."

Titius sat down. "Our art is tenfold." He counted off on his left hand. "The five abilities: distraction, disguise, sleight of hand, silence, quick kills."And then his right hand. "The five qualities: power, endurance, healing, knowledge, loyalty."

Caleb held out his hands, fingers splayed. "Left is distraction, disguise, magic, silence, death. Right is power, endurance, healing, knowledge and loyalty." He clasped his hands together. "When the two become one, the assassin is unbeatable."

Titius smiled.

"You're creating a monster," Cleopas snarled inside. *"He'll be the one who sends you to me."*

For two weeks they worked on the ten basics of the assassin's art. He then brought in others who were fluent in different languages to work out the finer points of pronunciation. At first Caleb stuttered like a goose trying to clear the water, but he improved as the days passed.

Titius spent mornings with his charge, then, as the Greek olive merchant, roamed the market. One day he stopped by the fish vendor.

Titius boldly sampled the pickled fish. "The finest in Galilee," he declared in flawless Greek. "It could be even better than what we have in Corinth."

"This dealer gets orders from all over the world," the vendor affirmed. "I can get a crate sent to your door, for the right price."

Titius took another nibble. "All the way to Corinth? That's a deal. Any way to work out a deal with the master himself?"

"Maybe… if you can wait three days," said the vendor. "There's a delivery then."

Titius looked around. The awnings rippled like a sea in the breeze. "Is this a man I can trust?"

The vendor smiled. He leaned over his fish. "You can trust this dealer, but his representative is not a man. It's a woman, as smart as she is beautiful. Looking into her eyes, you forget about how much money she's asking for."

"I'll be careful. I hope my olives will entice her as much as her fish entices me."

"Come mid-morning," said the vendor. "She only stays long enough to do business."

Titius nodded and walked away.

"*Don't go back,*" said Cleopas. "*She'll capture you with her eyes.*"

"I always loved her eyes," Titius said.

"*She has a partner,*" Cleopas countered. "*Live on your memories. Let her go.*"

"If there's anyone I'd like to let go, it's you."

The morning of the appointed day with the fish vendor, Sestus met with Titius and Caleb to review their training regimen. The update was short and Sestus seemed satisfied with the progress of his cross maker turned assassin.

By the time Titius excused himself, changed, and reached the fish vendor, Abigail was gone.

"She came early this morning," the vendor said, shrugging. "She needed to be in Magdala by nightfall."

"*Fool!*" Cleopas howled. "*Shamed by a woman again!*" When will you learn?"

"It's that wretched centurion," Titius said aloud. "Do the two of you conspire against me?"

The vendor stared. "I assure you, sir, I conspire with no one, especially a centurion."

Titius charged into the rush of people moving through the agora. "Wretched spirit," he said. "You're going to get me chained up like a zealot demoniac. The whole world will think I'm a lunatic."

Cleopas laughed again. "*Soon the whole world will know who you really are. Your disguises don't fool any of us who see you for the fraud you are.*"

"You keep saying 'us,'" Titius responded. "Never mind you. I need more help."

Titius sat with the baker to consider his options. The baker was a grizzled veteran who'd travelled with many Roman legions.

"Who's ready to help me train a new assassin?" Titius asked him.

"Jason of Thessalonica, the tiler, has proven himself in the arena and on the battlefield. He's due an easier task. Though I'm not sure he will be patient with inexperience."

"Who else?"

"Sosipater of Sparta, the stone mason, is stronger than three men together. Unmatched in stick fighting, boxing, and sword combat. He could teach your man something if he didn't kill him first."

"Get him for me," Titius said. "Caleb needs him and I could use the workout myself."

Titius met with Sosipater the next day and hired him to lead Caleb's fighting drills. He also sought out Lucius Flavius, a champion in wrestling and the bloody sport of pankration. In pankration, nothing was forbidden except eye gouging and biting. The mixed martial art was often lethal.

Flavius demonstrated his skill for Titius and Caleb by facing down five strong legionnaires and six slaves, one after another. He unleashed powerful kicks to the heads, elbows to the jaws of others, and brutal blows to ribs and limbs. Blood spattered Flavius' chest, fists, and feet.

"You can go," Titius said to him. "We've seen enough." The fighter turned without a word and sauntered away past the carnage.

Caleb physically trembled. "I can't do that," he said. "I can't destroy people for no reason."

Titius watched Flavius wash his hands in a fountain. "Pankration follows naturally from close fighting. If you ever lose your weapon, these arts are essential to survive. Learn them and pray you'll never have to use them."

The next afternoon Titius and Caleb set themselves to the task of learning to be ruthless and heartless. They wrestled, punched, and kicked large leather bags filled with sand. Their skin scraped away and blood flowed.

After that Caleb said, "I'm finished with women."

"Why do you say that?" asked Titius.

"What woman would love a man who would destroy someone so easily? She'd live in terror of him. What love could they share?"

"Perhaps," Titius replied, "we should learn only enough to protect ourselves."

"I don't know about you, but I want a woman who loves me."

Titius wrestled with this. Why become a man everyone looked up to if the woman you loved wouldn't have anything to do with you?

By the second rooster crow next day, Titius and Caleb were already running northeast toward Damascus. Cattle stood still in the dewy grass under the day's first birdsong. A few early workmen shouted their greetings. Titius and Caleb ran for two hours, noted the distance they'd covered, then turned back to Sepphoris.

"A champion has to build endurance," Titius coached. "We need to run until we can't run any more, and then run twice as far."

Caleb took another deep breath.

"Pain will become your friend," Titius added. "Some days you'll wish you were dead. That will remind you you're still alive."

The next day they ran northwest along the coast for two hours and returned. The third day they ran southwest toward Caesarea for two hours and returned. The last day in the cycle, they ran south toward Samaria for two hours and returned.

After four days they took a day off, then started the cycle again, always working to increase their distance. For a month they ran in the morning, lifted weights in the afternoon, and practiced fighting in the evening.

Titius marked the days until this assignment would be done.

Abigail would be visiting the fish vendor after three more cycles of running the roads, two weeks away.

This time nothing would stop him from meeting her.

33

Morning rain didn't shorten the line of carts jockeying to get into Sepphoris. Titius noticed that the usual cluster of Hebrew carpenters was missing, and when the ram's horn sounded he rightly surmised that another Jewish holiday was underway.

The legionnaires anchored their sandaled feet against the gate house and waved traders or travellers into the city without inspection. Titius noted the security breach to tell Sestus. The tax collectors didn't miss a soul.

As Titius stretched himself before a run, Sestus approached him and confided that he was taking Caleb to Jericho and then Jerusalem.

"Be outside the Antonia Fortress in two weeks," he ordered. A legionnaire brought his mount. *"No one* must know you're there. Zealots will be busy this Passover."

The Antonia Fortress in the heart of Jerusalem was an easy three day ride from Sepphoris. With Caleb gone, Titius had ten days to himself. He meandered around the market watching the fish vendor's stall in case Abigail showed up early. Dressed as a shepherd, he asked the vendor when the pickled fish arrived fresh from Magdala.

"I thought you shepherds swore to live on goat's milk and cheese," the vendor joked. "This fish is fresh every day. The supplier will bring more in two days."

Two days later Titius, playing the olive merchant, set up an observation post near the fish vendor. Under a drizzling rain carts moved in and out of the market.

Within a few hours, a man greeted the fish vendor familiarly. He was a young man with bushy black eyebrows and a big nose above a scruffy attempt at a beard. Powerful shoulders rippled under his tunic as he unloaded a basket of fish onto a scale.

"The rains are making the roads difficult," he said. "But praise the Almighty for good harvests coming."

The fish vendor nodded at Titius, who slipped into the vendor's stall.

"Peace to you," he said, "I am Porpherus of Corinth." He took off his blue cape and smoothed a wrinkle on his white tunic's sleeve.

The young Hebrew set his basket on the ground. "Peace to you. I am Emmanuel of Bethlehem."

Titius watched the fish as the vendor poured it out of the scale into his own basket. "My friend tells me," he said, "you help bring him the best pickled fish from Magdala."

Emmanuel nodded. "The fish belong to the Almighty. My uncle Isaac knows the secret of pickling. I'm a salesman and sometime escort."

"You escort fish?" probed Titius.

"I escort one who benefits our business," Emmanuel replied. "Because she's a woman. I was supposed to teach her the business but she's already shrewd."

"I trade in olives. I believe we can help each other," said Titius. "Can you take me to this dealer so we can talk?"

Emmanuel shook his head. "She's done so well that we've sent her to Jerusalem to open the markets there, for Passover. She knows people there to host her."

"She has no husband?"

Emmanuel laughed. "If I weren't betrothed, I'd be first in line for her hand." He checked the coins the vendor gave him. "She's given her heart to someone for whom she waits. She spurns all who court her."

Titius' heartbeat quickened. "May the new year bring blessing to you and your business."

"May the Almighty give you your heart's desires," Emmanuel responded, with a nod.

Titius's clenched and opened his fists, trying to relax. Cleopas was quick: *"She has given her heart to another. Leave her. She spurns all men."*

Titius nodded to Emmanuel and the fish vendor. "I'll take my leave and consider my options," he said. "Thank you for your service." He wandered away among the stalls.

"Forget her," Cleopas chided.

"Emmanuel blessed me," Titius responded under his breath, "by asking the Almighty to give me my heart's desires."

"You don't even believe in the Almighty," Cleopas countered.

"Keeping my options open," he said.

The next morning, clouds parting and the sun streaming, Titius borrowed a stallion and began his trek to Jerusalem. He dressed as a Roman noble to avoid any questions about where he got his horse. The roads were full of pilgrims heading for the Passover ritual.

Titius rode slowly, enjoying the beauty around him. Wildflowers bloomed everywhere. Hawks, pelicans, pheasants, ravens, and songbirds dotted the skies as if the sun freed them from hidden prisons.

He passed Nazareth and headed for Nain. The barley and flax harvest was underway and people were busy in the fields. Cart after cart of grain clogged the road.

By horse, it took only a few hours to reach the village of Nain southwest of Mount Tabor. Green pastures lay, a grassy sea, in all directions. The first signs of the wheat harvest rose from the rich red soil. Titius imagined how much Abigail would have enjoyed the journey.

The main houses in Nain sat above the sepulchral caves where the ground fell to the plain of Esdraelon. He let his steed drink briefly outside the city. He filled his gourd with the cool, clear mountain water and walked his horse down the village road.

At a small market he bought dates, figs, and apricots. An old woman shuffled toward him with a small bag. She held it to him. He smelled aging fish. "Roman! Roman!" she called. "Pickled fish, from Magdala... fresh for you."

"When did you get it?" asked Titius, trying not to turn away.

"Only a week ago," she said, smiling. "Still fresh for you."

"Who sold it to you?" he asked. He tightened his grip on the reins.

"An angel," she said. "As beautiful as Abraham's Sarah."

Who Abraham and Sarah were he had no clue, but only Abigail could be compared to an angel. He declined the old woman's offer and pressed on.

As he came through the Jezreel Valley he noticed that most traffic had veered east, to the Jordan Valley. Passover pilgrims wouldn't defile themselves by crossing Samaritan lands. The Carmel Ridge rose to the west and the mountains of Jerusalem rose majestically straight ahead.

He was within a stone's throw of Sabaste when he heard shouts. "Hail! The Messiah lives. Praise be to the Almighty, the Messiah lives!"

Titius called to a man, bone-thin and waving a wad of rags: "What are you saying?"

The man jumped up and down. "The Messiah lives! I am one of ten lepers he healed!"

Titius dismounted and approached the man. "There's already someone claiming to be the Messiah in Capernaum. How many Messiahs can there be? One for Galilee, one for Samaria, another for Jerusalem?"

"I know no other but Yeshua of Nazareth," shouted the man. "Yeshua of Nazareth healed me. He's my Messiah."

Titius backed his horse away from the ragged man and looked around. A crowd had gathered. "Yeshua's here? In Sabaste?"

One of the onlookers shouted, "Herod the Great may have named this city Sabaste but we still call it Samaria."

"Hush," said Titius. "This is Judea. You're still Samaritans. Was the Jewish Messiah here?"

"He was close by two days ago," said the former leper, scratching new stubble on his chin. "He spoke and we were healed. For the first time in seven years I can be with my family."

"Why are you here then?" asked Titius.

"They've gone to Passover. They don't know yet that I'm clean. Praise the Almighty!"

"Why don't you go too?" Titius asked.

"I have to complete the days of purification," he said. "They'll be back and we'll celebrate!"

That didn't make sense to Titius. If the man was healed, he was clean. What a strange religion.

The leper continued through the streets and the people made way for him.

"The disease has gone to his mind," Cleopas said. *"No man can cure leprosy."*

"Perhaps this Yeshua is more than a man," Titius mused.

"Better be obsessed with a woman than think such things," Cleopas responded.

Titius took some refreshment and booked an inn for the night. This Messiah was not going to be a problem for Rome just in Galilee. He'd have to find a way to report it to Sestus.

And soon he'd be closer than ever to Abigail. She was out there selling her fish in a sea of one million Passover pilgrims.

34

The innkeeper sent a maid with fruits, bread, and cheese for breakfast, with a flagon of cheap wine. Titius washed, then dressed again in his Roman nobleman's tunic.

As he walked to the stables, the innkeeper called: "Roman, wait!"

Titius instinctively looked around for a possible ambush. "If what I paid you is not enough," he said, "I can give you more."

"No, you've been generous." Titius watched his hands and eyes. The man betrayed no ulterior motive. "I want to warn you. A few days ago a centurion and his helper came this way. They were ambushed by Barabbas and other Sicarri. You may be in danger, a wealthy Roman on a horse."

"What happened to the centurion?" asked Titius.

The inn keeper smiled. "You care about the centurion but not yourself? Somehow they survived. I think Barabbas got away, but two of his men did not."

Titius looked toward Jerusalem. By horse, Abigail was half a day away. "Will you look after my horse if I decide to walk?" he asked the innkeeper.

The innkeeper nodded. "A good choice."

Titius repacked, leaving behind half of the supplies he'd carried on the horse. The pack he carried bulged with tunics, hairpieces and shoes. He'd replenish in Jerusalem.

"You know she'll be gone by the time you get there." Cleopas whispered.

In a grotto out of sight of the inn, Titius dressed as a Galilean shepherd, with a full beard and a shepherd's staff.

At the Jordan River he met high levels of rushing water. He examined the banks on both sides for anyone watching. Seeing no one, he removed his tunic and stepped into the strong currents. He successfully kept his tunic and pack above water. He slipped only once but kept from going under. On the far bank he dried his body with another robe before redressing.

He heard laughter. He quickly stuffed his pack. Three families with young children were passing toward Jerusalem. One father led a donkey carrying his daughter and one walked beside a donkey cart carrying two women, three children, and supplies. A third father walked beside a donkey carrying his wife and a young child.

"Peace to you," Titius called. They returned his greetings. "I'm travelling to Jerusalem for Passover. May I join you?"

The man beside the cart spoke up. "I've never seen a shepherd walk this road alone. Not without sheep."

"My brother's in Jerusalem preparing flocks for Passover sacrifices. He sent word asking me to join him. I began alone but was warned that there are zealots and bandits ahead."

"Very well," replied the man. "We could use someone else to keep us safe from those zealots and bandits. We go as far as Jericho tonight, to Jerusalem tomorrow."

Titius entertained the children with stories of his exploits with lions, bears, leopards and wild dogs.

"Which one had the biggest teeth?" a child asked.

"That's difficult to know," he said. "I was too busy running to notice."

The child laughed. "You should have used a slingshot," he said. "My daddy can kill a wolf across the road with one stone. Shoot your slingshot for us."

"I left my slingshot with another shepherd," Titius lied.

"Don't worry. My daddy will protect you," the child assured him.

Sometimes, with so many different personalities and disguises, it was hard to remember what he'd told people. The man leading his daughter on a donkey was listening more closely than Titius had realized.

"So you're from near Cana but you keep your flocks near Sepphoris? Your accent doesn't sound like that. You sound Greek or Roman."

Titius responded with a laugh. "You have a good ear, my friend," he said. "I have a Roman master who is trying to warp my tongue with Latin lessons. And my mother spoke Greek."

This seemed to satisfy him. The trip to Jericho passed without further incident.

As the travelers neared Jericho they saw camel caravans and elegantly-robed Arabs. A high tower sprouted above the date palms. Women carrying pots on their heads hauled water from a well near the main gate. Legionnaires stood on duty near a tax collector's booth. Ravens scavenged in the garbage dump. The freshness of country air became a memory.

The families bid him farewell and Titius explored the market. At the fish vendor's he noted that the pickled fish were not like the ones Abigail brought from Magdala. He ate his supper and settled down for the night among the sea of tents.

As he rested Titius thought back to his early days with the cross maker. Caleb had worked hard to get away from Sestus, but without success. The centurion had a hold on him, as he did on so many others. After burying the zealots' bodies in a shallow grave outside town, Titius had enjoyed playing the blind man and following his charge to the docks in Caesarea.

He tapped his cane right into Caleb.

"Old man," Caleb had called out. "I'm here. Where do you want to go?"

Titius remembered what followed. Caleb had been standing on a log and leaning against a warehouse.

"I'm Rome's eyes in this city," Titius had declared. "I saw you take on those zealots. I saw you ready to make a deal with the devil."

Titius remembered noticing the knife hidden under Caleb's carpenter's apron. He'd tapped Caleb's ankle with his cane and, when the cross maker looked down, Titius had stolen the knife. Moments later, when Caleb had reached back to get it, there was nothing there.

"If the devils possess you, old man," Caleb said, "go prophesy at the shrine of Pan. Leave me. And give me my knife."

Titius had smiled. "You're not as alert as you think. I was sent to keep you alive for Sestus." Titius held the knife up out of Caleb's reach.

"Give me the knife!" Caleb demanded.

"Take it!"

Caleb reached for it, but the knife disappeared. Titius held out an empty hand. Caleb grabbed for him and found himself spun around, the knife at his throat. "Things are not as they appear, carpenter."

"I hope for your sake that's true. What do I have to do?"

"You will learn to listen to my stick," said Titius. "It will tell you what's happening around you." He held out the knife so Caleb could take it.

Caleb stepped down and backed away. "I don't need any more training. I've tasted enough death for a lifetime. The Almighty can find other hands to do his work."

Titius had spoken carefully. "This 'Almighty'. Does he fight only for the Jews? Will I have to contend with him in our training? Will Rome have to conquer him?"

Titius kept his eyes closed. His hands moved warily before him like a wrestler ready to grapple.

"The Almighty cannot be conquered!" Caleb declared. "He is not a god to betray and anger! He claims to be the Creator of all things. His Temple is open to the people of all nations, but some of his followers will kill you if you try to enter."

"What must we do to silence these zealots who rise against us?" Titius asked. "Can we just kill them, or do we have to take their Temple and their land as well?"

The memory was as clear as yesterday to Titius. Now he was a day away from the city where the Almighty held sway. Where zealots, religious fanatics, Messiahs, and people from many nations mixed in a tension that Rome barely kept under control.

He had to guard a man who made the crucifixes they feared. He had to take his vengeance on the Roman noble who'd stolen his estate. And he had to find the woman he loved.

35

Shouts and celebration of visitors in the streets delayed his sleep. Traders' shouts and the grunts of camels and donkeys woke him early in the morning, but Titius lay still until roosters began crowing.

He dressed as a shepherd again and picked up food from the market. As he left the apricot vendor, he noticed three familiar faces: Sarah, Issachar, and Timna from the zealot camps. They walked beside a donkey carrying large baskets of apricots.

Sarah watched the Syrians guarding a grand gold-and-blue-curtained litter. She stumbled over a loose paving stone and caught the donkey's neck. Issachar pulled the startled donkey toward the apricot vendor while Timna scanned the crowd.

Titius circled a potter's stall, a carpet dealer, a wine merchant, the fish vendor, then back toward the fruit stalls. He backed toward the apricot dealer, pretending to examine some figs. The canopy helped block him from view.

"What do you mean you can't give us the same price?" Timna asked intensely. "This fruit is as good as the last we brought you."

The vendor's voice shook. "A centurion was here two days ago. He said if he finds out my fruit comes from anyone to do with Barabbas, he'll see that I'm crucified."

"He was trying to intimidate you," Issachar mocked. "Barabbas almost got that centurion in an ambush. We're trained and ready."

"I need to lay low for a while," the vendor insisted.

"What about the oath you took for the cause?" Timna said.

"They took six of your people from this market and sent them for crucifixion in Jerusalem," the vendor replied. "And several more on their way *to* Jerusalem. That's not how I'm spending Passover."

"Amnon, please," Sarah said. "You know we have more people here all the time. The fig dealer, the carpet weaver, the potter. I can send my cousin to be your assistant. She looks just like me."

The silence was too long. "When can she come?" Amnon asked.

"It will take a little time," Sarah responded. "I'll send her with the next shipment."

Titius waited until the fig dealer was busy and then slipped away. He noticed that the potter was watching the apricot booth very closely.

Within an hour Titius had joined a caravan heading toward Jerusalem. The heat was intense as they climbed the hills. An old man, already weary from the journey, lay atop several baskets of figs in a cart and covered his head with a shawl. His grandson on the front of the cart drove a donkey as boney as the old man.

Titius appreciated his physical fitness, which made the long hot journey seem a stroll. He'd be in the same city as Abigail and the cross maker by sundown.

Titius fell into step with three young men. Like them, he wore simple leather sandals, a plain brown tunic, and a shepherd's headscarf. The traders and travelers welcomed him easily.

Benomi, Saul, and Crissus were students of a young rabbi named Gamaliel. Most of their discussion seemed to be about finer points of the Jewish law, but within a half hour discussion turned to the new Messiah.

"Did you hear what that inn keeper said last night?" Benomi probed. "He claimed Yeshua of Nazareth took seven loaves and a few fish and fed four thousand people in the Decapolis."

"Do you think it's true?" Crissus asked. "Or just another version of the Messiah feeding five thousand men with five loaves and two fish near Bethsaida?"

"Two separate miracles," Saul answered. "I checked. The details are different. This Yeshua is reaching out to more than our people."

"Why would he go into the Decapolis?" Titius asked.

Benomi threw a stone into the trees. "Good question," he said. "Nothing over there but pagans tripping over themselves to be Greek or Roman or whatever is fashionable these days."

"Don't forget the zealots," Saul added. "Some go there to get away from the Romans."

"He doesn't act like a Messiah should," Benomi said. "He was in Caesarea near that shrine called the 'gates of hades' and told his followers that they'd even overcome such a place of evil someday."

"In Capernaum he healed a centurion's son," Crissus noted. "And in his own synagogue he told people that God's favour was on outsiders. He said that during Elijah's time God spared a widow in Sidon and during Elisha's time he healed Namaan the Syrian's leprosy. No wonder they tried to kill him."

"Should the Messiah be only for the Jews?" Titius asked.

"You've been in Galilee too long," Benomi said angrily. "Be sure, he'll be in the Temple again causing more trouble. Last year he turned over tables and chased the moneychangers out of the court of the gentiles."

Crissus asked, "Didn't he say the Temple was meant to be a house of prayer for all nations?"

Saul looked back – they'd gotten ahead of the caravan. "Let's wait. There've been attacks in this next section of road. We shouldn't leave these merchants unprotected. That old man and his grandson aren't going to fight bandits."

Crissus turned to Titius as they waited. "What do you know about the Messiah?"

"I look for truth wherever I find it," Titius said. "I saw him give sight to a blind man in Bethsaida. I saw him fill a fishnet to overflowing. I don't know how and I don't know what it means."

Benomi stamped his feet. "No! No! No! He is possessed by devils. How else could he do such things?"

Saul touched Benomi's shoulder. "Calm, calm brother." He pointed toward Jerusalem. "Perhaps if we talk to this Messiah we can convince him to use his powers against tax collectors and prostitutes. Instead of befriending them he should teach them more about Moses' law."

Titius fell back to walking with the merchants and their donkey carts. The three students kept talking, unaware he'd gone.

By the time the group crested the hill that looked down on the Temple's glistening white limestone walls, they were all ready for a moment of awed silence.

The old man raised his bony arms and opened his toothless mouth in a sob. His shoulders shook and the young man beside him put his arm around the frail body. "He thinks this is his last Passover," the young man said to Titius. "He's come every year since Antipas's father began to build this Temple. He fears the Romans will destroy everything if the zealots give up."

"What hope do so few have against so many?" Titius asked. "The Romans have unending armies, like the waves of the sea."

"But we have Messiah!" the son replied.

A great cheer rose up around Titius. "Soon we'll sing the Great Hallel at Passover!" Saul shouted. "We'll sacrifice a lamb on the same Mt. Moriah where God gave Abraham a ram. Let us sing!"

"Praise the Lord!" they sang. "Praise, O servants of the LORD, praise the name of the LORD. Let the name of the LORD be praised for evermore…"

Titius didn't remember the words. He went to the old man's cart and pretended to weep along with the pilgrim and his son. The Passover travellers sang or wept. Foreign merchants stopped to admire the view.

Benomi, Saul, and Crissus continued their singing chant as they hurried toward the masses gathering at Jerusalem's gates. From the hilltop it looked like the whole sea of humanity was pouring into a small limestone box.

They hurried down the Mount of Olives into the valley. The donkeys brayed, the camels grunted, the pilgrims wept, and the merchants cursed as their loads shifted and threatened to fall under the thousands of feet converging on Jerusalem. Titius helped the grandson tug the donkey up the paved street toward the Roman fortress tower by the market. Then he left them.

Bread, goat cheese, lamb and a generous cup of tea satisfied his stomach that night in the upper loft of a horse stable next to the Damascus Gate. The smell of hay reminded him of a certain night when he was young.

His father had been away at war. His mother busy with her books. The others were off on errands. There was no one around except Cleopas. The Hebrew slave had just begun to teach him to read.

During the lesson, Cleopas excused himself. Titius caught sight of Cleopas creeping past the great room where his mother was. Titius followed him. The slave opened the stable door and went inside, leaving it open. Titius followed.

Titius smelled horse dung and hay. He walked to the door and listened to voices inside. He could hear Cleopas whispering and a woman giggling. She sounded like the cook. He crept further into the dark stable.

A gust of wind blew the door shut! He stumbled and stepped on someone's foot. Terrible screaming sounded near his ear. His own screams joined the others until a hand covered his mouth and pushed him under a pile of hay. A heavy weight fell on him. He thought he would suffocate in the dust. He kicked, struggled and screamed. No help came. By the time he managed to get up he was shaken to the core. A servant had opened the door and pulled him into the light.

His mother forbade him to go into the stables alone again. "There are ghosts and demons in the dark," she said. Soon after that Abigail and her sister had come to keep watch over him.

In those first months, anytime Abigail thought no one was around she'd cry. He often saw her with red, puffy eyes and her sister would make excuses for her. On his ninth birthday Titius took a rose from the cook and dropped it into Abigail's lap as she sat on the stairs near the garden. She'd picked it up, smelled it, and smiled.

He'd do anything to see that smile one more time.

36

Sestus had made it clear that Titius was to be unnoticed and unidentifiable in Jerusalem. There were zealots from the Decapolis who knew him; traders and fishermen who could recognize him from Sepphoris, Capernaum and Bethsaida; and there were pilgrims from Nazareth, Caesarea and Cana who might sense something familiar about his face or his walk. He needed a disguise no one would notice but which would still leave him free to watch over the cross maker and search for Abigail.

He decided that dressing as one of the city's thousands of slaves would be best. He must appear credible in the markets as he looked for Abigail, but not tempt others to issue him orders, so decided to wear a privileged house servant's linen tunic, like Cleopas used to wear.

On his second day there, Titius stepped out of the stables into Jerusalem's midday crowds and headed for the markets in the Tyropoeon Valley. The linen tunics he must buy were closer to the Temple. For one day he risked wearing his shepherd's garb. The smoke and incense from Temple sacrifices floated down the hill and mixed with the smells of spices, sweating bodies, rotting vegetation, and sewage in these streets cramped between walls.

Jerusalem dealt with the huge influx of pilgrims by setting aside several areas for vendors. At his third market, Titius found the stall he desired. A linen awning, better than the usual woolen one, sheltered it from sunshine or rain. He hovered near a wall and watched shoppers paw through the merchandise. He listened to merchants and customers haggling for tunics.

A tall Nubian held up four tunics. "Lord Cretius is in residence with Herod. He needs these for his servants," he said.

An Egyptian woman raised an armload of linens. "Lord Cretius needs these for his household."

An elderly Jew raised a single rag. "Lord Cretius needs this for his pig." Several bystanders erupted in laughter. The Jew threw the rag at the Egyptian slave and hobbled away.

Sestus had given him plenty of money, so he counted coins from his tunic pocket. He quickly picked up what he wanted, laid down the money for the merchant and walked away without a word.

Back in the stable, Titius dressed in a fine knee-length tunic with an embroidered neckline and put on his best sandals. He paid a young woman near the stables to trim his hair and his beard.

"*You're planning something,*" Cleopas whispered.

"I must find out if there's a way to ambush Cretius," Titius snarled. "If that coward dares show his face away from his armed escort, my mother will have her revenge. Cretius must die."

"*Your mother is with me,*" Cleopas said. "*She doesn't need revenge.*"

Titius pressed his temples with his thumbs. "For Abigail, then."

"*You mock me in that tunic,*" Cleopas said as Titius started walking. "*My life was not a charade played in a city of fools. And the prayers to the Almighty at the Temple... they hurt my ears!*"

Titius turned toward the Fortress Antonia where Sestus would be stationed. He'd written a long account of his observations and he gave a boy a small coin to deliver it to one of the legionnaires on sentry duty. As the boy made his way toward the fortress, Titius hid himself in a doorway a short distance away.

The guards, dressed in full battle gear with bear-head helmets and sharpened javelins, would intimidate the bravest zealot. The boy walked tentatively toward the third sentry, the one sitting on his helmet and lounging against the wall; the one who Titius had pointed out to him.

The sentry examined the scroll, strained to see where the boy pointed, then motioned to another soldier and handed it off. Titius slipped away. The message would be delivered.

Back in the market, Titius found six fish vendors near the Sheep Gate, all selling fresh, pickled, salted, and dried fish: carp, sole, trout, bass, tilapia, perch, and sardines. No one had the Magdala pickled fish he wanted.

Titius ambled through the food vendors and picked up eggs, emmer bread with salt, honey, goat's milk, a roasted pigeon, olives, cheese, and grapes. He bartered for a blanket and a cloak for cooler weather before leaving everything at the stable. His step quickened. He would make a special meal for Abigail.

He spent the afternoon in the baths. The massage and scrape from a muscular slave was reviving after his long journey. Full and refreshed, he began to scour the city for Caleb's workshop. He started with the shops closest to the Fortress, but those he questioned knew nothing about a new carpenter.

Emerging from a warren of alleys, he saw deep purple ribbing a brilliant orange and red sunset. It seemed the whole city had come to a standstill. Priests and peasants alike stood in awe. Merchants and customers stopped bartering. Donkeys and dogs were silent.

With the sun down he blended with slaves, workers and pilgrims gathering around random fires in streets and alleys. Hovering, he'd listen to a conversation and then move on. He picked up a carpet left by a doorway and carried it on his shoulder.

It was the fifth fire where he settled. It took one word and one voice to convince him that this was the place to be. The word was "Barabbas" and the voice was that of the old zealot leader, Hosea.

37

Titius set down the carpet he was carrying, as if to rest. Hosea faced away from him, toward the fire. Five men huddled around the sparking logs warming their hands and sharing cups of wine. Skewers of lamb rested on a clay platter. Their laughter rolled easily. A sixth man stood in the shadows nearby; Titius recognized him as their sentry.

The sentry watched as Titius retied his sandal and examined the carpet's edging. Hosea spoke quietly: "Barabbas wants us at the Bethlehem vendors by sunset in two days." His next words were too quiet to catch.

When the sentry took a step out in his direction, Titius set the carpet back on his shoulders and walked around the corner into a dark alley. Three men appeared behind him, but he slipped quickly around another corner and disappeared up some stairs onto a flat roof. Voices and footsteps below intensified for a few minutes, but then faded.

"You're playing with fire again," Cleopas warned. *"You burned down that shed at your house. You blamed me and I took the whipping, but I know it was you."*

"That's what you get for scaring me, and for forcing the maid to go with you," Titius whispered. "I knew what you were doing. I heard the maid crying to Abigail's sister, Lydia. You forced her."

"At least I knew what to do with a woman," Cleopas replied. *"If a woman cries around you, you melt like goat's cheese in the sun. A woman needs to learn her place."*

"I have a chance to change things," Titius said. "I can become strong. You can't."

"The way you live, you'll be with me before you get near a woman," Cleopas sneered. *"If Barabbas doesn't slit your throat, Cretius or one of his assassins will. You can't hide forever."*

Titius stayed hidden for another hour. He left the carpet, peered over the knee-high wall around the roof's perimeter and, seeing no one, went down the stairs and slipped into the diminishing stream of humanity. A circular route back to the stable took longer, but no one seemed to be following him. He was grateful for a peaceful place to spend the night. Sleep came easily; not even Cleopas could keep him awake.

The rooster had finished crowing by the time he eased himself out from under his straw comforter and washed up. A clean linen tunic and he was off to visit the nearby wood market to see if Caleb had set up shop. There was no sign of the cross maker.

Since Abigail's fish vendor and Caleb's carpenter shop were not at the lower markets, he decided to walk through the Jaffa Gate and visit the upper markets near Herod's Palace. The surge of humanity in this area was as thick as at the markets near the Sheep Gate.

He passed Herod's three towers at the edge of the Palace. Above everything, the Temple stood blazing white on the highest plateau of land. He took a moment to look to the left of the Temple at the high observation perch in the Antonia Fortress.

Cleopas spoke up. *"You can be sure the centurion is up there now, watching you chase a woman instead of find that cross maker. You can't fool him for long."*

The fish vendors were easy to find. One of the stalls did seem to have Isaac's famous pickled fish. He tasted a few samples until the woman at the stall picked up the weights for her scales.

"Are you going to eat them all now or at least buy a few?" she asked, putting her hand over the basket. "They're the best from Magdala, fresh in yesterday." A long wisp of hair had escaped from her headscarf and lay across her nose. Her brown eyes crossed as she looked at it. She blew gently from an extended lower lip but the strand of black hair didn't move. She shook her head and finally brushed it aside with her hand.

Titius picked up a handful of fish and placed it on her scale. "The woman who brought them to you, is she returning soon?"

The woman took his coins and added a few more fish to his purchase. "Do I look like a prophet? My husband is usually selling." She wrapped the fish in a small rag and handed it to him. "I'm only here while he's at the Temple. If you ask me, this pickled fish isn't natural. No person with good taste will feed this to their family."

Titius snacked on the fish; likely it was an acquired taste.

As a Gentile — a slave and a non-believer — he knew the Temple was off limits to him. He wandered by the Hippodrome, where the chariots raced, sitting in the Temple's shade. Smoke from sacrifices drifted down. He tasted iron, like blood, on the back of his tongue.

During the Passover, energy and attention were focused on the Temple. *Perhaps Abigail was in the court of the women saying her prayers. Perhaps she was in the courtyard listening to the Messiah teach or expound the Torah. Perhaps Caleb was there. What would it be like to belong to a people like this?*

Cleopas dismissed it: *"They'd kill you before they let you in."*

Titius shuddered. "You're right." He left the Temple and passed the pool of Siloam and the Temple of the Freedmen. As he examined the building, a small girl holding two roses emerged from a nearby garden.

"Peace," he called.

"Peace," she replied. "Would you like a flower?"

Titius took it and inhaled: images of Abigail in the rose garden. He smiled. "Where did you find such a beautiful flower?" he asked.

She pointed to a path leading behind the Pool. "A beautiful woman gave it to me. In the garden. There are more flowers than you can count."

"Thank you," said Titius. He hurried down the path. Who could it be but Abigail?

The garden was almost hidden by a wall and a hedge. When he saw the sea of red he stopped. The same awe as when he'd seen the sunset reached into him.

He looked around. A bent woman using a cane to take painfully slow steps moved from flower to flower.

"Excuse me!" he called. "Peace to you."

"And the peace of Passover to you as well," she said.

"I'm looking for a woman who gave two roses to a little girl," he said. "She's has long dark hair, strong shoulders, a noble walk."

"Why, thank you," said the old woman with a smile. "I gave the roses to the girl. I see she gave you one."

Titius was speechless. Where was Abigail?

The woman tapped her cane on the path. "It seems my beauty is not enough to sway you," she said. "Are you looking for the woman from Galilee who walks these paths every evening?"

"Yes, perhaps, I am," he said. "Every evening, you say?"

"Yes, while she was here."

"What do you mean?"

"In this garden she used to sing of one she loved. She told me that in another garden, long ago, she gave her heart to someone. It's been many years since she's seen him."

"Did she say where? Who the man was? What did you mean 'while she was here'?"

She smiled. "Such noble songs about a noble man, out of her reach but always on her mind. If you've set your heart on this woman, save your tears. She wasn't singing about a servant like you."

Titius wanted to confess his life to her. "Thank you for the flower, the time, and the story. One day I'd like to meet the beautiful woman who sings in this garden."

"Yes, only last night she got word that a man was looking for her in Magdala. She's gone to see for herself."

"When will she return?"

"Only the Almighty knows," the woman said.

38

On the third day after meeting the woman in the garden, Titius heard Caleb's distinctive flute as he strolled by the sheep pool north of the Temple Mount. The sound came from a limestone hut. Three planks of rough cedar and a large burl of olive wood nestled against the wall by the door.

Titius, dressed as a carpenter, walked quickly to the door and peered in. One side of the room was filled with assorted squared cedar logs. The other side had a small open fire with a pot suspended above it. The far wall held a curtained doorway. The work bench was full of chisels, adzes, saws, squares, and planes.

Caleb lowered the flute and polished it with an oily rag before looking up. "How long have you been hiding around here?"

Titius walked to the far curtained door and pulled aside the curtain: a straw pallet, a few blankets, some scattered tunics. "Do you share this room with anyone?" he asked.

Caleb laughed. "You know my record with women. If Sestus hasn't told you, the last woman I got close to he made me *crucify.*"

"I know what it's like to crucify someone you care about."

Caleb set the flute down. "Would you like a drink?" he asked. "Hot goat's milk with cinnamon and honey? There's some pickled fish on the workbench, and apricots and dates."

Titius accepted the hot drink, shifting it from hand to hand as the clay mug cooled. He sampled the pickled fish and knew it immediately. "Where did you get this?" he asked, searching Caleb's face.

Caleb raised his eyebrows. "Something wrong with the fish? It isn't poisoned, is it?"

Titius shook his head. "No. It tastes like the fish you get in Magdala, at a friend named Isaac's."

"Small world," Caleb stated. He picked up a few of the tiny fish and popped them into his mouth. "A week ago I met a woman coming into the city. She was looking for a fish vendor to sell her wares to." He crouched down and stirred the spiced milk, then set the pot on the floor. "I took her to the upper market where I knew someone. They bought all she had."

"What did she look like?" Titius asked.

"Do I sense something more than curiosity here?" Caleb probed.

"I may know her," Titius replied. He took a flute from the workbench and ran a finger along its holes.

Caleb smiled as he stood. "She's been like an angel filling my dreams the last few nights. I think she went home for more fish. I wonder if she needs help finding another vendor…"

Titius leaned back against the work bench. "She's given her heart to another," he said.

Caleb stood looking out the door at passing pilgrims. "Whoever he is has had long enough to claim her," he said. "She needs a man who can appreciate her for who she is. A woman like her shouldn't have to wonder if she's truly loved."

"What about these crosses?" Titius asked.

Caleb turned to his half-finished work. "Sestus crucified six zealots and six bandits the first week we were here. There are a few more condemned in the Fortress, waiting for these crosses to be done. Passover's finished. Sestus is off chasing Barabbas."

Titius dipped his mug into the steaming pot for more milk. "Do you think he'll ever catch him?"

"If he doesn't, someone will. No one can hide forever."

Cleopas whispered. *"You can't hide forever."*

"I can try!" Titius said aloud.

Caleb looked at him strangely. "You? Why should you hide?"

"It's the art," he said. "A thespian assassin bets his life on his ability to hide."

"You'll need to work on this disguise," Caleb said. "Your beard's too short and neat. Your shoulders not broad enough, your hands not calloused enough. Come work with me for a few months and you can become the kind of man that a woman might look at some day." He put on his cloak. "I need to check the market to see if my angel's come looking for me." And he walked out.

Titius picked up the flute and blew on it as he'd seen Caleb do. It emitted a shrill squeal. He spotted a gob of sap seeping from one of the cross beams. He broke it off and stuffed it into the end of the flute. "I need to see if my angel's looking for me," he whined mockingly.

The fish vendor had told him Abigail was back in Magdala, so he didn't bother chasing Caleb. The cross maker might be Abigail's countryman. He might be broader, more muscled and of saner mind. But she'd given her heart to someone in a garden long ago. Who could that be but Titius?

Four people stopped by asking about carpentry jobs; Titius told them to come back another day. The last was a well-proportioned priest needing a stronger chair. "I'm not sure the carpenter on duty here can make what you really need," Titius said. "Perhaps we need the Messiah's help. I hear he's also a carpenter."

The priest's face reddened as he squinted and shook his jowls. "Don't you know who I am?" he said. "You insult me twice and think you'll thrive? If you follow this so-called 'Messiah', Yeshua of Nazareth, we'll destroy both of you."

"Perhaps the shop's owner can make you a better deal," Titius said. "You should come back tomorrow."

The priest huffed and chugged out of the shop.

"Oh, Cross Maker!" Titius said aloud. "I think you'll need the help of any angels you can find."

39

After three weeks shadowing Caleb, the only interesting thing Titius noticed was a young woman named Suzanna stopping by the shop for flute lessons. Sometimes she'd sit and talk and sometimes she'd dance to Caleb's playing. Suzanna's clear flirtatious interest in Caleb had Titius dreaming about meeting Abigail.

Every day he went to the market and asked whether the pickled fish dealer from Magdala had come by. By the third day the vendor saw him coming and simply shook his head.

Pentecost attracted a massive influx of pilgrims for the harvest rituals. The Messiah had been in the Temple teaching again but had withdrawn to Caesarea with a small band of followers. An informant told Titius that one of Yeshua's followers had actually proclaimed his master the "Son of the Living God", the same title Augustus had adopted.

"He can't survive long," Cleopas said. *"Rome won't endure competition with Caesar."*

"This time I think you're right."

Titius perfected six disguises to add variety to his days: the upper-class slave, the Grecian olive merchant, the shepherd, the carpenter, the blind man, and the corpulent bearded Pharisee.

When Caleb worked, Titius slipped away to probe the city for zealot activity. It didn't take long to find. Men loyal to Barabbas gathered around fires, tables, bath houses, and certain vendors to make their clandestine plans.

Once a week he would hire a messenger to drop off another scroll at the Fortress. Twice he saw Sestus hurry out when a scroll was accepted, but Titius avoided being seen. Orders were orders.

Titius could see the results of the intelligence he submitted. Each night legionnaires raided the zealots' secret meetings and more were put in chains to wait for Caleb's crosses. The peace from the power of the cross soon began to spread over Jerusalem. Rebel gatherings and zealot activity in the city halted.

The zealot daggermen focused their terror on isolated targets outside the capital. Roman centurions began to chase them down.

Sestus was frequently away, leaving Caleb free to wander as he willed. Titius was relieved that, once Caleb had sorted out the disagreement with the priest, there were many orders from the High Priest's family, from the nobility, and even from the palace. The cross maker had become a carpenter again and, looking at the traffic at his door, a very successful one.

Titius analyzed the fat priest's mannerisms and speech patterns. He learned to mimic his voice, his walk and his temper. He kept track of which market stalls the priest frequented. Finally he decided to test his impersonation at the market.

When Titius stepped among the stalls, the date vendor reacted with the enthusiasm he always did when the priest walked by. So did the young man who roasted goat over a charcoal fire. The woman selling oranges and lemons frowned at him curiously and Titius moved on quickly.

An hour later, Titius went to Caleb's shop and ordered four stools. Caleb hardly stopped working long enough to take the order. "Bartholomew," he said, "the Almighty must be blessing you with many guests. It will take a few days but you'll have your stools. Greet your beautiful daughters for me. May you be blessed one day with a son."

On his way home, Titius considered confessing to Caleb to avoid another angry confrontation between carpenter and priest. "Cleopas, do I tell him?" he asked aloud.

There was only silence.

Playing the priest satisfied the actor in him, but no one spoke around a priest; they bowed and murmured or looked away.

Sitting near the linen vendor, however, Titius the "priest" was readily ignored. Some of his best information came from servants who gathered there. His knowledge of many languages helped him decipher the whispers the servants shared in secret.

An Egytian slave tested a linen stola. "My master bought two Gauls today to work in our kitchen. One of them used to work for Herod in Sepphoris."

A Greek maid picked out several towels. "My mistress is hosting a great banquet for the governor and his wife."

A Galilean cook picked out two new frocks. "The Romans almost found the zealots hiding in our house last night. I had to stall them!"

Near the end of that day two broad-chested warriors, swaggering distinctly like assassins, stopped at the stall. "We serve Sestus Aurelius, Legate of Judea." They sounded Ephesian, Titius noted. "His personal bodyguard often comes by here. When did you last see him?"

"Do you wish to buy this bodyguard a tunic? I need to know his size."

"He's my size," the shorter of the two said. "You wouldn't recognize him. He'd be dressed like an old blind beggar, a household servant, or a harlot. He answers to the name 'Titius Marcus Julianus.'"

The merchant chortled. "Are you saying that a top Roman warrior has a blind beggar or a harlot for a bodyguard?" the merchant said. "The only people here are the people who are always here. Perhaps that priest will satisfy you."

The larger assassin took a step toward where Titius, well-stuffed into his priest's regalia, rested under a canopy.

"That old drunk is not who Lord Cretius is looking for. Mounting that head on a pole would likely get our own heads stuck on a pole. Keep your eyes open."

Titius burped and slumped against the wall. The assassins left.

The early autumn rains fell with no sign of Abigail. Caleb and his girl, Suzanna, continued their flute lessons, dancing, and walks, so much so that Titius no longer worried about the carpenter's old fixation on the woman from Magdala. Plowing was underway in the fields and the Feast of Trumpets, Day of Atonement and Feast of Tabernacles arrived. Little booths sprang up everywhere around the city as residents moved out of their homes to re-enact their ancestors' wilderness wanderings.

Titius couldn't miss the uproar from the Temple Courts. He joined the stream of men coming through the gate to find out what had happened. Yeshua had arrived from the Galilee without his usual contingent of followers.

"Did you hear Yeshua?" asked a Saducee. "He says he'll be here only a little longer and then we won't find him anymore."

Another replied, "Not only that, he said that if people believed in him, streams of living water would flow out of them."

"They're calling him a prophet" a third said. "And Messiah, Son of David."

"Yeshua clearly is possessed by demons," the first chimed in. "People are going mad watching his miracles. Rome won't tolerate it. They'll take the whole city from us if we do nothing."

"I can't believe he got away again," the second said. "I bent down to pick up a stone to throw at him and when I looked up, he was gone."

"The people seem to love him," the third observed. "They flock to him here every day, drinking in his every word."

"The people are ignorant," the first growled. "No prophet comes from the Galilee. The Messiah comes from Bethlehem, from David. They know nothing."

Playing a privileged household servant, Titius walked freely through the markets. When the throng poured out of the city after feast days, the tables were fewer and the vendors less attentive.

Once a week he stopped by the rose garden.

"Still looking for your angel?" the old woman with the cane would ask.

"Still looking!" he'd say.

"She probably won't be here until the flowers come back," she said after the third week. "She told me once she had friends in Bethany. Please, call me Elizabeth."

"Glad to know you. I want to make sure I don't miss my chance," he replied.

The next day he watched Suzanna lean coyly against Caleb's

doorway. Titius' hunger for Abigail overcame him. Too many years had passed.

The next Sabbath evening, just before the city went quiet for its evening of worship, Titius changed into his shepherd's garb and bolted for the gates. He ignored the sentries' glances, descended into the Kidron Valley and climbed the Mount of Olives. Farmers were travelling home from their fields. Before dark he settled himself in Bethany.

As Titius slurped up the porridge and cheap wine the innkeeper offered, he talked with a businessman.

"I'm coming home to Galilee," Titius said. "I've been in Jerusalem for six months and need some room to move."

The businessman smiled. "Name's Lazarus. My sisters and I have a little business. Been pretty good since Yeshua ben Yuseph started staying here."

Titius sat upright. "You mean that new Messiah?"

Lazarus reached for another glass of wine. "That's him. We thought he was going to come and take Jerusalem back from the Romans and put us in control again."

"Isn't that what everyone expects of every Messiah?"

"Yes. But this Messiah says he's going to be crucified."

Titius picked up his cup and sipped. "Your priests, rabbis, and teachers of the law may stone him before the Romans get him."

Lazarus raised his eyebrows and shook his head. "You don't understand this man's power. He opens blind men's eyes. He calms storms, and raises the dead to life. He feeds thousands on a handful of loaves and fish."

Titius dropped two coins on the counter. "This Messiah interests me," he said. "He raises the dead, yet claims that he will be killed. Your leaders have talked openly about killing him, yet he persists on tormenting them with his teaching. The people worship him almost as an Emperor. You know the Romans won't tolerate that much longer."

"He's on a mission from the Almighty," Lazarus said. "I've had enough. Too much talk will only bring more trouble for Yeshua."

"I intend no trouble," Titius assured.

"I wish you peace," Lazarus said, standing.

"I wish you peace as well," Titius responded.

All that night images clashed and battled for control in his dreams. Romans, led by Sestus, chased him down with javelins as he tried to escape his oath; zealots, led by Barabbas, lunged at him with daggers trying to avenge Phoebe and Jonathan; slaves, led by Cleopas, pursued him with hammers and nails, threatening to crucify him. Every time, just as he was grabbed the Messiah would say "Stop!" and the dream would fade.

Cleopas undermined every positive thought he had about the Messiah. Titius drifted off to sleep dreaming happily of hundreds of fishes swimming into a net, yet woke sweating and in terror, dreaming he was surrounded by rock-throwing Pharisees and Sadducees.

By sunrise he was well on his way to Jericho.

40

Dust billowed from under Titius's sandals as he walked away from the Jordan. Jericho's high walls appeared through a gap in the date palms. As Titius descended the last slope toward the city, a lone rider galloped up behind him. "Peace to you, shepherd," called the rider, slowing his mount to a walk. "Have you sold your flock and walked from Jerusalem already?"

"Peace to you," Titius said. "I started early. I need to reach Galilee."

"Not even the bandits are up this early," the rider noted. "But I love the early light on Herod's palace." He pointed to it. "Even Antony and Cleopatra did nothing to improve it. Augustus was wise to return it to Herod."

Titius scanned the public buildings and the Hippodrome, clearly Roman additions. Date palms grew everywhere near the numerous oases where camels and caravans loaded, unloaded, and reloaded. Tax collectors, under their overseer's eye, badgered coins from all who passed.

Two bodyguards stepped in front of Titius and the horseman as they neared the gate. Titius handed over the expected coin for the personal tax. The short man who accepted it held it up to the light and bounced it gently in his hands. "Feels real enough."

"Zaccheus," the horseman bellowed, "good to see you again. My friend and I have come from Jerusalem. He's tired. Let him get some rest."

"Elkanah," Zaccheus replied. "I hope your friend isn't a zealot.

The Romans are busy today. Five were taken from the market this morning."

"My friend is neither a zealot nor the son of a zealot," Elkanah said. "If you find a dagger on him you can charge the tax to me."

The well-dressed enforcer, who stood not even to Titius's chest, motioned to his henchmen and they took Titius' pack and pawed through it. They nodded to Zaccheus and he waved Titius in. The horseman who'd accompanied Titius was left uncinching his saddlebags for tax agents looking for anything that might get them an extra coin.

Titius bought himself food and filled his gourd with fresh water. The early winter clouds filtered the harshest sunshine, so before the noon meal he was on the way to Magdala.

The remains of a wild boar killed by a lion lay a stone's throw from the path. Titius calculated how much daylight he had left. With a predator so close, he decided not to travel after dark.

By mid-afternoon the next day he'd crossed the Fara River and neared the juncture of the Jabbok and Jordan Rivers. At dusk he dropped his mat by a tree and rested against it. The deer wandering toward the river reminded him of the last time he'd rested in this place.

He'd been wrestling with Phoebe's marriage proposal. Would he become the brother-in-law of Barabbas and infiltrate the zealots more deeply or would he run back to being a Roman assassin? The zealot women had shown great trust, letting him guard them while they bathed; the young men had shown great trust, letting him teach them the art of warfare; the elders had shown great patience, letting him live and work among them.

But his deeper passion for Abigail, for avenging his mother's death, and for staying loyal to Sestus compelled him to run for his life. Among these very bushes he'd changed his clothes before pressing on toward Sepphoris.

From atop a tall tree he looked across at the zealot camp. He spotted the hill where he and Jonathan had sat, waiting for the elder's decision, just above the village.

"You should have married that zealot woman," Cleopas said.

"If I'd married Phoebe, Barabbas or Sestus would have killed me by now."

"If it's not her that gets you it'll be another woman," Cleopas said. *"Just don't let it be Abigail."*

"Why do you abhor Abigail?" Titius asked. "Mother sent her away because of Father, not you."

"It wasn't only your father," Cleopas said. *"He liked her in the garden. She was with* me *in the shed. Your mother found us."*

Titius almost lost hold of the branch he was on. "You wicked, evil, liar! I should have crucified you twice and burned down that shed with you in it."

"And you thought you *were the man in the garden she loved,"* Cleopas mocked. *"I told you women were your weakness. They were your father's weakness as well."*

Titius remembered several times seeing Abigail and Cleopas exchange glances. Before now he'd thought her looks were fearful. Now he wasn't so sure.

"Shall I tell you what she's like... as a woman?" Cleopas asked.

"No, no, no!" Titius yelled. "Get out of my head!" He reached into his pack and took out a rope.

"You know what you should do with that rope, don't you?"

"I'm going to kill myself!" Titius roared. "Then I can come and get you!"

Titius wrapped the rope around a sturdy lower branch and made a noose. He looked across at the zealot hill and slipped the noose around his neck. "I'll never have Abigail or Phoebe," he thought. "My real weakness isn't a woman. It's a slave."

As the shadows crept deeper in the forest, he slid off the branch and plunged.

Darkness and light twisted together in a whirlpool: trees, bushes, river, ground. He felt swallowed, as if in quicksand. Everything in his stomach fought to be free. The world spun and he faded into the same darkness he'd known with Jaennus at the bottom of the training pool.

And all the time Cleopas spewed hideous ghoulish laughter.

Light finally came. Someone held Titius' shoulder, shaking it, and poured water on his face. The panic of drowning seized him for a moment but he sputtered and tried to sit up. Strong arms held him down.

"Peace. Be at rest, shepherd," a familiar man's voice said in Hebrew. "You're safe now."

"The lion is dead," another gruff voice said, also in Hebrew. "Although it looks like there were other attackers before the beast arrived."

The two men propped Titius up. His neck burned with pain. Someone held a damp cloth to his head. He saw, hazily, a lion's body less than six strides away. He shook his head to clear his vision and almost screamed from the furious pain. His hand rested on his lap and felt a rope there.

"I'm Issachar, this is Simon," the first voice said. "Our friend, Timna, shot the lion with an arrow and then went looking for your attackers."

Titius shuddered. He looked carefully at the closest face and knew. These were two of the young zealots he'd trained. He'd been found out!

"You're fortunate your attackers didn't tie the rope properly," Simon said. "Your neck will hurt, but didn't break."

"If you take me to Barabbas," Titius said in Aramaic, "let me wash my wounds first?" It hurt a great deal to talk and his voice was raspy and hoarse.

"What do you mean, shepherd?" Issachar asked. "We don't follow Barabbas."

""You're sold out to Barabbas," Titius said. "I know Phoebe. Elizabeth. Jonathan, Hosea, all of you."

Simon yanked the rope away from Titius' feeble grasp. "Explain. We're no fools, falling for reckless accusations."

Titius struggled to his feet. "No strength to fight. No reason to resist. I'm the one you knew... David. On the other side of the Jordan."

Simon drew his sword. "You don't look or sound like David. David was murdered."

Titius stood with the cloth over one eye as blood trickled down his face into his dirty beard. "Do I look murdered?"

"Almost," Issachar said. He gently wiped blood from Titius ear. "Whoever hit your head and tried to hang you was merciless. The beast must have chased them off just before it turned on you. It is your fortune that we arrived in time. Where have you been?"

Titius put the rag over his other eye. "Story's too long. Let's go now."

"We can't take you," Simon said.

"Why?" Titius asked.

"We don't follow Barabbas anymore," Simon replied. "We all went one day to see Ethan's crazy relative. It changed our perspective forever."

Issachar broke in: "The Messiah was there." He pointed northeast, toward Gadara. "He cast out a legion of demons. Another time he fed four thousand of us. Even though some of our people had attacked his village, killed carpenters... he fed us."

"*It's a trap,*" Cleopas hissed. "*Leave these lunatics.*"

Simon handed Titius a fresh rag. "We're leaving Barabbas to follow Yeshua," he said. "We felt an urgency that we must not wait until morning. When we crossed the river, we found you. Come with us to see the Messiah."

Simon carried Titius' pack, then helped Issachar support Titius as they started down the trail. The evening shadows were swallowing the landscape, but they kept moving. Timna soon joined them.

"It's David!" Simon said. "He's not dead!"

"You kept your shooting skills strong," Titius said hoarsely.

"I'm pleased to serve again," Timna replied. "Let me run ahead and find a safe place to make camp." The young man ran off on the darkening path ahead.

41

Through the night, on the hard earth they'd cleared for his blanket, Titius tossed and turned. The phantom pain of the noose around his neck choked him, leaving him gagging and sweaty.

Timna, Simon, and Issachar had all taken turns stoking the fire and walking the camp's perimeter. Cleopas was relentless, predicting destruction and taunting Titius for walking into a trap.

The first morning birds were a relief. Titius tested his muscles in case he'd have to fight. He'd taught the young freedom fighters well. The remaining zealots might track and attack these deserters.

None of Titius' weapons were in sight but he was skilled in wrestling, boxing and pankration. He could even fight like a Spartan, and bite or gouge out an eye to save his own life. Cleopas wouldn't be satisfied today: Titius would fight to live. But his painful neck wounds left no question that he wouldn't be at his best.

Simon began to make breakfast. The spark of dry wood catching flame was a comforting sound.

"Come, David," Simon said. "I've prepared our jentaculum to start the day: biscuits, cheese bread, apricots, honey, dates, olives and bacon."

"You provide well," Titius said. "Most Romans have only a cup of water."

The young zealot nudged his comrades awake with his foot and waited for them to stir. "Timna learned from a Roman that every legionnaire has wheat, bacon, fish, a bird, cheese, fruit, vegetables, olive oil and wine almost every day, so he's fit to fight."

"Timna worked hard to make him talk about his secret diet. They have salt, eggs, berries too."

Timna and Issachar gathered around the fire. They warmed their hands and stretched stiff limbs. Simon walked to the Jordan for more water. He poured some on a cloth and gave it to Titius to wipe his face. The cloth turned red from blood that had dried on his face and neck.

Titius burned with anger at Cleopas, but Cleopas wasn't going anywhere. Perhaps he could make a run for it and the zealots would kill him quickly.

"David, what do you know about this Messiah?" Issachar asked. "Our brothers in Jerusalem say the authorities are looking for ways to kill him before the Romans take the Temple away. He makes trouble there during every feast."

Titius took a bite of bread and chewed thoughtfully. "His words mesmirize people. His magic confounds religious leaders. His compassion confuses them... those who want to overthrow Rome. He speaks as if he knows men better then they know themselves."

Simon crouched down to sort out his pack. "That's what I saw in him as well. We couldn't point to anything he'd done to help the Romans enough to deserve a dagger to his throat."

"People said he healed a centurion's servant from far away by just speaking," Issachar said. "But how can you prove it enough to cut a man's neck?"

"Hosea sent us to investigate the Messiah over and over," Timna said. "We were supposed to find some reason to encourage him to overthrow Rome, or we were supposed to attack him quietly when no one was around. He always had followers close by."

"Except when he prayed," Issachar said. "I saw him alone one night and tried to get close. There was strange power around him as he called to the heavens. My hand couldn't grasp my dagger."

Titius considered this improbable, but Issachar was clearly sincere. After Titius' own encounters with Yeshua, it was clear some kind of power rested on this man.

"So, now we'll follow him," Simon said. "Maybe he'll destroy the Romans with his words or his magic. Maybe we'll die trying. It's better than slithering around trying to figure out what Barabbas wants next."

They set out on the road. Titius limped along. The vision in one eye was blurry and his head hurt in ways he'd never felt before. Even the vicious blows of Sestus or Jaennus to his temple, as he'd learned to fight, didn't hurt like this.

The young men took turns updating him on life in the zealot camps. Sarah had sent her sister to Jericho; the Romans had captured most of the zealots posing as vendors there. Phoebe had been courted by two big men who everyone suspected were Roman infiltrators. They'd called Barabbas, but the men left before anyone could expose them. Jonathan was now betrothed to Phoebe's cousin, Tamaris. Hosea was coordinating zealots in Jerusalem along with managing the opening of the trade route Barabbas had established with the Parthians.

Titius heard the words but could hardly absorb the information enough to remember it for Sestus. Black phantoms floated across the field of vision in his left eye and the pain felt like a drill driving into the back of his head.

The four of them continued until Titius had to stop for a rest. His back, neck and shoulders burned with pain. Issachar frequently jogged to the nearby river to resoak the rag with fresh water. Titius was grateful.

"David, where did you go when you left us?" Simon asked.

"I was on a mission," Titius responded.

"Why didn't you take any of us?" Issachar asked. "We would have done anything for you."

"It was time for me to leave."

"I found that blood-stained tunic you left," Timna said. "I had to show it to Phoebe. I've never seen a woman weep so loudly."

"What's that?" Issachar said, turning around.

Timna shouted, "Romans! Run!"

The cedar forest they were passing through swallowed his zealot helpers. Titius sank to his knees. A moment later he heard the unmistakeable pounding of hooves on the road. There was no where to go so he rolled off the path into a shallow ditch.

A dozen horsemen thundered to a stop beside Titius. He heard Sestus shout: "Check out that shepherd!"

A legionnaire dismounted and knelt beside Titius. The soldier turned him over, moved aside his shepherd's head covering, and ran a rough hand across his face. "Been beaten badly," the man reported. "No recent cut to his throat. He's had some care. Probably abandoned as too weak to walk."

Sestus spoke up. "Bandits! Zealots would have cut him deep. Can he talk?"

The legionnaire asked him in Aramaic, Greek, and Hebrew, "Have you seen three zealots around here?"

Titius feigned unconsciousness but groaned for effect when the soldier shook him.

"Leave him!" Sestus commanded. "We need to get to Sepphoris and then back to Jerusalem. I have empty crosses to fill."

The soldier left Titius and the troop charged down the road in pursuit of zealots. Soon Simon called from behind a fig tree: "Are you still with us?"

Titius rolled over and propped himself on one elbow. "See any Romans?" he asked.

Issachar reached him first and helped Titius get to his feet. "Come. Quickly, in case they come back."

Titius set a hand on the zealot's shoulder. "They won't be back. I know that centurion. They're on their way to Sepphoris and Jerusalem."

Timna jogged down the road toward them. "They're gone," he declared. "Blessings to you David for not giving us up."

Taking turns, two of the three would put their arms around him and lift the weight off his legs. The third man would carry the extra pack. In this way they made good time and reached the towers of Magdala just after the sun reached its zenith.

"I'm grateful for your help," Titius said. "Isaac, my friend, works in the fish sellers' building. He pickles fish. I'd like to speak with him."

Timna and Issachar eased out from under his shoulders. "You're a free man," Timna said. "Do you want us to wait for you here or in Capernaum with the Messiah?"

"I'll only slow you down," Titius said. He needed to look for Abigail without these men.

"Very well," Simon said. "We'll stop for the noon meal and enjoy this pickled fish. If your host wants you to stay, we'll press on. Lead on."

Titius had hoped to disguise himself as the olive merchant to meet Isaac, but with his bloodied appearance, his full beard, and the three zealots with him, he'd have to find another ploy.

"I feel weak," Titius said. "Isaac's business is by the stream. Simon, could you ask at the counter if the owner is there? Tell him his friend Porpherus will meet him in Capernaum."

"How fortunate. We're also going to Capernaum," Issachar said. "If Porpherus is your friend, he can introduce us to the Messiah."

"Porpherus is a Greek olive merchant," Titius said. "Not with the Messiah in any way. Isaac employs a woman who may know the Messiah, but I'm not sure."

"You'll see," Simon said. "Soon everyone will be following the Messiah. I'll go and pass on your message."

42

Simon returned before the rest had finished eating. He brought a small bag of pickled fish. "The vendor says Isaac's gone to Jerusalem and the woman's gone to Capernaum to hear the Messiah."

Titius' heartbeat quickened. Abigail was only hours away. He struggled to his feet and took the cane that Timna had fashioned for him during the brief stop. He nodded to the zealots. "Hurry ahead. I can get there on my own from here."

Simon hoisted Titius's pack and stood aside. "You didn't abandon us to the Romans. We're not going to abandon you now."

Titius stumbled. "I've trained you too well," he said.

The road to Capernaum grew dense with human traffic: donkey carts, horses, camels, and hundreds upon hundreds of people walking. Titius choked on the dust and wrapped a damp shawl around his face.

The zealots finally stepped off the road and rested on a fallen log near to the lake shore. "Let's walk along the shore," Issachar suggested. "There'll be no dust and fewer people."

Simon took a few steps down the slope and examined the footing. "We'll have to support David even more down here," he said. "This ground is rough."

"We can do it," Timna encouraged. "We can still make it before the sunlight is gone. We need to find this Porpherus. He can help us find shelter."

As the zealots chatted among themselves, Cleopas started in: *"Fool! It's all going to backfire when they find out there's no olive merchant waiting for you."*

"I can handle it," Titius retorted. A flock of pelicans landed on the lake.

"It's insane to chase after that woman," Cleopas said. *"You should've hung yourself properly. You can't do anything right."*

"The Messiah will change the world," Titius said aloud. "The Messiah is the hope for all of us."

"Yes!" Simon shouted. "The Messiah will save us all." He grabbed a stone and hurled it as far as he could into the water.

Three fishermen stood near a boat nudging the rocky shore a short distance away. They were examining a net for holes. One of them turned to Titius and the zealots. "Peace to you, strangers," he called.

"Peace to you," Simon responded. He put down the two packs he carried and waved both arms above his head.

"Where are you travelling?" the fisherman asked.

"To Capernaum, to see the Messiah," Simon called back.

"Come with us," the fisherman invited. "We need help with our nets and we can take you to Capernaum in exchange."

The three zealots discussed this without talking to Titius. "We'll come with you," Simon said, "but our friend isn't well."

"He can rest in the back," the fisherman offered. "We have room. We're just fishing for sardines."

Clouds tumbled across a blue Galilean sky. Gulls and cormorants and fish eagles drifted effortlessly on the wind.

Issachar looked into the boat and went back to Titius. "David, we're going to put you in the back of the boat like a log. Grit your teeth while we move you."

Titius stiffened and they handed him up to the fishermen. The fishermen set him down in the back of the boat with a blanket and then helped the others on board. Two fishermen jumped off and pushed the boat into shallow water. They climbed on board, rowed into deeper water, then hoisted the sails.

The wind was boisterous as they bobbed up and down through the choppy water. The fishermen shouted orders to the zealots and between them they kept the ship on course. Two of the fishermen hurled nets into the water. The first waves of nausea hit Titius not long after. He was soon leaning over the edge of the boat vomiting as water splashed his face and sloshed into the boat.

"Don't you think the fish are fat enough?" one of the fishermen yelled.

Titius remembered his last meal of tilapia and vomited again.

Figures on shore grew smaller as the wind pushed them into the middle of the sea. Timna pointed toward the dark clouds racing toward them. There were shouts and commands. Bodies strained and groaned against ropes and sails. The fishermen focused on keeping the ship on course. The sail lowered. A sheet of rain joined the wind in churning up the whitecaps.

Titius held on in a white-knuckled death grip as his side of the boat pitched toward the water. "Get away from the side!" one of the sailors warned. "Lie down!"

Titius let go. His side of the ship jerked skyward. He flew over the keel and plunged into the deep. He let himself twist, sink and rise. Light and dark spun up, down and around. His training in the assassin's pool with Jaennus kicked in. He relaxed as his body was pushed violently down and then slowly surfaced.

"Come to me," Cleopas called. *"You've waited long enough."*

"No, come to me," another voice said. "Strip and swim."

Titius pulled off his tunic and stroked his way toward the surface. The skills Jaennus had taught him now served him well. He bobbed into the air and waved. A net landed perfectly around his head and caught his hand. He held on as they dragged him like a fish to the boat.

Wearing only his sandals, they pulled Titius up and he flopped into the middle of the boat. He stayed there, seasick in the sloshing pool of water, sheltered from the sharp whistling overhead. His companions took up oars and joined the seafarers pulling the vessel toward shore.

Titius thought of Caleb's big Persian slave. Would Nabonidus still be in the gladiator arena or rowing in a warship's galley? Was Caleb still safe without his guardian? What would Sestus say when no messages came to the fortress? Surely Poseiden would claim his life before darkness swallowed them whole.

He wrapped his arms around his knees and prayed in his spirit to the god of the storm. The boat's captain commanded the crew, and his orders drew shouts of confirmation. Titius was thrown helplessly side to side. He locked his arms around his head and curled into a ball. The water sloshed over him, around him, under him. Time seemed to stop.

Cleopas raged and mocked until Titius wanted to be thrown overboard like Jonah. Dry heaves convulsed his body. He hugged his ribs to keep them from breaking.

There was a horrendous grinding – they'd hit land. The boat jerked sideways and Simon plunged over the edge.

Titius tossed off his saturated blanket and pulled himself up to the rail, worried about the zealot gone overboard. Simon scrambled to his feet on shore less than a javelin's throw away.

A manic laugh erupted behind Titius; he was sure Cleopas had resurrected. When he turned, it was only one of the fishermen laughing at the wind and shaking his fist at the sea.

Titius didn't wait for anyone to hand him over the edge. He lowered himself off the listing, shuddering vessel and dropped into the shallows. He scrambled across the rocks and almost lost a sandal. Then he lay on the shore, watching the fishermen trying to anchor the ship as it bucked like a wild stallion.

Simon, his eyes wide with awe, pulled Titius to his feet. "Can you imagine? The Messiah calmed a storm just like this one with a single word." He handed Titius a sopping tunic. "Come, we have to see him. Capernaum is only five stadia away."

43

Simon, Issachar, and Timna formed a wedge ahead of Titius as they pushed through the crowds approaching Capernaum. The gentle breeze was a welcome experience after the storm.

The homes in Capernaum were rough basalt blocks stacked on each other, designed to withstand strong winds. People pushed their way into sheltered courtyards to get their evening meal of soup or porridge.

A large fisherman pushed his way through the zealot trio. Titius was elbowed into a wall. A patch in the wall, a few stones and a wad of mud, fell to the ground. Stone stairs led to flat roofs made of beams covered with mud and thatch.

"Where's the olive merchant?" Simon asked. "We need shelter."

Titius shrugged. "It's too late now. The markets are closed. We can shelter at the inn."

Four homes huddled around a covered courtyard where tradesmen, merchants, and vendors gathered to eat and get out of the wind. This was the village inn. Titius pushed in through a narrow doorway in the wall, ignoring the stares and whispers of those huddled around three fires. Doorways let in the last of the evening light. The north side opened on a dining area.

Clay pots, plates, an olive press, and a few grain mills sat neatly along the walls. Several dozen clay lamps flickered.

"You look even worse in here," Timna said. "If I didn't know you were David I'd swear I never met you."

"Let me get you a dry tunic," Issachar said. He disappeared inside. A few moments later he returned with a tunic and a blanket.

"Thank you." Titius accepted it, throwing off his wet clothes and putting on the warm, dry garment.

"You're lucky we're following the Messiah now," Issachar said. "The innkeeper said he'd never give anything to a zealot or a Roman."

Simon carried over four bowls of soup, some bread, a few sardines. They ate as if they hadn't eaten for days. Even Titius felt his stomach settle as it filled. He accepted a mat and curled up near a wall, not far from a fire. Sleep came quickly.

In the early dawn, Titius slipped away from the inn. He walked to the sea. Clouds as docile as sheep grazed the heavens. Gulls, pelicans, and fish eagles twirled and whirled through the breezes over the waking village.

Fishermen were already out in numbers all over the sea, tossing nets and hauling in their catches. A middle-aged woman stood quietly gazing at a group of boats not far from shore.

"Peace, to you," Titius said.

"And peace to you," she responded, turning. "I see life hasn't been kind to you recently."

"I'm David," Titius said. "I hope the Messiah might change that."

"I'm Salome, wife of Zebedee," the woman replied. "If you mean Yeshua ben Yuseph, then yes, he can help you." She looked back at the boats. "I'm his aunt, his mother Mary's sister. He's out there with my sons, James and John."

Titius watched the group of four boats working as a unit to gather their catch. "I heard the Messiah lived in Nazareth."

Salome sighed. "He did. The ungrateful wretches tried to throw him off a cliff. He left and came down here to be with family."

"So he lives here now?"

"I actually can't tell," Salome said. "He's here a few days and then off with my sons to the Decapolis, or Caesarea or Jerusalem… wherever God wants him to go." She pointed at the four boats. "Fortunately our fishing business is good. We can help support him. We mostly pay for food. He sleeps wherever he can find a place to lie down. I've never walked so much in my life."

"So, you are a follower of his?"

"Now that's a good question," she said. "I used to think everyone in this part of Galilee was his disciple. Now, Pharisees, zealots, tax-collectors, lost women… all surround him. It's hard to know who's for him and who's out to get him."

Titius nodded. The fishermen hauled in their nets and then rowed to shore. Shouts and laughter drifted easily across the water.

"Come meet my nephew," Salome said, "the next king of Israel."

Titius followed her along the shore until they neared the men hauling in the boat. The catch was transferred into reed baskets. They draped the nets over a rack to inspect them for tears.

It was easy to recognize the Messiah. He was the focus of attention; everyone stepped aside and made room for him. His step was confident and almost dancelike as he met those who rushed to greet him. His smile was constant, his face filled with wonder.

As Salome called out to Yeshua, Cleopas began to scream. *"Run! He'll destroy us!"*

No one looked bent on destruction. There was only the confident, peaceful Messiah walking beside his aunt.

"Run!" Cleopas screamed along with a hundred other voices. *"Run!"*

Titius knelt. The screams in his head tempted him to smash his head on the stony beach. He pressed his hands against his temples. The noise refused to quiet. The crowd closed in.

The Messiah walked up to him. "The play is over," Yeshua said. "Be free, be at peace. When I set you free you will be truly free."

Yeshua touched his shoulder and lightning jolted him to the core. His body shuddered. Then he was immersed in an inner silence, a peace so deep he wanted to drown in it. Stillness. Emptiness, yet fullness. No voices, no confusion, no guilt, no fear, no shame. Only silence. His body felt strong and whole.

"I must go to Jerusalem," Yeshua said, pausing only a moment. "Hurry, while you can. Go there. Your friend will need you soon."

But Abigail was here. His newly-converted zealot friends were here. Was this the time to go back to Jerusalem? Something powerful inside urged him that it was. And this time, it wasn't Cleopas.

Titius left notes with both the fish vendor and the innkeeper, addressed to Abigail in care of Isaac. He left a note for Simon urging him to meet the Messiah quickly. Before the town was awake he was on the run toward Jerusalem.

Without Cleopas, he was left with his own thoughts. He remembered the Messiah's words: "Your friend will need you soon." Which friend? Caleb? Sestus? He wished it were Abigail.

As he passed Magdala, pounding hooves sounded behind him. He slowed to let the Romans pass. Instead, a squadron of fully-armed zealots galloped by. The last horse stopped beside him.

"David?"

Titius looked up. It was Jonathan.

"David, you're alive!" he shouted. "Climb on! We must hurry."

Titius climbed up behind the young zealot. The rest had moved down the road and were almost out of sight. In a few strides the stallion was thundering again. Early travellers scowled, shook fists, or cowered by the roadside.

"Where are we going?" Titius shouted.

"Barabbas needs us!" Jonathan yelled back. "That Roman centurion has him trapped. We have to save him."

44

Titius hung on tight as Jonathan galloped between the caravans and foot traffic near Tiberius. The recent rains kept the dust down. A single eagle rode the thermals overhead.

Titius' mind remained clear and quiet as the horse gained on those ahead of it. By the time the troop dismounted three hours later, a line of early Passover pilgrims was already lined up at the crossing to ford the river. Titius, wobbly and weary, dropped to his knees at the water's edge and quenched his raging thirst.

The horses' sides heaved. The men walked restlessly back and forth along the bank, waiting for the path to clear. More and more pilgrims joined the line. The zealots dug into their saddle bags for dates, apricots, figs, and bread. Jonathan and an old shepherd approached Titius.

"Peace to you, David," Hosea said. "Are you a phantom raised from the dead or just a coward on the run?" He waved his dagger inches from Titius's nose. "Barabbas will be interested to meet the man who broke his sister's heart."

Titius looked into Hosea's fiery eyes. "I was dead in ways I can't explain," he said. "I met the Messiah. I'm here now."

"I'd run you through myself," Hosea said, "but we need every warrior we can get. I know you can fight."

"I appreciate your mercy," Titius said. The one thing he wanted least right then was to fight.

"It's not mercy. I don't dare deprive Barabbas of the satisfaction of avenging his sister."

Several zealots led their horses to the river's edge and started to cross. Jonathan handed Titius his share of dried fruit and a chunk of barley loaf. "Eat quickly. We're going now," he said. "We'll change horses in an hour at Aenon."

Titius considered bolting, but the Messiah's words kept him focused. "Hurry to Jerusalem. Your friend will need you soon." It was almost as if Yeshua had arranged the transportation.

The change of horses at Aenon meant another brief break. Some of the warriors flopped on the ground in a small grove of oaks. They guzzled water or wine from their gourds and refilled them from a village well. Others walked to the Jordan and dunked their heads in the cool water.

Titius sat with Jonathan and looked for a way to escape. When he saw Hosea watching him he lowered his head and left his fate to the gods. Could even the Messiah help at this point?

They gave Titius his own horse for the rest of the ride. The men were tired and anxious. They wouldn't be much help to Barabbas against Sestus and his legionnaires.

The zealots rode hard along the road closest to the Jordan. Shouting usually worked to clear travellers from the path ahead, but as they neared another river crossing the path was glutted with ox carts, donkey caravans, and families with little children. The lead horsemen pulled off the path and they galloped across the grasslands.

One of the horses stumbled and threw its rider into a heap on the ground. The rest of the group pulled up as pilgrims rushed over to help.

"Stay back!" Hosea shouted. "Keep moving!"

"What's wrong?" Titius called to Jonathan.

"Looks like the horse broke his leg," Jonathan replied.

Hosea looked over the riders. "Keep going," he commanded. "Jonathan, David, go to Alexandria. Shem will meet you there with fresh horses and take you to Barabbas. The centurion is still waiting for his reinforcements." He walked toward the thrashing horse and pulled out his sword. "Hurry!"

The dust thickened as the landscape dipped lower and lower. There were fewer plants and animals. Titius wrapped his head scarf across his face below his eyes and tucked it into his tunic. The late afternoon sun blistered down; sweat drenched his neck and back. Pain pierced his legs and buttocks but he kept riding toward the ravine in the Jordan where Sestus and Barabbas were about to do battle.

Which friend did the Messiah think needed his help? Was it Sestus, the centurion who'd pressed him mercilessly to become a thespian assassin? Was it Barabbas, the zealot who fought for his people's honor? Was it Caleb, the cross maker who he'd been assigned to guard?

Shem led Jonathan and Titius through the ravine along the Jordan. It twisted and turned but Shem knew every step as the shadows fell. They reached a larger cavern and he hooted like a screech owl. A similar cry echoed from the left passage.

"Wait," Shem ordered. He stepped into the shadows. Soon he was back with a torch. "This way," he called, waving toward a break in the cliff face. "Barabbas says the Romans will attack at dawn. Their reinforcements have just arrived. We'll attack tonight."

Titius's stomach twisted as he anticipated the battle. He took three deep breaths, as Jaennus had taught him, to focus his mind. He must find a way to warn Sestus.

Titius kept his face covered as they moved into the zealot camp. Dark canopies anchored to the cliff waved gently in the breeze and deflected plumes of smoke from small cooking fires. The aroma of roasted meat filled the place. Voices rumbled softly.

Jonathan walked confidently up to a large warrior in a group examining a parchment. The men moved to make space for him and greeted him with nods.

Barabbas huddled with Jonathan and then waved the new warriors to one side of the grotto. They dropped their swords and javelins in a pile nearby and their horses were led away.

Jonathan came back to Titius sitting against the cliff. "Let me handle this," he said. "If Barabbas realizes you're the one who left his sister, it might be a distraction. Just fight and make him glad you're with us."

A dozen men huddled around a fire as Barabbas drew in the dirt with a stick. A light rain fell, muddying the map. There were nods and gestures as the men worked to understand their roles. Titius moved closer and stood under a tarp so he could see the scratchings on the ground. He kept his head bowed whenever he thought Barabbas might look at him.

Barrabas was focused and confident, the young men around him patriotic and energetic. When the discussion was over, Jonathan gathered his group together. Titius stood with the other men.

Jonathan picked up a stick and drew their current location, then drew the Romans' location nearby. "Listen carefully," he said. "We'll travel up this cliff and approach from above." He pointed at some of the men. "Half of you will shoot flaming arrows and toss pots of hot oil on the Roman tents." He pointed at Titius and the men beside him. "You men will throw javelins at the sentries and then boulders down on the camp."

"What will the others do?" someone asked.

Jonathan pointed to a section on his drawing. "The others will ambush from this side. The grotto they're hiding in will trap them." He dropped the stick. "We aren't waiting for morning for this fight. We do this now."

The energy was palpable as men dispersed and collected supplies. Each fighter carried gourds of oil, arrows, and a sword. An owl's hoot above silenced the camp. Jonathan led his fighters to the edge of the cliff while others dispersed into the darkness.

Titius had little trouble climbing the cliff. He tucked his sandals into his tunic so he could use fingers and toes to hold the rock face. A few fighters behind him slipped and slid down; there was considerable noise for the first half of the climb until they figured out how to stay quiet. With all that noise no one was going to be surprised. The last thing Titius needed was for Sestus to see him.

Once they all huddled atop the cliff, they lowered ropes and hauled up javelins and more jars of oil. Scouts scurried ahead to check for sentries. They returned a few minutes later. "The Romans are all down below," they reported. "No one up here."

They divided the supplies and passed them up a human chain to their attack position. Looking over the edge of the cliff, Titius could see that most of the Roman troops were inside their tents below. The cliff top was bowl-shaped, with a piece of the bowl, as it were, broken away. The Roman sentries guarded that entrance, but not the heights above them.

Something wasn't right. It secmed too easy. Titius waited in a dark dent in the rock. He gripped his oil. Could he really pour it on Sestus? Or should he pour it out on the ground and hope he got away? Would he shoot a legionnaire if Jonathan were being attacked? Would he let the gods decide who lived and who died?

He remembered Jaennus' words: "Death is the only way to be free from the thespian assassins. Either the death of the emperor, the death of your commander or the death of yourself." If Sestus died, Titius would be free. But Sestus was the only one who could retrieve his ring from the assassin's death pool. Or was he?

More zealots crept closer to the precipice and readied their weapons. The camp below appeared totally unaware.

Was he still free if he killed his own commander? The legion's standard bearer and two bodyguards stood by a tent below him. He gripped the gourd of oil more tightly. Could he pour it on Sestus' tent?

At the owl signal, Jonathan whispered a command. Open gourds of oil fell on the Romans, followed by flaming arrows. Titius held his gourd and watched. Well-aimed javelins skewered two of the sentries and rocks soon showered down on the helpless legionnaires emerging from their tents. The horses below whinnied and reared as fire surrounded them. Supply wagons burst into flame.

Warrior cries shattered the night. Romans without breastplates, helmets, or shields stood shoulder to shoulder against a mob who attacked from above, from in front, from the sides. Battle adrenaline surged through Titius' veins. The glory of men dying for their cause blinded him to the attack's insanity.

Titius watched Barabbas and three of his men move along the edge of the grotto toward Sestus' tent. They wore black and disappeared in the shadows. The chaos in the burning camp distracted attention from them. Finally, Barabbas crawled out of the darkness toward Sestus' bodyguards.

The two legionnaires turned to face the intruders and were shot with arrows from above. The first sentry crumpled to his knees. Another arrow pierced his neck, felling him. The second sentry yanked the arrow from his lower back and looked up. Barabbas sprang from nearby and thrust a sword into his side.

Sestus, still strapping on his armour, stepped out of his tent. He wore his distinctive horsehair helmet. Barabbas and the three charged him. Titius didn't throw oil. He didn't scream in warning. He didn't throw javelins. He hunched in the darkness and watched.

Roman reinforcements streamed into the fight. The thunder of their hob-nailed sandals, the banging of swords against shields, and the roar of their death chant echoed off the grotto walls and rushed past Titius into the night sky.

Barabbas and his companions speared Sestus repeatedly. The rebel leader put a dagger to the centurion's throat. Titius watched him struggle to take off Sestus' helmet, but the Roman reinforcements surged toward him.

Barabbas left his three companions and slipped back into the shadows. Titius tracked him climbing up the cliff face. He saw him reach the precipice on the far side and disappear.

The battle below was brief. Dozens of zealots died, but many others ran away, leaving the Romans standing around their dead commander. Only then did Titius throw his gourd of oil down into the fire consuming Sestus' tent.

Several legionnaires began climbing the cliff. Titius and the zealots slipped back down the ropes on the other side. Titius had prepared his horse for a quick escape, but this was too close. Ten feet from the ground he jumped and landed amid rocks. He slipped and tumbled through the mud to the bottom. Ignoring the pain, he ran through the bushes to where he'd hidden his horse.

Barabbas had killed a leading Roman centurion. Rome's rage would be strong. If the Messiah had sent him to help Sestus, he'd failed. If the Messiah had sent him to help Barabbas, he'd failed.

Titius mounted his horse and galloped away. Fewer than two dozen horsemen were with him. He glanced back to see archers drawing their bows. The sound of swords clashing together split the night.

Rome wouldn't rest until Barabbas hung on a cross. Until that happened, the Romans would kill and capture as many attackers as they could. Caleb would soon be needed.

45

More than forty zealots rendezvoused near Aenon. Barabbas was not among them, but Jonathan and Hosea were. Titius was warming his hands by a fire when Jonathan joined him. The Romans weren't the only ones who'd taken prisoners.

"I can't believe what a captured legionnaire told us," Jonathan said. He kicked a stray coal back into the flames. "He said we defeated them only because the centurion and the rest in the grotto were sick with dysentery. He said the other soldiers were elsewhere so they wouldn't get sick."

A flock of Egyptian geese, flying south to the sea, flapped furiously a few handbreadths above the Jordan's surface. "That sounds reasonable. I've never seen Romans fight so poorly."

"Don't let Barabbas hear you say that," Jonathan said. "He's waited a long time for this day. We lost a lot of good men."

Some of the zealots changed into regular pilgrims' clothing. Others were repacking their bags and loading their horses. Weapons were packed into an ox cart's false bottom, then covered with bricks and a tarp.

"Soon the Romans will come, without mercy," Titius said. "We should scatter and hide for a while. I'll go to Caesarea."

"Is that what you did last time?"

"I did what I had to do," Titius said. "Can you watch my horse for a moment while I, um, use the bushes?"

Jonathan led the horse to a small copse of trees. "Hosea said to wait here until Barabbas and the others arrived."

While Jonathan brushed the horse's neck, Titius slipped away. He ran hard toward the river and dove in fully dressed. He stayed under, swimming and drifting with the current. Then a quick breath and back under, swimming hard to get as far away as possible without being noticed.

He had a bruising experience in the shallow rapids, avoiding the boulders. The water, icy from the winter runoff, chilled him to the bone. He hoped the water was too fast and too cold for crocodiles.

After a long drift down the river, Titius looked for a good place to get out near Jericho. He swam to shore and listened: a leopard snarling, frogs croaking, crickets chirping. A hippopotamus' loud snort from the other shore. No sound of horses coming after him.

He slipped back into the river and rode it until the first light of dawn tinged the horizon. The road to Jericho finally appeared around a bend in the river and Titius swam to the bank. He slipped into a grove to wring out his tunic and redressed behind some bushes. From the road he heard voices.

A large merchant caravan, accompanied by Passover pilgrims from Galilee, chanted and argued. Titius waited until they were out of sight and then continued along the road.

By the time he'd stepped through Jericho's gates, the noonday sun had dried him. His money was back in his horse's saddlebag, with Jonathan. He couldn't beg – that would draw attention to him. He drank from the town well and waited.

A short man approached him boldly. "Peace to you. I'm Zaccheus, chief tax-collector. My man says you didn't pay your personal tax at the gate."

Titius looked into the dark sparkling eyes. He'd run across this man here before. "I've always paid my tax," Titius said, "but this time I have no money. Nothing. I ask for mercy."

Zaccheus eyed him for a moment and then pointed at a stall against the far wall. "The Almighty demands charity for the poor. Eat your fill there and tell them I sent you."

Titius was shocked. He hadn't seen charity like this. In Rome, gold bought relationship, agreement in trade, war and peace alike. Those with money ruled and those without served. Titius bowed and backed away from the tax collector.

The vendor by the wall hesitated only a moment when Titius told him Zaccheus had sent him. . He gave Titius two barley loaves, cheese, figs and salted fish, with a mug of tepid water.

As Titius reclined under a canopy, the sound of hundreds of hobnailed sandals echoed off the Jericho walls. Rome was on the move. Barrabas was going to face Rome's rage.

Merchants and residents disappeared like snow on a hot day. After the roar marched past, the streets slowly filled up again.

That afternoon a camel caravan passed through the gate toward Jerusalem. Its riders wore white headcloths and earth-colored tunics. Titius slipped out with them and jogged along behind. The Arab traders moved quickly, camel bells ringing. The steep ascent was wearying in the hot sun but Titius kept pace with the beasts.

One of the men dropped out and waited until Titius caught up. "Peace to you," he said. "We're Bedu from Perea. The master wishes to understand your business."

Titius nodded. "I only seek protection with your caravan. I'm walking alone to Jerusualem. I mean no harm."

"Consider yourself one of us. I am Shaban."

Titius thought through his catalogue of names for a new identity. He licked his lips and swallowed. "I am Titius, son and senator of Rome."

The Arab chuckled. "The Bedu are people of honor and we speak truth to each other." He pointed at Titius' feet. "No man of power would wear a beggar's sandals."

Titius smiled. "Not unless he had to walk through camel dung in front of him."

Shaban looked ahead. "We dishonor you. Come, walk with me in front of the camels."

From the caravan's head, Titius could hear men singing to their beasts. He didn't understand the words, but understood how music calmed those far from home.

"What do you know of the new Messiah?" Shaban asked. "My father told me that, when he was young, he met a great caravan who'd seen the star announcing his birth."

"I've met the Messiah," Titius said.

"You've met such a great king?"

"This king wears sandals like mine, a robe like mine." He pointed to Galilee. "He terrifies Jerusalem's religious leaders, but in Galilee he heals the blind, the lepers, the demon-possessed. He multiplies bread for the masses, turns water to wine, and fills fishermen's nets with a word."

Shaban rubbed his beard. "Such a powerful man will surely lead his people well. What do the Romans say about him?"

Titius considered his response. "Rome wants peace. They think they can get peace only through the power of the cross."

"So Rome will crucify the Messiah?"

"It's a difficult time for this country," Titius replied.

"I must tell the others," Shaban said. He jogged back to the other camel drivers and they began a vigorous discussion. Titius walked alone, contemplating. Would Rome crucify the Messiah?

The caravan reached Jerusalem as the sun kissed the horizon. Rome's full power was on display at the city gates: squads of fully-armed legionnaires searched every pilgrim.

The camel riders turned aside to a caravansary for shelter. Titius slipped through the Sheep Gate and up to Caleb's carpenter shop. No one was there. He stepped inside and curled up on the bench for the night. If the Romans planned to crucify the Messiah, the cross would probably be made in this room. He could make sure that didn't happen.

In the middle of the night a hand grabbed Titius' ankle. He grabbed the attacker's wrist, squeezed and twisted his foot out of the grip. He put a choke hold on the man. A gourd of wine dropped to the floor. Wine splashed on Titius's foot.

"It's me!" the captive howled. "Caleb!"

Titius released him and they lit a lamp.

"Sestus is dead," Titius said. "Barabbas killed him."

"I know," Caleb said. "I was at the fortress. The centurion Cato came and told me." He cleared the carpenter's bench. "How did you find out?"

Titius picked up a few shavings to feed the glowing embers in the firepit. He added more wood as the flame grew. "Big news travels fast," he said. "They say his cohort had the fever and couldn't fight. Barabbas could never have gotten him any other way."

Caleb put two big pieces of cedar in the fire. "All I know," Caleb said, "is the Romans will have that zealot soon and I'll make a special cross for him." His expression hardened. "I'll have vengeance for my father."

"I met the Messiah," Titius said. He took bread and cheese out of the cupboard. "You knew Yeshua growing up, didn't you?"

Caleb sat on a stool and stirred the fire with a stick. "Yeshua loved adventure." He nudged a coal back into place. "Yeshua loved to laugh. He worked hard. He honored his parents."

"Did you know that he'd be the Messiah?"

"Every mother in this land thinks her son will be the Messiah," Caleb said. He joined Titius at the workbench to eat. "Every son wants to make his mother happy."

Titius lifted his bread. "I praise the Almighty. He healed my mind."

Caleb stared and sat up on his workbench. "What are these words, coming from a Roman like you?"

Titius tore off more bread. "He healed my mind."

Caleb shook his head. "Suzanna follows the Messiah. She tells me not to hate Barabbas."

Titius joined Caleb on the workbench. "It sounds like you're getting closer to her." He waggled his eyebrows.

"That's the problem. I should have been there for Sestus, but I was walking around Jerusalem with a woman."

"I'm your guardian. You're a cross maker." He touched Caleb's wrist in affirmation. "You're not a guardian."

"You trained me to fight. I almost got Sestus killed. I've been useless here."

Titius thought before he spoke. "I used to believe in fates imposed by the gods. I thought we were at the mercy of their vanity and vengeance." He poured wine into a mug. "Listening to Yeshua, I think the Almighty has other plans. Even you aren't more powerful than the Almighty's designs for us."

"What good am I if I can't help bring peace?" Caleb paced to the door and leaned against the frame.

"I've never seen so many crossbeams in your shop," Titius said, patting a pile of squared timbers.

Caleb scowled. "Cato told me that we'd soon have a message to send to these zealots. Sestus always believed the power of the cross would bring peace here. Soon we'll find out if he was right."

Titius slid off the workbench and crouched by the washbasin. "Perhaps one day we'll gain peace without needing the cross."

"I'd love to see that day," Caleb said.

"You need your sleep," Titius said.

Caleb disappeared inside his bedroom. Titius set his empty wine cup near the fireplace. What would a world without the cross be like? How would the powerful bring peace? Perhaps he and Abigail would meet before that great day. Titius curled up on the workbench and went back to sleep.

At dawn, Titius fed the fire again. When he heard leather sandals approaching the shop door he hid under the workbench.

Suzanna entered with a tray and put it on the workbench. She stirred the fire, poured some water into a pot and set the pot to boil. She pushed aside the curtain and peered in. After a moment she turned and searched a basket beside the workbench. She returned to the curtain and began to play a haunting melody on a flute.

A few moments later Caleb emerged and embraced her.

Suzanna tried to keep playing as Caleb squeezed her to him. She finally spun around, giggling, and backed away as the carpenter spread his hands and slowly stomped toward her.

"You tease me, woman," Caleb said.

"I brought you breakfast," Suzanna replied. "You need your strength. I'll pick up the tray later. There's water boiling for you."

Titius heard her sandals leave the shop. The aroma of fresh bread and oranges drew him from his hiding place. He split the food in half and ate his share.

"I spent half the night dreaming about Barabbas," Caleb said. "My stomach is sick from the thought of his freedom. He killed my father and he killed your centurion. How can you eat?

"Justice will find its time, my friend," Titius assured.

Caleb threw his food onto the floor. "Just leave me alone!" he yelled, his face red. "My father is dead, Jaennus is dead, Sestus is dead. The only person who isn't dead is Barabbas. Go find him and I'll make his cross."

46

The next two days went quickly as Titius kept watch for Abigail at the fish vendor and the rose garden. The pickled fish tray lay empty. The old woman, Elizabeth, shook her head when she saw Titius over her rose bushes.

The upper city was full. All the empire's languages reverberated off the limestone walls as people jostled to and from worship. The Messiah and his followers had found some other place to hide. The priests seemed peaceful and confident as they fulfilled their duties in the Temple.

The lower city was the same. Titius leaned against a wall near the Damascus Gate, a stone's throw from Caleb's shop. The streets were packed as tightly as pickled sardines with Passover pilgrims searching for food and shelter. A growing rumble echoed off the walls. Titius stopped to listen.

Massive waves of chanting and cheering swept like an ocean down the Mount of Olives and into the city:

"Hosanna!"

"Blessed is he who comes in the name of the Lord!"

"Blessed is the coming kingdom of our father David!"

"Hosanna in the highest!"[1]

People all around Titius began to move toward the sound. He pressed back against the shop wall to avoid being trampled. What insanity possessed the people? Even Herod wasn't welcomed like this. Surely, it couldn't be Caesar himself.

Caleb pushed his way through the crowd. Titius followed the carpenter until they reached the Antonia Fortress. Titius turned back toward the Temple Mount. He'd promised to keep his presence a secret. He'd get a report from Caleb later.

Titius scaled a garden wall and watched as a man, looking like Yeshua, rode a donkey into the Kidron Valley and then up toward the gates. A green pathway of palm branches lay strewn before and after him. Pilgrims had stripped the surrounding trees.

"It's the Messiah!" a man standing on a nearby roof shouted.

This was not a good time for the Messiah to be stirring up the people. Someone must warn him to get back to Galilee.

The shouting poured into the city. Several women danced around the approaching Messiah. One caught Titius' attention: she held her headscarf stretched between her upraised arms and twirled with an angel's grace. Her long dark hair spun out from her upraised face, which wore an expression of umimaginable joy. She wore a rose behind her ear.

Color swirled around her. The rose fell and was crushed by the donkey's hoof. Several men pushed past the dancers, stepped up to the donkey, and pointed animatedly at the crowd. The man on the donkey simply nodded.

The human river moved uphill. A dozen pharisees stepped onto the edge of a roof, blocking Titius' view. Others gathered around him. "We should have killed him when we had the chance," a voice declared behind Titius.

Titius sidestepped to regain his view. The woman was nowhere to be seen.

Titius scanned the top of the Antonia Tower. Caleb was with one of the Roman centurions looking out from the parapet. The centurion pointed toward the Messiah going up to the Temple. The donkey and its rider disappeared in the masses.

When Titius got into the street, the crush pushing toward the sheep market swept him along like a river. He worked hard to escape and finally got down an alley leading toward the Damascus Gate. Thousands were pushing in from there but he forced his way past the tangle of arms and legs, away from the hypnotic chanting and the acrid tang of smoke and fresh blood.

He was sure the woman with the rose was Abigail. He'd never get close to her if she was in the Courtyard of the Women at the Temple. No man, and definitely no foreigner, could enter it. He'd have to wait until the Feast was over. Not a Jew in the world would understand if he approached a woman and tried to convince her to come away and talk.

Through back streets he navigated to the carpenter shop. Two Roman legionnaires waited outside the door. Sweat streamed down Titius' back.

"Who are you?" they asked him.

"Titius Marcus Julianus, former aide to Sestus Aurelius, Legate of Judea, Champion of Rome."

One legionairre nodded. "He was a good leader." He pointed toward the Antonia Fortress. "You'll be glad to know we've captured his murderer, Barabbas. The Centurion Cato commands crosses be prepared immediately for the zealots."

Titius bowed. "I'm the cross maker's guardian," he said. "I'll let him know you need a special cross immediately."

He stepped past the soldiers into the shop and made himself something to eat. A small bowl of pickled fish made him consider wading through the crowds one more time in search of Abigail, but the crowd outside was still thick. Caleb would be back soon and he might need some help.

Caleb charged into the shop well after dark. His eyes were haunted. "Where've you been?" Caleb said. "They have Barabbas. He's finally going to pay for murdering my father. I need to make a crossbeam that will bring him to his knees."

Titius looked at the pile of crossbeams against the far wall. "You have enough to choose from."

Caleb shook his head. "No," he said. "I need a heavier one, as heavy as Sestus. Only an olive beam will do."

"Get some sleep and then decide," Titius said. "The sentries outside will protect you. There are big olive trees in the Garden of Gethsemane."

"Did you see the Messiah?" Caleb asked.

Titius nodded. "It felt like a new-crowned Caesar coming to claim his throne. But. no emperor would display such humility before his people, dressing in common clothes and riding a donkey. "

"He isn't acting like the boy I knew in Nazareth but he isn't acting like a king. I can't figure him out. Today, in the Temple, he threw over the moneychangers' tables, freed the doves, and chased out the sacrificial animals."

"Why?" Titius asked. The Yeshua he'd seen healed people. Yeshua had freed him of Cleopas. He cared for people; he didn't deliberately create trouble.

"I didn't see him do it," Caleb said, "but I heard he said the Temple was supposed to be a house of prayer for all nations."

"And yet inside the Temple you have a sign declaring death to foreigners who try to come near."

"It's our way to protect the Temple's purity," Caleb said. He walked to the crossbeams and ran his hands along the top one.

"Suzanna's been telling me about this Messiah. He's not as I would've expected. Maybe he can bring us peace despite Rome's terror."

"Was Suzanna one of the women dancing around Yeshua?" Titius asked. "I might know one of the women who was with her." He poured a cup of wine and handed it to Caleb.

"She was there," Caleb said, accepting the mug. He stepped outside and ordered something to eat from the sentries. One of the legionnaires left.

"When will you see her again?" Titius asked.

"Not until I finish the cross for Barabbas," Caleb said, resolve in his voice.

Titius felt trapped in the shop, sentries outside and a preoccupied cross maker inside. How would he find Abigail? Maybe the Messiah was now possessed, a danger to his people, accepting their praises and walking into a confrontation with Rome.

Titius didn't volunteer any information about the dancers and Caleb didn't ask. When the legionnaire returned with the food, the two ate quickly, then doused the torches. Titius curled up on the bench with a blanket once Caleb went to bed.

Titius rose early and stirred the fire into life. In the dawn light, Caleb stuffed handfuls of parched grain into a fold of cloth. His hands shook. He spilled some wheat on the floor, then picked up a hammer from his workbench and threw it against the wall. It bounced against the ceiling, breaking off the head. The handle fell near the fireplace.

Titius jumped away from the bouncing hammer and stood on a cross beam. Caleb turned away without even an apology.

"Shalom, my friend," Titius said.

Caleb put on his apron over his carpenter's tunic. He rubbed his thumbs against his temples and twisted his head back and forth. Titius heard his neck bones crack across the room.

"How will you get the tree back here?" Titius asked, hoping to focus Caleb's mind.

"The Almighty will help me," Caleb said. "If justice isn't dispensed soon, the people will get restless and think Rome is weakening. Peace won't have a chance if we don't work the crosses."

"You sound more Roman than I," Titius said. "Truly you have drunk Rome's poison from Sestus."

Caleb eyed Titius briefly, then grabbed a few tools and set out into the flow of humanity scurrying by the shop toward the markets.

[1] Mark 11:9-10 NIV 1984

47

Jews from Egypt, Libya, Mesopotamia, Parthia, Asia, Galilee, and Rome piled into the rose garden like pickled fish in a basket. Titius pushed his way through a gap in the hedge that kept the curious on the cobblestone path among the flowers. Word of mouth had drawn people there, the only place in Jerusalem to get away from the overwhelming smoke of sacrificed lambs.

Titius nudged his way past a huddle of young women looking at a yellow rose bush. The widow of the garden wasn't with them, nor with the next four groups he saw. He found her near a limestone hut, perched on a stool in a patch of sunshine. Her eyes were closed and a faint smile teased the corners of her mouth.

"Peace to you," he said.

"And peace to you," she replied," her wrinkles soaking in the warmth. "Who might you be today?"

Titius was wearing a white tunic, blue sash, and tall sandals. "I am who I always am."

The women's eyelids flickered and her smile widened. "Is this the same man who seeks the queen of roses? Your voice is different. Perhaps my news is meant for different ears."

Titius stepped forward until his shadow fell over her. "Elizabeth, I've waited long enough. I can't enjoy your games."

"Did you find the beauty you sought?"

"I wouldn't be here if I'd found her." He touched her hand holding her cane. "Has the singer from Galilee come recently?"

The widow smiled. "Ah, so this time you come as you are, without hiding. Perhaps this time you'll find her."

"When was she here?" He couldn't believe he'd missed her again. Was he cursed to always be looking and never find?

The old woman groaned as she rocked herself back and forth and stood. She opened her eyes and looked into Titius's face. "Move out of my sunshine."

Titius stepped back and watched Elizabeth close her eyes and lift her face once more to the sun. She rocked gently back and forth. He waited. Perhaps she was a prophet listening to the Almighty. Or perhaps she'd forgotten he was there.

There was a screech and they turned and saw a hawk diving after a pigeon. The smaller bird dove into shrubbery and the hawk soared back into the heavens. "Two days ago," she answered. "The woman you're looking for went to Bethany to see the Messiah."

She couldn't be far. Titius nodded and left the old woman.

Titius pushed against the tide of humanity surging into the garden. When he finally emerged through the hedge behind the pool of Siloam, he headed past the perfume factories toward the nearest city gate.

Titius followed the road below the city and skirted the outside of the huge walls toward the upper city. The constant stench of burning trash, human waste, animal carcasses, and criminal corpses in the Valley of Hinnom made him gag. He walked as quickly as he could.

Rounding the corner below the Temple he saw a group of Pharisees huddled tightly together. Titius moved slowly toward them and faded into the shrubbery. None of the black-clad, heavily bearded men looked in his direction. Their voices carried in the wind.

"The whole world is following him. We must kill him before the Romans shut down the Temple."

"How? He avoids every trap we lay. He's never alone."

"Is there a woman?"

"No! You see him. He wouldn't fall for such an old trick."

"Perhaps there is a follower we can bribe to betray him?"

"There may be one." A wind rustled the leaves, drowning out their words. Then the Pharisees stepped apart and the first speaker said. "Let me try."

A small caravan of merchants broke up the huddle. Titius blended in with them and went on his way. The religious leaders seemed to be talking about Yeshua. How strange that the Messiah so loved by the people could be so hated by their leaders.

The pathway round the wall was crowded with pilgrims. It was soon apparent there was no quick way to get through the Tyropoeon and Kidron Valleys to the Mount of Olives. A squadron of Roman Cavalry charged down the road, scattering pilgrims on both sides. A gilded carriage bounced along behind the horsemen as they headed for a main gate near Herod's Palace.

Titius cut through the Garden of Gethsemane. Caleb the cross maker was wrapping a golden rag around a tree, claiming it for Caesar. Titius waited for an inner voice to comment, but there was only silence. He shook his head and went on his way.

Dark clouds leapfrogged across the hills and charged toward the Temple. The sun stood high. Swallows skittered over the graveyard against the towering walls. Wildflowers bent before the strengthening wind.

He hurried up the hill to Bethany. Near the top he sat and watched the shadows surround the Temple. Ant-sized figures crawled into the warrens of the city that never slept. The religious leaders in their ceremonial black robes bowed and accepted sacrifices, pronouncing the Almighty's forgiveness on his people. They thought no more of killing the Messiah than they thought of killing their lambs.

The priests, he realized, acted out their piety better than he himself had ever acted. Something had changed inside him – he could never pretend like that anymore.

Once in Bethany, Titius sat at the community well and waited. The village seemed lighter and less windy. A young girl with a clay jug approached. She hesitated, stopped, and took two more steps in his direction.

"Peace to you," Titius said.

"And peace to you," she replied. "Are you here for the festival? You look Roman."

"You are perceptive for your years," he said. "Who might you be?"

"I am a servant of Lazarus." The girl bowed her head, almost hiding her midnight-dark bangs and chocolate eyes.

"The one the Messiah raised from death?" Titius asked.

"Yes, the same." She tied the rope to the jug and lowered it.

The jug slapped against the water. "Was he truly dead?"

"Yes, for four days," she said without looking up.

"The Messiah healed me, so I believe."

"Yes, he heals many." She drew the jug up to the rim, untied it, and set it on the rocky lip. "Right now he teaches his followers. Perhaps you can see him tomorrow."

"Do you know if there's a young woman from Galilee among his followers? A singer?"

She glanced quickly at him, then lowered her gaze. "There are many women from Galilee here." She turned to go.

Titius blocked her path. "The one I seek wears roses in her hair."

Her eyebrows furrowed for a moment. "I may know someone like that."

Several onlookers started toward them. "Was she one of the dancers who led the Messiah into Jerusalem?"

The girl seemed to sense the onookers. "I'm here to serve, not to observe."

"Please, if you see a woman who wears a rose, tell her the noble man she seeks has come to her from the garden in Rome."

She took a step around him. "I must get this water back. Maybe the one you look for will come get her own water."

Titius watched the young woman walk toward a big limestone house. Two large tents beside it rippled in the breeze. The people huddled in them prepared to eat their evening meal.

An old man with a cane hobbled, accompanied by two big young replicas of himself. "If you're here to see the Messiah, you'll have to wait until after Passover," he said. "If you're here searching for zealots to betray to the Romans, then leave. Now."

"Peace to you," Titius greeted, his hands open.

"Keep your peace," the old man snarled, waggling his cane. "We have enough trouble."

"I'm waiting for someone I used to know," Titius said.

The young men reached for Titius' arms. He stepped back out

of their reach. They grabbed for him again, but Titius ducked and put out his foot, tripping one. The other charged and Titius flipped the aggressor over his hip, flat onto his back. He felt the cane whack his calves and rolled away.

When he sprang to his feet, all three men held knives. Dozens of villagers had formed a hedge around them. The first sprinkles of rain fell, but only a few observers moved away.

Titius saw a space in the wall of people. He thought he could get through, but a broad-chested man closed the opening. The man's face was familiar. Titius's peripheral vision caught flashing steel and he stepped sideways to avoid a knife blade from one of his first attackers. He moved fast as a cobra, grabbing the wrist, holding it and elbowing his assailant in the stomach. The knife dropped to the ground.

"Stop!" the fisherman commanded. "How is this a welcome for our guest?"

"This is no guest," the old man bellowed. "He's a Roman hunting for zealots."

"I came looking for a friend," Titius said. "The Messiah healed me and I wanted to share my news."

"I'm here."

48

Titius stepped back at the sound of the woman's voice. The fisherman stepped aside.

Abigail's raven hair was almost hidden by a shawl. Her eyes glistened as she briefly looked at Titius and then looked down. Her hands trembled. In her right hand she held a rose. Droplets of rain fell from it.

Titius stared. "I found you," he said.

She kept her head bowed. "I'm here," she said. "Is it true Yeshua healed you?"

"I have so much to tell you," Titius said. "Do you remember the garden in Rome?"

She nodded and whispered. "I'll never forget your garden." She held up her rose. "Wherever I go I seek its beauty and peace. Why are you dressed like a servant?"

Titius smiled. "It suited my purpose. I'm not the child you knew."

"And I'm not the girl you knew," she replied. "Come inside. I don't remember rain like this in Rome." She looked into his eyes and smiled.

The rain poured like a waterfall and the villagers scattered. Titius followed Andrew, the fisherman and Abigail toward the tents beside Lazarus' house.

Titius and Abigail were both drenched by the time they ducked under the large white tent beside the house. Rain trickled from

Abigail's nose and chin. She wiped her cheeks but kept looking into his eyes.

He saw nothing but her: raven curls hiding shyly under her headscarf, eyes bright and questioning. Titius drank in her face. "I have looked for you everywhere."

"I've been waiting," she said, tucking a stray curl back under the shawl. Her eyes examined him. "You look so much like your father. You're so tall, so strong."

Titius shook his head. "Thanks to your Messiah, I'm nothing like my father."

A middle-aged woman bustled about handing out towels. "Dry yourselves," she said. "Then come and eat. No guest will die of starvation in this house."

"Thank you, Martha," Abigail said. "No one does hospitality like you. I'll be there to help you in a minute."

"Mind your guest, Abigail," Martha replied. "The dishes won't go anywhere." She nodded at Titius and hurried away.

"I hardly believed this day would come," Titius said. He wiped his face and hung the towel across his shoulders.

"I hardly believe it still," Abigail replied. Raindrops and tears intermingled on her chin.

"You still have the heavens in your eyes!" Titius whispered.

"You still have the earth in yours," Abigail replied.

Titius was jostled by a heavy shoulder. "Man, stand away from her," a male voice boomed. "Woman, he's a Roman! Consider the Almighty. At least wait until the Messiah comes back and gives his wisdom."

Abigail blushed and backed away. "I need to help Martha with the food. Don't go away."

Titius reached for Abigail but a strong grip crushed his wrist. He brought an elbow up into the man's jaw, and the man crumpled at his feet. Two more approached him, but his raised fists and the fire in his eyes stopped them long enough for the fisherman to intervene again.

"What is it, Roman?" Andrew held up his hands. "Will you fight for every woman you see? Come! You and I need to breathe before it gets too hot in here."

Abigail was nowhere to be seen so Titius went out into the rain. He draped his towel over his head. He saw Caleb's friend, Suzanna, at an open doorway, watching him closely.

"As soon as the rain stops, the Messiah will be returning from the Temple," Andrew said, putting one hand on Titius' shoulder. "Is Abigail the friend you spoke of? How do you know her?"

Titius shrugged the hand from his shoulder. "Are you her father?" he said. "She's a free woman who deals with her own affairs."

"She's a follower of the Messiah and it's my job to guard her," Andrew declared. "She's now my sister and I'm her brother. If you wish to speak to her, you'll speak to me first."

He could subdue the fisherman, but Abigail would resent her guardian being ignored. "I understand," Titius said and wiped his face. "Peace to you and to your house."

"And peace to yours," Andrew replied. He kept walking.

Titius pulled on his head covering and kept pace. "I'm Titius Marcus Julianus, son of Senator Julianus, former owner of Abigail on our estate in Rome."

"So, you come to claim your slave?"

"No!" Titius said, his hands open in sincerity. "I've cared for her since I was young. We've been separated for many years. I come to speak to her. To see the desires of her heart."

Andrew ran his hand through his hair. "But you're a Roman Senator and she's a Jewish slave. How can such things be?"

"The Messiah touched my mind," Titius said, "and now I'm surer than ever what I seek."

Andrew stepped back. "She's never mentioned you." He stepped around a muddy patch in the road. "Now, you've seen her. Go back to Jerusalem and wait until tomorrow." He pulled his shawl back over his head. "I'll talk with her to see what she wants. Meet me tomorrow at the Sheep Gate and we'll talk."

"I'll stay and speak with the Messiah," Titius said.

"Tomorrow!" Andrew replied. "That's soon enough. Go home and get dry. We have enough people here already."

He hadn't come this far just to be put off, but this was the man he had to impress. "Before I go," Titius said, "I've heard the religious leaders saying things that could mean harm for the Messiah."

"What have you heard?" Andrew asked.

"The Pharisees are looking for someone to betray him." Titius looked into the fisherman's bearded face. "They want to kill him."

"We know," Andrew said. "The people have welcomed Yeshua as their king and the rulers are jealous. There will be trouble. The Messiah warned us."

"If there's trouble, please keep Abigail away from it," Titius said. The tent was no place to hide from the Romans. "I can take her to a safe place."

"Tomorrow! See me tomorrow." Andrew turned away and slogged toward the tents.

The torches flickered weakly as a bedraggled Titius limped into the carpenter's shop. Caleb was planing a cedar cross beam and talking to himself.

"You sound like me before the Messiah touched me," Titius said, remembering how Cleopas had plagued him almost every waking moment.

Caleb jumped and released his plane. "So, you still live! Were you out chasing a woman and forgetting the job your centurion gave you?"

Titius moved to the firepit and took off his tunic. He threw a chunk of discarded cedar on the flame and draped his soaking garment over a crossbeam. "My duty is done when there is either the death of the emperor, the centurion, you or me." He picked up a stick and nudged the log into the flames. "So, since Sestus is dead, I'm free."

"So the woman rejected you," Caleb said with a snort.

"The last woman I saw was Suzanna," Titius replied, grinning broadly and wrapping his arms around himself.

Caleb picked up the plane and hurled it as he charged, head down. Titius sidestepped and brought his fists down on Caleb's back. Before the cross maker could get off his knees, Titius grabbed his wrist and put him in an arm lock, pressed against the wall near the workbench.

"Let me go!" Caleb yelled.

"Do you remember this position?" Titius asked.

Caleb struggled, then stilled. "The warehouse in Caesarea, when I was with Nabonidus. It was you. Get away from me."

"I've guarded you over and over," Titius said. "I've fulfilled my oath." He released Caleb and stepped away. "We need to work together for the Messiah's sake."

"What do you know of the Messiah?" Caleb growled. "You're a Roman. He's the Jews' Messiah."

"I know what I know."

Caleb grabbed a spare tunic from his room and threw it at Titius. "Cover yourself. Some decent woman may pass this way."

Titius chuckled. "At this time of night? I doubt it."

"The Messiah could be in danger," Caleb said. "I've heard rumours."

"So have I," Titius said. "That's why I say we work together. I can find things out and you can tell the Messiah's followers so they can protect him."

"The people love Yeshua," Caleb said. "What can the Romans do to him?"

"It isn't the Romans," Titius said. "The religious leaders intend to bribe one of his followers."

"It won't work," Caleb declared. "Those men would follow him to their death, they're so loyal. And I have to get these crosses done. Maybe after Passover we can plan a way to protect the Messiah."

49

Just after the rooster crowed a second time, Titius backed up against the wall outside Caleb's shop. It had been three days since the Messiah had turned Jerusalem into a boiling cauldron of intrigue. Titius' ears couldn't keep up with the plots and plans. Some wanted to make the Messiah a king and overthrow the Romans. Some wanted to destroy the Messianic pretender before the Romans destroyed everything.

When Titius had slipped out before dawn, the cross maker had been asleep with his head on the olive beam designed for Barabbas. Now, as he returned with sardines, oranges, cheese, and olives for breakfast, he heard Suzanna's voice inside.

"Why would the Romans be tense?" she asked.

Silence hung like a morning cloud over a lake. Finally, Caleb spoke, "The leaders who murdered my centurion will be crucified in two days. They're worried about how the people will react." Titius heard tools being dumped on the bench. "Thanks for the soup. I need to finish this crossbeam."

Suzanna cleared her throat. "I've never seen a crossbeam made of olive wood," she said. "The grain looks so beautiful. It's hideous to think about its purpose." She groaned. "Don't you think it'll be too heavy?"

"This one is specially designed," Caleb said, "to send a message that people won't soon forget. We must show them the terror of the cross."

Titius clutched the food and slipped away. Abigail might go to the market to buy things for the Passover meal. It was the day of Preparation for the Feast of Unleavened Bread. To avoid Andrew he needed a significant disguise.

Instead of women heading to market, the streets were filled with men moving toward the Sheep Gate, all shoulder-to-shoulder, tight as stones in a wall. At every intersection two Roman legionnaires stood on the rooftops, owls peering down on passing rodents.

Titius put on a scribe's clothes and joined the flow. "How will you choose your lamb?" he asked a merchant scuffling beside him.

The man knit his brows and shook his head. Titius spoke in Hebrew. "How will you find the right lamb?" he asked.

Again the man frowned. "I will take what I'm given," he said. "Same as always."

Titius nodded. He was like flotsam being tossed toward a beach. Abigail could have been anywhere in the market and he was stuck with guilty men hoping some sheep would wash away their sins.

A shout echoed from ahead. The vortex of men pulled Titius up to a blood-stained garment covering a body. Large stones sat close to the covered head. Screams of rage vibrated into the cobblestones. Passersby spat on the corpse and hurried by. "Roman spy!" yelled the old man ahead of him. "No non-Jew is welcome in this place."

"There's no lamb for that kind!" the young man beside him shouted. "Imagine, pretending to be a Jew at Passover!" He spat and moved on.

A shudder convulsed Titius and he was sure it would give him away. No one seemed to notice and he slowly began to push his way out of the river of bodies.

At the Sheep Gate the momentum slowed as the men offered

money and received lambs. Jubilant at their purchases, they shouted for joy, almost drowning out the bleating.

Titius was still pushing out of the crowd when a strong hand grabbed his shoulder. He turned and stared into the eyes of the fisherman, Andrew.

"Come, this way," Andrew shouted. "I've been waiting for you."

"What about your lamb?" Titius called back.

"Others will get mine," Andrew said. "We dine with the Messiah for Passover tonight."

Titius looked down at his clothes. "How did you recognize me?"

"I was coming to help that poor man and I saw your eyes," Andrew said. "I saw fear, not hatred. I knew it was you."

Titius followed Andrew slowly against the flow of traffic until they reached a small perfume shop. "We can meet here," Andrew said. "One of the sisters in our group owns the shop."

"Thanks for coming," Titius said. "I wasn't sure what time."

"I didn't say," Andrew said, stepping inside the shop. The walls were lined with vials and jars. "I asked the Almighty to bring you." He leaned back against a tall cupboard.

Titius breathed deeply: jasmine, frankincense, rose petals, many other smells. "Can you really ask the Almighty to bring someone to you?"

"I did." Andrew looked toward the ceiling and bowed his head for a moment. "Now, I talked to Abigail." He looked at Titius. "She says she hasn't seen you since she was young. She can't tell me who you are now. So, who are you?"

Titius sat on a stool. "You ask a hard question," he answered. "I'm not who I seem to be, but I'm not who I used to be."

"Tell me about your family."

"My grandfather was a great Roman general and my father was a senator," Titius began. "Abigail served in my house, a servant to my mother. We were great friends... until one day, my mother sent her away."

"Why did you want her sent away?" Andrew sounded harsh.

"I never wanted her sent away," Titius said, standing. "She was my best friend! I believe my mother saw my father trying to take advantage of Abigail and sent her away for her own protection."

"Who did you marry?"

"I never married."

"Why not?"

"My soul was attached to one woman and I came looking for her." Titius sat with his head down. "I almost found her at Isaac's pickled fish shop in Magdala. I *almost* found her every place I've been, but I always seemed a step too late. I've never been with another woman."

"You're a Roman, a man of violence," Andrew said. "And you never seem to be the same person twice. How can you be trusted?"

"It's true," Titius acknowledged. "I've been working for a centurion, guarding a cross maker. I've done many things I regret. But I met the Messiah and I'm a different man."

"Becoming a different man takes time."

Titius examined Andrew's swarthy face. "You've been with the

Messiah for years. Surely you've seen how men are changed with a single touch."

Andrew nodded. "Why would you force a Jewish slave to marry a senator determined to destroy her people?"

Titius winced. "I'd never support anyone who wants to destroy her people." He rubbed his sweating forehead with his sleeve. "I don't even know if I can be a senator. Herod's assistant, Cretius, stole my family estate and I have to get it back to qualify for a senatorial position. I also have to retrieve a family ring that may be forever lost."

"What would you be willing to do to get your estate back?"

"I don't know," Titius said. "I don't know much anymore. So much is changing."

Andrew stepped toward Titius and extended his hand. "She wants to talk with you."

Titius took the offered hand in both of his. "I want to talk with her."

Andrew turned to the back of the shop. "Abigail."

50

Abigail, her head bowed, stepped out from behind the counter. A scarlet shawl draped down over her eyes. A few dark curls showed near her temples. She wore a long white stola and a leopard-skin belt.

"Abigail," Andrew said, "your only Master now is Yeshua. You have no fear of man. Just tell me and I'll remove this man from your presence."

Abigail raised her eyes slowly and looked at Titius. "Is it true? You've never taken another woman?"

Titius looked away. "Do you think me less of a man for ignoring other opportunities?"

Abigail smiled. "Not at all," she said. "It makes you special. Apart from eunuchs, a few slaves, the Messiah, and some of his younger followers, I know no other man who survives without women."

Andrew stretched his arms between them. "Speak the truth," he said. "How is there such intimacy and desire between two people who haven't seen each other for years?"

Titius tore his gaze away from Abigail and glared at Andrew. "I told you, she was my mother's servant and my childhood friend. Her magic captured my heart. Her beauty stole my will."

"Is it true, you never wanted me to go?" Abigail said.

Titius' mouth dried up like a desert. He struggled to free his tongue. The words came out in a whisper. "I wanted to protect you."

Abigail examined his eyes again. "Why would your mother send me away if not because of you?" Her brows knit. Water filled the corners of her eyes.

Titius wanted to run but his feet wouldn't move. "She saw you with my father in the garden."

Her face flushed red. She bit one knuckle and turned away. Sobs wracked her; she held herself in a tight embrace. Andrew put a hand on her shoulder.

"Go!" Andrew said to Titius. "Go! And don't come again."

"No!" Abigail said, straightening up. "Please, let me talk alone with Titius. He needs to know the truth about my life."

Andrew stepped away. "I'll be right outside," he said. "Just call and I'll bring down the wrath of the Almighty on this imposter."

Abigail wiped her eyes with her sleeve and smiled feebly. "And I thought the Master said James and John were the 'sons of thunder,'" she said. "I should talk to him again."

Andrew backed out the door without another word.

"I am a sight," she said to Titius. "Weeping like a harlot on her wedding day." She slumped onto a stool and propped her chin on her fists. "No, no, no," she said, shaking her head. "I've spent so many years thinking you loved my sister, you loved the cook's assistant, you loved anyone but me."

Titius knelt at her feet.

She looked at him, tears still streaming. "Your father was my master. What could I do?"

He put his hand on her shoulder but she shook it off.

"You have to believe me," she said. "I never let him have me." Abigail stood and walked to the counter. "My sister gave herself to your father, to Cleopas, and to the gardner, just to protect me. I've never forgiven myself or let myself get near another man."

Titius stood. "My mother sent you away to protect you," he said.

She faced him. "Now I see that." She grabbed her headscarf and threw it across the room. "How could I have known that when I was so young?" she shouted. "Everything I knew, everyone I loved was taken away. I was sent to a place they told me was home. Made to live with others they said were my people."

Titius took a step toward her. "I'm here," he said.

"Yes, you're here," she said. "Just when I'd convinced myself you were a dream that I'd never love again, that I'd be the woman apart."

"I'm sorry," Titius muttered.

"It's not your fault," Abigail said. "The Messiah took my stony heart and melted it before you came back. I thought all my love would be only for him. Now here you are and I'm more confused than ever."

Titius leaned against the counter next to her. "The Messiah healed my mind so I could love again. If I'd found you sooner I may never have been able to know the joy of watching you dance before the Messiah."

"You saw me dancing?"

He smiled. "Like a butterfly in a garden. A swallow in the wind. You were a rainbow unleashed."

"It felt like that," she said. "I felt like a little girl in your rose garden again. I could see all of creation in the clouds. I could hear forest songs in the people's celebrations."

Titius picked up a small bowl of frankincense. "I went to your rose garden in the city," Titius said as he held it out to her. "Not even the best incense can match that haven."

"Here?" Abigail accepted the bowl, passed it under her nose, and set it on the counter beside her. "Did you meet Elizabeth and Hannah?"

"I met a young girl and an old woman if that's who you mean," Titius replied.

"Did you talk with them?"

"The old woman told me about a maid from Magdala who waited for her nobleman to come and claim her."

The sun passed its zenith and started its slide toward Passover. "I told Elizabeth about the nobleman my first time in the garden, to stop her questions," she said. "And as I walked there and remembered your garden in Rome, I began to believe maybe I truly was waiting for someone. When I met the Messiah, I thought the love I needed was spiritual instead of personal."

"I think I've visited every fish vendor you've ever sold pickled fish to," Titius said, laughing.

Abigail went behind the counter and began to collect her bags. "I have another sack if you want some. This fish definitely does not smell like roses." She set a small sack on the counter.

"I hear it's an acquired taste. Uncle Isaac still thinks the Romans will soon be shipping them all over the empire."

Andrew stepped in. "Abigail, we need to go. Things must be changing in our favour. I saw Judas talking to some of the priests. Even they were contributing to our cause. He must be on an errand for the Messiah."

Titius put his arm in front of Abigail. "Where are you going?" Titius asked.

"We need to get supplies at the market for the Passover meal," Andrew replied. "Titius, I'm sorry you can't join us. Abigail can see you again after the holiday." He picked up Abigail's bags and turned to go.

Titius turned to Abigail, "But we've only just begun to talk."

Abigail retrieved her shawl and put it back on, nodded politely, and stepped out the door.

Titius followed them, but they were quickly swallowed by the crowd. "When will I see you again?" he called.

His only answer was a braying donkey coming straight at him.

51

The donkey coming down the hill clearly pulled a cart too heavy for it. The young boy holding the reins screamed warnings as the cart bounced along the cobblestones. Its load of heavy stone tilted dangerously and the cart plunged toward the orange vendor. Titius leaped to the donkey's neck, wrapped his arms around it and dug his heels into the ground. This slowed the cart down enough so that two other men could grab it and keep it upright until it did stop.

The boy thanked him. "The centurion needs these stones right away at Golgotha. You saved my life."

Titius surveyed the load. "Be at peace, slow down." He examined the donkey's hoof for damage. "Golgotha? Isn't that where the Romans crucify zealots outside the city?"

"I just deliver," the boy said. "I don't ask what people do with them."

Titius hurried back to the street where Abigail and Andrew had headed, but they'd disappered.

Dejectedly he wandered the streets. How could he prove himself worthy of Abigail? His dreams that night were filled with Abigail driving runaway carts he could do nothing to stop. He woke, shaking and sweaty, before falling into a peaceful sleep.

Dawn tickled Titius' eyelids during his morning dream: Abigail curled up on a marble bench in the rose garden in Rome. The light brushed her hair as it flowed over her shoulder. A hawk drifted in descending circles closer and closer to where she lay.

She shrank until she was small as a mouse… and then the hawk dove.

"No!" Titius bolted upright. He opened his eyes and saw a rooster on the edge of the roof where he'd slept. Confusing dream and reality, he hurled a stick at it as it stretched and flapped its wings. It hit the rooster and it sailed off the building. In the distance another rooster crowed. And then another.

Titius stretched, then walked to the roof's edge and looked down on the streets already filling with slaves and worshippers. Passover had arrived.

Titius had been left behind by Andrew and Abigail and then realized that Caleb had filled his shop with other Passover guests. So the roof of a centurion's house had become Titius' refuge while Jerusalem celebrated. As a non-Jew, Titius felt unwelcome.

The weather had been cool, but a carpet and a few blankets on the roof had provided all the comfort he needed. He had no trouble buying dates, figs, bread, cheese, meat, oranges, and pomegranates. The noise of celebration had kept him awake most of the night. Alone on the roof, just the stars for company, left him feeling alone, as if he could never belong to anyone, anywhere. Even Cleopas might have been a welcome intrusion. But something deeper urged him to take comfort.

His disguises now seemed pointless, but he wasn't sure how to ignore the training that compelled him to absorb everything happening around him. So he put on a scribe's woolen tunic to head out among the religious pilgrims.

He had a good stretch, but felt unwashed and unclean. Well, there were more than a hundred pools and mikvahs around the city. It was no problem to set that right.

About to leave, he took one last look over the roof's edge to locate the fallen rooster. He saw a group of five women rushing toward the city gate. They looked like a group he'd seen with the Messiah. One of them looked like Suzanna. The women disappeared into a nearby alley and Titius turned and went on his way.

He washed at a fountain with a stablehand and a kitchen slave, using a cloth for his face, his mouth, his hair, his feet, his armpits. As he sat to put his sandals back on, he noticed two of Yeshua's close disciples running in the direction from which the women had come. Their eyes were frantic with fear.

Then a loud hum, like bees gone mad, took over the streets. A legion of hobnailed boots pounded all the way from the Antonia Fortress to the Upper City. A swell of people began to move in their wake, away from the Temple, toward Herod's Palace.

Titius returned to his perch on the roof to see what was happening. Two young men ran up the stairs to watch from the high roof with him.

"What's happening?" Titius asked.

One took off his prayer shawl and turned in amazement. "Where've you been?" he asked. "The priests arrested the Messiah. The Sanhedrin condemned him. They're taking him to Pilate to have him crucified!"

Titius shuddered. Yeshua? Surely not. Titius watched a crowd gather in a courtyard. "Why would Pilate crucify the Messiah? The whole nation declared him their king just a few days ago."

"They're fighting for the survival of our nation," the other man said. "What will the people do if the Romans crucify both Barabbas and the Messiah?"

Titius raced down the stairs. He pushed through the crowds to the carpenter shop. The olive crossbeam and several others were gone. Caleb was nowhere to be seen.

He pushed his way to the Antonia Fortress. The legionnaires from Gaul refused to listen to him as he called for the lead centurion. Being dressed as a scribe didn't help, even when he spoke in Latin and Aramaic. His name meant nothing to the men on guard.

He worked hard against the crowds to reach the shop again, where he changed into carpenter's clothes. Abigail would be distressed, but he didn't know how to reach her. The street to the perfume shop was beyond the crowd, so he could hurry past the sheep gate to reach it. The place was locked up.

Shouts reverberated off the limestone city walls: "Barabbas! Barabbas!" over and over. "Crucify him! Crucify him!" The people had spoken: Barabbas, the head of the Sicarii, was done. The serpent would be slain; Sestus would be avenged. Even the Jews knew justice.

Titius sat on a wall outside the perfume shop and waited. Watching Barabbas die didn't interest him. Once Pilate released Yeshua, the city would return to its rhythm and someone would come and tell him how to find Abigail.

As time passed the population moved as one outside the gates to watch the gruesome executions. The power of the cross would be demonstrated again and Caleb would have his revenge, watching Barabbas die.

Titius watched a sparrow pecking at seeds in the dirt. What would Phoebe think when she heard her brother was dead? How would the zealots respond? Who would rise up to fight for the homeland? As Rome's massive python prepared to squeeze Judea's hero in a death grip, where was Hosea?

And where was Abigail?

52

Titius had no stomach for watching Barabbas get executed. He knew Phoebe loved her brother and that the zealots believed in their cause. They were as dedicated to each other as any of the Romans or Jews he knew.

While everyone else was leaving the city for the place where Caleb's crosses would be used, Titius hiked up the Mount of Olives and kept walking, right past Bethany. On his way back he stopped at the home of Lazarus, Martha, and Mary to see if Abigail was there. The place was deserted.

As he sat looking over the Temple and the city, an unnatural darkness wrapped itself around the sun, then around everything below. A fearsome tremor rocked the hills; Titius had to grab a nearby oak to stay upright. The wind howled. The city's limestone blocks, once a glistening gem welcoming the world, now seemed to quiver. Terrified shouts erupted from all quarters.

Behind him there was light. In front of him there was complete darkness. Sweat soaked his brow and trickled down his back. It looked like the heavens had poured a cask of tar down over God's very dwelling place.

He stood at the brow of the hill watching and waiting. The ground stilled. A finger of light lifted a corner of the blanket of darkness. The first birds sounded. A rabbit raced past. A baby cried. Even Cleopas seemed normal compared to this.

The intense quiet felt like a hand on his jugular. He'd heard from Caleb about the plague of darkness on Egypt; this must have been similar. Surely the angel of death had come to claim a soul, if not everyone's soul. Who hovered around this holy place and what was he doing?

Slowly Titius started down the hill toward the garden of Gethsemane on his right. He took half steps, willing his sandalled feet to find the next step. The way had been packed hard by millions of pilgrims and he could easily feel when he strayed from the path.

Halfway down the hill he stepped on something that moved – there was a yelp, a snarl. The dog bit into his arm right above the wrist and he brought his forearm down on its snout. It yelped again and ran away.

Titius crouched, clutching his arm. His senses were on high alert. This dog was clearly not like the wild dogs he'd encountered outside Nazareth. He was in the darkness, as dark as a forest at midnight on a starless night. Evil slithered, prowled, lurked closer and closer.

"Help me, Yeshua!" he called out.

Thunder rumbled across the heavens. Once again he felt as he had at the bottom of the pool where Jaennus had tested him. Something bigger than he pulled him... and he was up and free and gasping for breath. Fire burned in his stomach. He hugged his knees and held on.

His soul had been bathed.

A hand shaking his shoulder startled him. "David! David! What are you doing here?"

Titius looked up into Jonathan's curly dark beard and chocolate eyes and said, "It was so dark."

"The Almighty has worked his judgment on the Messiah," said

Jonathan. "The authorities will be rounding up his followers. Hurry! The Romans will crucify us all if we don't run."

Titius uncurled and stood. "What are you talking about? It was Barabbas they crucified."

"No!" Jonathan said. "The people chose to have Pilate release Barabbas and crucify Yeshua. He's dead. It's over."

"They killed the Messiah?" The last dark clouds faded from over the city.

"Yes! Now come with me," Jonathan urged, grabbing Titius' arm. "We have to run."

Titius wrenched his arm away. "No! I have to find someone. You go. I'll find you when I can."

Jonathan tried one more time to grab Titius by the sleeve, but when Titius resisted, Jonathan rushed into the stream of humanity rushing away from the city. Panic, hopelessness, and terror filled their eyes.

Titius took a step toward Jerusalem, his arms outstretched. What was happening?

Titius skirted the masses, stumbling over gravestones and small bushes, down the rest of the hill. He ignored the shouted warnings from others desperate to get away. He breached the gate and walked into the tomb-like city.

And the hob-nailed sandals began their horrifying rhythm, reverberating off the cobblestones and walls. "Barabbas is alive and Yeshua is dead," Titius said out loud. "Yeshua, if you're dead, how did you help free me?"

The heavens remained silent. Streets began to fill again with everyday worshippers moving toward the Temple. But Temple guards blocked the entrances. People were turned away. Angry shouts echoed up the hill. Something had gone terribly wrong.

As evening shadows began to fall, Titius pushed his way toward the crucifixion site. A carpenter as fit as Yeshua might last days on a cross. There were too many questions that needed answering. What did one say to a Messiah dying on a cross?

He rounded a small rise and saw a group of women weeping by the path. A religious leader hurried by with a sack. The smell of myrrh and aloes filled his nostrils. Vultures circled overhead. He must hurry.

He approached the crossroads where they crucified people. The tops of three crosses appeared above the bushes. Three crosses? He hoped they hadn't crucified Yeshua's followers with him. Surely not Andrew and Peter. He stepped out into the open.

The crosses were empty.

Titius saw two legionnaires cleaning up the site. He ran to them. "I'm Titius Marcus Julianus, guardian for our former centurion Sestus Aurelius, legate of Jerusalem," he panted as he raised his right arm. "Where are the men who were crucified today?"

The legionnaires held out the bloody nails and rope still in their hands. "If you wanted to help, you're too late. We've already broken their legs and dumped them in Gehenna to burn with the trash."

"All of them?" Titius asked.

"No." one answered. "Two religious leaders took down the one who said he was the Messiah and put him in a tomb."

"Which cross did the Messiah die on?" Both pointed to the center cross.

Titius took a step closer: the cross made of olive wood. Dark stains marred much of the grain's beauty.

"This was the strangest crucifixion," the other soldier said. "I always thought they wouldn't defile themselves with the dead, but for this one they didn't hesitate."

Titius stood by the center cross and looked toward the city. "Didn't his followers try to stop this?"

The first paused halfway up a crude ladder leaning against a cross. "Most of the ones here were women. The religious leaders just made fun of him. I think they'd have pounded the nails in themselves if we'd let them."

Titius stared up at the cross. "How could this happen?"

"Do you follow him?" the second asked.

"I'm a Roman," Titius said, "Why would you think I'm his follower?"

"Be at peace," the legionnaire replied. "People from many different nations once praised him. No doubt this nation's hope is broken and we can now have peace."

"The power of the cross," Titius said.

"Exactly!" the other legionnaire agreed. "The power of the cross has triumphed again. Rome is supreme."

"Do you know the cross maker?" Titius asked.

"Caleb ben Samson?" responded the first soldier. "Yes. He claimed the nails for the Messiah. He took responsibility. He wept as much as the women."

Titius nodded and marched quickly off. He had to find Caleb

right away. There was no Cleopas to respond. And now there was no Messiah to answer his questions.

53

Abigail stood in a huddle of women hugging each other. Her shoulders shook from sobbing. Titius watched helplessly from a wall nearby. The crucified Messiah's followers hid in the shadows close to the tomb of David. Others stood watching them.

One of them made eye contact with Titius and moved quickly to the circle of women. Several grieving disciples spun in his direction and began to move quickly away. Abigail was among them until she looked over her shoulder and saw Titius.

Titius stood palms up, imploring her to come to him. She shook off a hand that tugged at her. Two tentative steps in his direction was all Titius needed to jump down and run to her.

They halted a few steps apart and stood looking into each other's eyes. "He's gone," she said, "they killed him."

"I know," Titius said. "Have you seen Caleb ben Samson?"

Abigail looked up at an upper room where several of the followers had gone. "The Lord's disciples are taking care of him."

"What are we going to do?"

"We have to hide until the Romans stop looking for us." Abigail looked into his face. "You're not going to betray us, are you?"

"How could I betray my own heart?"

"Some of the others say Roman hearts never change; that soon they'll destroy our Temple, as they did our Messiah."

Titius touched her cheek and she flinched. "They may be right," he said. "But the Messiah changed my heart. Now I'm neither Jew nor Roman. I'm someone new."

Abigail touched her own cheek where Titius had touched her. "Come with me! Elizabeth promised to hide some of us at the rose garden."

"We should run to Isaac in Magdala or to Capernaum or even across the Jordan. They'll find us here."

"You go if you want," Abigail said. "I will stay with the others. I can't run when Mary, Martha, and Lazarus will need me."

Titius shook his head. "I lost you once and I'm not leaving you again. I'll go with you."

"You don't understand. I could never live with myself if you're caught."

Titius grabbed her wrists. "Listen to me. I love you. I always have. I'm not going anywhere without you."

Abigail tried to pull away. "You can't love me." She hung her head when Titius refused to let go. "I'm a slave and you're a senator. They might stone me, but they'll behead you. I can't lose anyone else today."

Titius stepped back. "I'm going to Elizabeth's. If you care at all about me, or about yourself, then I'll see you there."

He walked toward the temple, where smoke still rose from the sacrifices. A dove flapped across the courtyard as he stepped around a cart and passed a garden. The flowers were bent over.

At the corner, a vendor and a customer argued over the price of sandals. Two women sat on stools weaving baskets. A child slept on a blanket near an open door. Titius looked back over his shoulder.

"Wait!" Abigail called. "I'm coming! We have to hurry."

Titius met her in the middle of the courtyard. The vendor and customer stopped arguing. A second dove joined the first and nestled on a post under a canopy.

They stopped by the market and Titius bought two of the rough tunics yard servants wore. In an alley, Titius led Abigail into a shadowed alcove. He gave Abigail her tunic and then shrugged on his new garment over his old.

Abigail found it difficult. Titius turned his back, as if once again guarding the zealot women at the bathing pool. In a few moments she touched his arm. As the sun slipped toward the hilltops they reached the garden and approached Elizabeth's shack.

"We have a special knock," Abigail whispered. "Wait here."

Seeing no one close by, she rapped three times softly, waited, knocked twice more, waited and then knocked three more times.

Elizabeth opened the door and ushered them in. Three men sat on carpets, their backs against the far wall. Four women stood near the door, two holding trays of food and drink. Four olive oil lamps hung from the ceiling and cast a flickering light. A clay vessel crammed with roses sat on a table near a side door.

Abigail exchanged hugs with the women and waited as the men stood.

"This is my friend, Titius," she said. "He's new to the faith."

One of the men extended a hand. "I am Thaddeus. It's strange to join a faith whose founder has just died."

Titius nodded in acknowledgement. "I knew Yeshua of Nazareth for two years while he was in Galilee. He healed me. I owe him my life."

Thaddeus said, "You're welcome to sit and tell us all your experiences with the Messiah. We'll wait here until the city quiets down."

For two days Titius and Abigail helped feed the waiting group. In the evening lamplight they shared the events of their lives during their separation. The memories they shared during Sabbath meditations, about their hope in the Messiah, gave them both joy and sorrow. Many others gave their own accounts of how Yeshua had changed their lives.

When Sabbath was over, Titius invited Abigail for a walk in the rose garden. They watched an oxcart meander down the side of the Mount of Olives, past the Garden of Gethsemane, through the Kidron Valley, and up toward the city.

"Ask me the question you dare not ask me," he said.

She looked away briefly toward the mountain and then faced him. "Why didn't you marry?"

"My father was arranging a betrothal. He was killed by the Germans before it was finalized. My mother talked with Lord Cretius about a business arrangement between his family and ours, but she died in childbirth."

Elizabeth emerged from her house with a tray of fruits. Titius took some dates. Abigail picked up a fig. They stood eating as Elizabeth examined their faces, smiled, and went back inside.

Titius touched Abigail's chin. "I suppose that smile means our secret is not such a secret."

Abigail turned back toward the mountain. "And what secret might that be?"

Titius cleared his throat and sighed. "I came here looking for you, but Sestus caught me." He touched her arm. "Why didn't you marry?"

Abigail looked into his eyes. "So you've never been with a woman?"

Heat rushed up his neck and into his cheeks. "My mother sent me a few slave girls after you were gone but I could think of no one else but you."

Abigail hung her head. "Cleopas tried to have his way with me until my sister intervened. When I was sent to Palestine, two sailors had their way with me. I couldn't stop them."

"The past is the past, for both of us."

"I don't blame you if you leave me. I wanted to jump into the sea and end my life but I didn't have the courage." She looked toward a hawk overhead. "Isaac and Yeshua gave me hope to keep going." She opened her hands to the heavens. "I thought I'd never have to think about love again." Tears trickled down her cheeks. "This is no time for love."

Titius turned toward the house. "What we have may not be much right now… but I urge you to think of love one more time."

Abigail followed him to the door where Elizabeth waited. Abigail sank to her knees. Elizabeth crouched down beside her as the tears streamed. "Daughter, the morning will come quickly. There's a mat by the other wall with the women. The Almighty will give you strength for your sorrow."

The internal ache wouldn't leave Titius when the lamps went out. He thought of how far he'd come to find his heart's desire. Now the Messiah's death had killed more than hope. He sat with his back against the wall until the fire in every muscle and joint wore him out. He lay on his side waiting for the night to end.

54

Elizabeth answered the faint knock at the door not long after dawn. Her shadow passed in front of a single flickering lamp in an alcove. She nudged Abigail, then the two of them slipped out into the waking city. A rooster crowed.

Titius leaned on one elbow and peeled back his blanket. Minutes passed, but the women didn't come back. Finally he roused himself and crept over the other sleepers. He eased open the heavy door. He heard only a final rooster crow, a donkey bray, an angry merchant shouting.

He couldn't see the women in the early clouded day. Titius dressed as an upper-class house slave and hurried through the rose garden to an alley facing the Antonia Fortress. He stopped when he heard a group of legionnaires parading toward him and scampered up the stairs onto a roof, lying low as the soldiers marched past. He wasn't sure where he stood with them anymore: was he a Roman? A guardian assassin? A follower of the dead Messiah?

All that mattered was keeping Abigail safe, and now he couldn't find her. His disguise meant he wouldn't be stopped by anyone but the soldiers. It was early for market stalls to be open, but it made sense that the women would go out to get supplies. Titius headed to the main market.

By the time Titius had searched the markets and gone back to the rose garden, panic knotted his stomach. Everyone knew who "Abigail the Fish Vendor" was, but no one had seen her. Strange rumours were floating around: early morning earthquakes, people seeing dead relatives, even a priest admitting that the Holy of Holies had been damaged in the massive Passover blackout.

A beggar told him he'd overheard a legionnaire say Barabbas might be raising an army of zealots to storm the Antonia Fortress before the pilgrims left the city. Not long before that, three women had run by saying someone had stolen the Messiah's body. Strange things were happening in the city.

Titius used the special knock and Elizabeth opened her door.

"What's the news about the Messiah?" she asked. "We hear he's alive."

"What do you mean?" Titius closed the door behind him. "I only heard that someone stole his body."

"Suzanna told Abigail and I that Mary Magdalene saw him alive. The men are mocking her, but they can't find the body. Some say they've seen angels."

"Where's Abigail?"

Elizabeth touched his arm. Her eyes sparkled. "She's gone to the tomb to see for herself. If you want to see her then go to the garden of Yosef of Aramathea near Golgotha."

Titius'spirit soared with yearning even while his heart threatened to strangle him with fear. He forced his feet to move faster and faster toward the skull-like hill outside the city.

He found her kneeling at the entrance to an empty tomb. She was running her hands along the edge of a huge stone, the governer's broken wax seal still stuck to it. Tears dripped off her chin and soaked into her blue tunic. She heard him and turned.

She stood. She held a single rose. She dropped it and came to him across the garden, accepting his embrace and hugging him. "He's alive!" she said. "He's alive... Mary saw him. He said to tell us to meet him in Galilee."

Titius worried they were all delusional. As if Cleopas were back to deceive them all.

Titius let go of Abigail and walked toward the tomb. Cedar trees seemed to leap straight up from the ground behind the sepulchre. He picked up her rose and handed it back to her. She tucked it behind her ear.

Titius's sandals crunched across the gravel pathway. He stepped into the tomb and saw a folded shroud. He could still smell the frankincense and other burial spices. Sunlight crept into the darkness and the place designed for death began to seem a place redesigned for life. For the first time in months, he felt peace.

He turned and saw Abigail watching him. He joined her outside the tomb, looking up toward the blue sky. "He's alive!" He pulled her to dance in a crazy circle of joy. "He's alive! If he told us to meet him in Galilee then we have to go to Galilee. He's alive!"

"Come," Abigail urged as she slowed the dance. "Mary, Martha, and Lazarus will give us provisions for the trip. If you go with me, I'll go."

Titius looked into her eyes. "Only if you agree to be my wife."

Abigail lowered her head. "You're my master. Whatever you command, I will obey."

Titius lifted her face to look into his eyes. "As your master, I free you." He took the rose from behind her ear. "As one who loves you, I beg you: be my wife because you *want* to be my wife." He held out the rose again.

"But how?" she asked. "No rabbi will join a Roman senator to a former Jewish slave."

"Andrew can be our rabbi," Titius said. "We're both followers of the Messiah. We'll set a new pattern for a world where those differences don't matter. Yeshua will break down those barriers and fill the gaps with life. Will you marry me?"

"If I'm really a free woman, then you need to make proper arrangements with Andrew in Bethany."

55

Titius ran up the hill, not slowing until he reached the Sheep Gate. The flowers were brighter and the rain drops, glistening like jewels, nestled in the broad leaves. A small pup by the road circled and barked with life.

Lazarus had promised to contact Andrew about wedding details. Abigail said she'd wait for all to be done properly before they left for Galilee. Food, clothing, and gifts had to be bought at the market.

As much as he longed to see Yeshua, his desire for union with Abigail was stronger. Since Yeshua was alive, they'd have their whole lives to be with him. Now it was time to set his life straight.

Titius was almost at the market when he neared four Nubians carrying a litter. The long cedar poles supporting the curtained golden carrier blocked his path. An Egyptian stood in front of it shouting, "Make way for Lord Cretius! Make way for Lord Cretius!" A group of debating men stood in the middle of the road. A cart and its recalcitrant donkey lingered at an angle in the road. The crowds were in no hurry to clear the space.

All thoughts of his wedding tasks evaporated from Titius's mind.

Cretius himself stretched through the curtains. He looked at the donkey and the men refusing to move. "Use the whip!" he shouted to the Egyptian. "How dare these peasants stand in the way of the king's counselor! This is the king's litter. Don't let them damage it."

The golden litter pushed ahead, the Nubians taking one patient step after another. The Egyptian snapped the whip overhead. An idea captured Titius and he raced for the clothing vendors.

A friend there, who supplied the Roman legions with special orders, napped on his stool with his head on a pile of black cloth. Rather than wake him, Titius took what he needed and left the money on the table. He slipped into a stable and changed into his new Roman military attire.

His upcoming marriage gave him new motivation to carry out his plan. By the time Cretius' litter reached Herod's Palace, Titius could see it again. He slipped up an alley and vaulted over a low wall before standing behind a hedge just a javelin's throw from the palace steps. Those passing on the street hardly looked in his direction. They were used to Romans everywhere.

The Nubians set the litter down and stood aside as Cretius clambored out between the curtains and toward the gates of the Palace. The sentries stood still as marble; the Roman lord hardly gave them a glance. Titius watched.

Once Lord Cretius was out of sight, the Nubians laughed and ambled off together toward the market. The Egyptian threw down his whip and wandered off toward the public baths.

Titius waited for the next shift of sentries. When the new legionnaires were in place, he walked up forcefully. "Where are my litter bearers?" he shouted.

One of the guards furrowed his brows. Titius stood nose to nose with him and shouted again: "Where are my litter bearers? You'd better find me someone to carry this thing or you'll be carrying it yourself."

"Where do you need to go, my lord?"

"The hippodrome. How dare you even ask?"

The legionnaire nodded and marched away toward the market. The three other sentries didn't flinch.

Titius paced back and forth, muttering about incompetent servants, before stepping into the litter and closing the curtains. Not long after, the Nubians jogged back into place, picked up the litter, and began to step quickly. The Egyptian was nowhere in sight.

The litter jostled back and forth. Titius took quick peeks through the curtains at the crowds parting for the "king's counselor". The people called vuglar names at Lord Cretius, names as foul as sewage.

As the Nubians began the steep descent to the hippodrome, some angry bystanders threw rocks at the passing entourage. Sweating slaves cursed the vigilantes. Rocks tore the curtains. Titius held up pillows to keep from being hit. They cursed him in many languages.

As the litter passed a narrow alley, Titius jumped out between the curtains and ran. He didn't glance back. The mob's angry shouts were enough to keep him running all the way to the stable. He changed into his servant's tunic and walked casually to Caleb's shop.

His satisfaction at the trouble he'd created for Cretius lasted only a few minutes. After all, Cretius had raped Titius's mother, stolen Titius' estate and hired thespian assassins to kill him. Titius would never be a Roman senator if he didn't get that estate back. Cretius had to die.

Pacing around the shop only increased Titius' hunger for revenge and darkened his plans.

Well past noon, Titius stepped out of the carpentry shop in his new military clothes and wandered through the market. Vendors' respect was clear as he picked up dates, figs and apricots. If he tried to buy wedding clothes or gifts for Abigail now it would arouse too much attention. He walked on.

He meandered toward Herod's Palace and hid behind the same hedge as before. He waited once more for the sentries' shift change. When the new group was in place he marched aggressively toward the palace, right past the guards.

Two burly centurions at an inner gate held up their shields. "State your name and purpose," one thundered.

Titius smashed his sword against the shields. "Move aside! General Maxim Julianus has come to settle accounts with Lord Cretius. I demand his presence immediately."

The shields lowered. "Your message has been sent."

Titius stood firm, sword drawn. A few moments later he heard a scream of terror in the halls. The two centurions stepped back. "You may proceed," the voice said.

The hall was shadowy, lit with two silver lamps. Thick smoke hung in the air. Heavy purple curtains blocked the outside light. Persian rugs soaked up any sound. The hallway narrowed like a funnel as he walked. It felt like a trap.

He waited while his vision adjusted. The smoke burned his eyes and irritated his nostrils. He sensed a presence to his right. He remembered the leopard on the road from Jericho as he prepared himself. He ducked to the left. Three javelins flew into the spot he'd been standing in. One pierced the curtain on the far side.

Titius seized a javelin from the rug and scrambled further into the the darkness beyond the burning lamps. Two shadows, just visible, by the flickering light, slipped into the hall. Titius' javelin flew straight into the closest figure's torso.

Amid the screaming, the second shadow slipped behind the curtains. Titius crept further into the darkness.

At the end of the hall Titius stayed low, moving to his right along the wall. Two curtains moved easily at his touch and he slipped between them into a room with faint natural light. Pillows and half-full wine flagons were scattered around the room.

The sound of voices drew him toward a door that opened onto a small courtyard. Two maids watered two small fig trees. Behind a low hedge a man cowered: *Cretius.*

Titius stormed into the courtyard, imitated his father as best he could. "Cretius, you pig! How dare you steal my wife and my estate!"

The maids scampered quickly away. The guards would be here quickly, thought Titius.

Cretius stood, his hands raised. "They told me you were dead!"

"Do I look dead to you? I was sent to find those who betrayed the empire. Now I come to finish my task!"

Cretius stumbled backward and fell into a pond. He scrambled out of the water. "Guards!" he screamed, racing away.

Two sentries, swords drawn, ran into the courtyard. "Lord Cretius is a traitor to the Emperor," Titius barked at them. He dropped his javelin and drew his sword. "Get him."

The centurions quick-stepped around the pond and disappeared in pursuit. Titius waved off a handful of household staff and noblemen who'd come to the courtyard. "Stay where you are!" he commanded.

Cretius's Egyptian bodyguard, his sword drawn, broke through the small group. "Where is my Lord Cretius?" he demanded.

Titius picked up the javelin he'd dropped. He held it to bar any way around him. "Your Lord is a traitor to the emperor! He must pay for his crimes."

The Egyptian pulled out his whip and snapped it. "I care nothing about that." He waved his sword and stepped toward Titius. "He pays my fees, and if you stay in my way you'll die by my sword."

Titius braced himself, sword in one hand, javelin in the other. "Today you'll meet your gods if you choose to fight. If gold is all you want I can satisfy you. If you want mortal combat both you and Cretius will never see another sunset."

The Egyptian hesitated; from somewhere, Cretius screamed.

The servant charged, snapping his whip and thrusting with his sword. The whip wrapped itself around Titius's javelin and yanked the weapon sideways.

Titius parried his blows, sword to sword. He regained control of the javelin and swung the butt end up under the Egyptian's chin. The warrior staggered back and snapped his whip at Titius's neck. Titius raised his elbow and deflected it. Blood flowed down his arm.

The Egyptian cracked the whip at Titius's ankles, distracting Titius from the sword that moved steadily closer.

"My battle's not with you!" Titius shouted. "Cretius runs, refuses to fight for himself. Stand down and you'll live."

The Egyptian smiled and brought his whip down again at Titius's ankle. "I never trust a Roman. I didn't survive the arena to be brought down by a jackal like you."

Titius jumped onto a bench and hurled his javelin at the Egyptian's belly. The Egyptian tried to deflect it with his sword but was too slow. He stood, transfixed by the weapon protruding from his body. Titius raised his foot and pushed the weapon in deeper. In the manner of gladiators, the Egyptian fell to his knees and bared his neck for Titius's fatal blow.

Titius left him and ran after Cretius. As he reached the stairs to the next garden, a legionnaire met him. "General, Lord Cretius chose to fall on his own sword. He is no more."

Revenge had been snatched from his hand. His stolen estate was now a victor's wreath abandoned on the track without competition. His mother's death was unavenged.

"Your wish, my lord?" the legionnaire asked.

Birds and butterflies flitted back and forth; fountains gurgled. City smells and noise belonged to another world. "Speak of my presence to no one. Lord Cretius chose to end his own life. Report his death at this own hand to his masters."

Titius knelt by a pool and washed the blood from his arms. He waved at a servant girl, who brought him a towel. He soaked the cloth and wrapped his arm. The bandage quickly turned red.

He walked past the still form of the Egyptian and tred deliberately back through another entrance. Palace staff bowed politely or prostrated themselves as he passed. Memories of his father absorbing public adoration after a victory filled Titius' mind, without any comment from Cleopas. A life of power and prestige could now be his.

As he passed on to the busy Jerusalem streets, the attitude toward him changed. The people looked at him angrily. An old man spit in his direction. A bony dog ripped at a dead rat near a garbage pile.

Four legionnaires appeared beside him. "Where is the rest of your legion, General? Should we march you back to the Fortress?"

A small crowd was now shouting obscenities at him. He looked across the valley toward the Mount of Olives and Bethany, where Abigail waited for her wedding. He looked back across the city toward the Antonia Fortress towering above the skyline beside the temple.

"To the fortress!" Titius declared.

56

Halfway to the Antonia Fortress, Titius and his escort walked through a market. A small riot near the fish vendor's stall drew his attention. Turning to the legionnaires, he commanded: "All of you, break up that mob."

The four lifted their shields, drew their swords and marched toward the group. Titius backed into a nearby dark alcove in an alley. He donned the carpenter's clothes he'd hidden there, applied a new rag to his wound, and slipped away. He knew the rioters would dissipate like morning mist. The legionnaires would eventually return to their post.

As Titius walked, he processed his combat with the Egyptian and his failed efforts to interrogate Cretius. Now he'd never know all that happened between Cretius and his mother. He clenched and unclenched his hands, still stained with blood. He stopped by another fountain to wash.

The streets were full of pilgrims loaded with supplies for their trips home after Passover. The Messiah's death would be big news for them to carry with them. Not all would know about the resurrection being proclaimed by his followers. As he watched the pilgrims, he realized he'd never bought the food and supplies for his wedding. He doubled back to the market where he'd changed his clothes.

He noticed two of the four legionnaires still near the entrance, keeping a keen eye. Titius kept his gaze lowered and wandered to the fish stall. "Enoch, what's the news?" he asked.

Enoch scooped several handfuls of dried fish into a pouch and made a great show of weighing them carefully. "Your plan with the Romans worked perfectly. No one was caught." He scooped a few fish off the scale and reweighed the rest. "Barabbas has gone to Jericho. The zealots are staying quiet after the latest crucifixions."

Titius pointed at the salted tilapia. "How are the fishermen doing with our troubled climate?"

Enoch bent down and spoke while out of sight. "They're going to Galilee. Yeshua called them to meet him there."

Titius knocked on the counter. "I'm getting married."

Enoch stood up. "Did you say 'married'? Praise the Almighty!" He added an extra two tilapia to the bag. "Will you return to Rome?"

"My bride is Abigail, who brings you pickled fish from Magdala."

"How can you marry a Jewess?" He glanced toward the two legionnaires and lowered his voice. "Who will perform the union?"

Titius noticed one of the legionnaires moving in his direction. "I'm going now to see. This food is for the wedding!"

Enoch also noticed the legionnaire. "Then this is your wedding gift. Take it. May the Almighty bless you!"

Titius slipped out of the market and hurried through back alleys and narrow streets toward another market, where he finished buying for the wedding. Before midday he slipped out the Sheep Gate, down the valley and up over the Mount of Olives to Bethany.

When Titius crested the hill on the Mount of Olives, he saw Abigail sitting at the well. She stood. A javelin's throw away from her he set down his load and she ran into his outstretched arms.

"You've come," she said. "I thought you may have changed

your mind when you didn't come yesterday." She buried her cheek in his chest. "Andrew's given his blessing. He'll meet us this evening, before he joins the others in Galilee."

"How did you know to wait for me here?" Titius asked.

"Servants brought three crates for you earlier," she said. "They said you were coming soon."

"I ask your forgiveness. I had to set some things right so this marriage will be good for both of us."

They gathered up the packages and turned toward the house, now in the midst of three white tents. "Everyone is preparing," Abigail said. The old man with the cane who'd accosted Titius earlier raised his hand in greeting as they passed the well.

"Is the chuppah, the wedding canopy, ready?" Titius asked. "I've never been to a wedding like this before."

"Come and see!" Abigail answered, giving a twirl. "I know I'm not supposed to see you before the ceremony, but I begged to be allowed to make sure you were safe. I must go get ready!"

"I brought the ketubah, the marriage contract." Titius held out a scroll. "Who do I give it to?"

Abigail ran her hand along his bearded cheek. "Lazarus." She took two of the bags he carried and walked quickly ahead of him to Mary, Martha, and Lazarus' house.

By the time Titius reached the house, Martha stepped out and took the rest of his bundles. "Do we assume now that even marriage will change?" she asked. "There was a time when we had a betrothal ceremony, and a proper time of preparation. So many questions I have for the Messiah!"

Andrew appeared and laid his strong hands on Titius' shoulders. "So, how will we do what's never been done before?" He pointed toward the chutzpah nestled under the center tent. "Will you build a room on your father's house for your bride? Will you take her from us to Rome?"

Titius nodded. "My father's home is now my home. Abigail knows it from her youth. It will be enough for her. If it isn't, then her every wish will be my command."

Andrew turned to look toward Jerusalem. "Will you keep the faith of our Messiah? Will you raise your children in the truth of Almighty God? Will you nurture your wife in true love and happiness?"

Titius looked into Andrew's eyes. "This is my heart's desire."

"Let me read the ketubah and see how you will keep your promises to Abigail and how you will compensate her guardians."

Titius handed over the scroll detailing the promises of his covenant contract with Abigail's guardian. He watched Andrew nodding as he read. Two turtle doves settled on a nearby myrtle tree. They jostled each other for position along a branch and then cocked their heads, as if waiting.

"It's a fine contract," Andrew said. "Generous and gracious. You respect Jewish custom and yet keep some of your own ideas. I will pass this on to Lazarus for official acceptance."

Andrew gave the ketubah to Lazarus and took Titius into a back room to change into his white wedding tunic. The three crates Titius had sent on ahead were stacked in a corner. A tray of dates, figs, cheese, fish, and bread was set out but in his nervousness he could do little more than nibble. Even the wine didn't tempt him.

As the evening shadows approached, torches and lamps were lit. Titius stood looking out a window at the perparations. Guests, wearing their finest, lingered in front of the house, sampling from trays carried by young women. Two lambs were roasting on a spit over a fire. The meat's aroma filled every nose.

When the time arrived, Martha escorted Titius to his place beside the wedding canopy. Lazarus arrived with Caleb and several others. Andrew handed them the wedding contract.

"What?" exclaimed an elderly bearded man. "He calls this a contract? In my day we knew how to value a woman."

A portly rabbi pushed his way into the huddle. "Surely, he can't expect us to give up our traditions. He should wait like everyone else has to wait."

Andrew raised his hand for silence. "On the other hand," he said, "Titius already has a home set up for Abigail and…" he waved his hand again. "And… he's been waiting a long time."

Another man stepped up. He was middle-aged, dressed in costly garments. "I have questions." He looked to the guests and they responded: "Ask the questions."

"Will you love her all her life? Will you give her children who make the Messiah proud? Will you live honorably wherever the Almighty may lead you?"

Titius smiled. "I will."

Caleb stepped out of the huddle to speak. "Hear me, before you let this Roman take a treasure from our nation. I too have a question." He held a small bag high over his head. "I know that this man is missing something that identifies him as heir to the Roman estate he claims. Titius, where is the ring your father gave you?"

Titius's stomach knotted. It was at the bottom of the assassin's pool.

Caleb swung the small bag back and forth. "You can see it on his face, my friends. He knows he's missing his family ring."

Titius stepped forward but Andrew held him in place. "Wait," the fisherman said quietly.

Caleb walked toward Titius. "Hold out your hand," he commanded.

Titius held out both hands.

"Did you not swear your loyalty to a centurion named Sestus Aurelius?" Caleb asked.

Titius nodded.

"Did he not take that ring and throw it into a pool where it could not be retrieved?"

Titius nodded, feeling heat race up his neck.

"And wasn't your centurion the only man who could dive to the bottom of that pool?"

Titius looked down.

"And wasn't this centurion killed by Barabbas?"

"Yes," Titius said. "Rome has never had a finer soldier than Sestus Aurelius."

"You speak the truth," Caleb said. "Three months ago, your centurion conquered the pool a second time and left you a gift with me."

Titius's heart raced. Caleb emptied the small bag into Titius' hand and there was his family ring: two rubies set in gold, the family crest of a lion clearly etched around the stones.

Titius' yell vibrated off the hills around Bethany. His belly laugh, mixed with tears, stalled the wedding ceremony for several minutes.

Lazarus gave his formal acceptance of the ketubah on behalf of Abigail and several men escorted Titius to the canopy.

The village men danced to a rousing psalm. Titius caught his breath when Abigail, a rose secured to her veil, was escorted in. She was beauty itself. He laughed freely as she and her maidens circled seven times around him.

Titius accepted the glass of wine from Lazarus and shared it with Abigail. He took the ring from Andrew and placed it on the first finger of the bride's right hand. Andrew officially read the ketubah and Titius joined him for the signing. Titius crushed a wine glass under his heel to confirm his commitment.

Then everyone present broke into dancing, dancing and more dancing!

Delicacies and wine flowed freely until Andrew and Martha brought Titius and Abigail together under the center of the canopy. "It's time for you to be husband and wife," Andrew said with a grin. "Some parts of marriage never change. We'll save some of this feast for when you're no longer busy."

Titius reached for Abigail's hand.

Lazarus ran into the circle of celebration. "Run!" he shouted. "The Romans are coming!"

57

Abigail turned to run but Titius grabbed her elbow and held her. "Stay with me," he said.

"But the Romans are coming!" She tugged to get away; Titius held her tight. "They killed our Messiah. Now that he's risen, they're coming for us."

Titius walked to a small crate. He opened the lid and lifted out a Roman short sword, a gladius, and a helmet. "If the others are going to make it to Galilee, we may have to provide a distraction."

"I don't understand."

"Trust me."

The faint sound of hobnailed boots echoed. Abigail and Titius vanished through a doorway.

"We'll need to change quickly." Titius handed an elegant purple chiton to Abigail. "Put this on." He turned and began to remove his tunic. They had to ignore personal embarrassment – the thundering of hobnailed sandals left little choice.

"I hope you remember my mother well. You must imitate her and stay by my side."

"I hope you didn't order these Romans to put off being with me," Abigail said, struggling to pull the white stola on. "It was easier to dress your mother," she said. "I hope you know what you're doing."

Titius laughed. "You make a fine Roman matron." He picked up his gladius, helmet, and cape. "I am a general and you are my wife. "Put up your hair." He walked toward the door, still carrying his sandals. "Prepare the wedding feast for our guests, Abigail. You're about to host your first celebration."

Abigail stared at her new husband as he crouched in the doorway tying his sandals. She turned to survey the reamaining food. "I hope they're too hungry to care what they eat."

She flew to her task despite the tight, ornamented stola. She combined half-empty dishes into heaping plates, put out clean cups, filled empty ones, straightened linens and tossed pillows into corners. "This better not be a habit of yours," she said, picking up the last of the used dishes. "There, how does that look?"

Titius smiled and put on his helmet. "You're a gift from the Almighty." He stepped out to meet the arriving army.

Titius stood in the road. Two centurions led the soldiers. Titius recognized one of them from Herod's palace, where Cretius had met his fate. Titius held up his hand.

"Halt!" the commander shouted. The column of thirty men stopped as one.

"Centurion!" Titius declared, "I see that you received the message. Your feast awaits."

The Centurion reached for his sword.

Titius stepped forward. "The feast to reward you for bringing justice to that charlatan, Lord Cretius. You did get the message at the Fortress, didn't you?"

The second Centurion stepped up beside the first. "Centurion Flavius Segundus reporting. We have orders to capture two zealots on this road."

Titius looked down the road. It was deserted. "Looks like they're gone," he said. "My wife has everything prepared. At least take a few minutes to enjoy my hospitality and appreciation. I have the use of this fine home only for the day. Your men are welcome as well."

The centurion looked down the road, glanced at his fellow centurion, and waited for the slight dip of the helmet. "The men will wait here while we examine the preparation," he said. Fifteen pairs of legionnaires stood like statues, red capes fluttering.

The two centurions and Titius ducked under the canopy's flap and examined the spread. It didn't take long for them to sample the food and swallow several cups of wine. Abigail stayed out of sight.

Segundus stuffed a pastry into his mouth. "Where are the servants? Where's this wife of yours?"

Titius clapped his hands twice. "The servants were purified Jews and couldn't remain with Romans. My wife is here."

On cue, Abigail stepped out in her Roman attire. Braided hair pinned up with sapphires topped a long white stola and a golden belt. Titius was transfixed.

Segundus nudged him. "You sure she's your wife? Looks like this is your first look at a goddess."

Abigail stared up at the centurion, a full head taller than she. "My husband, General Julianus, would usually be insulted that you compare me to something as ordinary as a goddess," she said in perfect Latin. Abigail brushed her delicate fingers above her ear as the centurion nodded. "This trouble with Lord Cretius has distracted him. Please enjoy this poor fare." She pointed to the table. "It seems this city is farther away from Roman delicacy than we realized."

Segundus took off his helmet and tucked it under his arm. "You honor us with what you have," he said, smiling at Abigail and nodding to Titius. "We'll be pleased to enjoy your hospitality. Then we must continue with our business."

Titius stepped out of the doorway. "The emperor's business must not be delayed," he said. "Please welcome your men."

When Abigail excused herself to freshen up, the Centurions signaled the thirty legionnaires to come in. The men were soon cramming food into their mouths while nodding politely and sharing appreciative grunts. Within minutes the platters were cleared and the flasks were emptied.

Segundus ordered the men back into formation on the road and returned to Titius. "General Julianus, my men appreciate the feast. We're happy to serve Rome any way we can. But we must obey our orders."

Titius unsheathed his gladius. "For the glory of the Empire and the true Emperor!" he shouted.

"For Rome! For Caesar!" the troops thundered. With that they marched. Their hobnailed thunder echoed off house and forest.

Abigail emerged from the kitchen. "Who is this man I married who's so respected by the oppressors?"

Titius allowed a smirk to cross his firm jaw. "I'm only who I am."

Abigail beheld the table and floor littered with chicken bones, lamb shanks, pits, and peelings. "I wonder what our dinner was like?"

Titius rested his hand low on Abigail's back. She shivered. "I'm wondering more," he said, "what *after* dinner is going to be like."

The bride pulled out her sapphire combs and shook out her hair. She put her arms around Titius and looked longingly into his eyes. "The marriage bed awaits us. We've waited long enough."

58

Soon after dawn, Abigail slipped out of the house on to the cobblestone patio. The two turtledoves pecked at crumbs scattered on the lawn. Otherwise, there were no dirty dishes, no leftover food, no unfinished wine.

Smiling, she turned back into the house. The floors and counters were clean. Her cheeks warmed as she remembered that the pleasures of the night before were enjoyed while someone outside the door cleaned up the remains of their wedding feast. She unwrapped a neat tray of dates, figs, and cheese that sat on a counter. "It is as they expected it to be," she said aloud.

"Is someone there?" Titius called out.

"No, my love. Only me."

Titius came into the kitchen, belting his tunic. "Who were you talking to?"

Abigail turned. "To myself, to God, to the turtle doves. You can't expect me to change old habits because of one night with the man I love, can you?"

Titius reached for her. "So, is it Rome or Galilee? Where will our life be?"

Abigail snuggled into his chest. "No matter how well I play the part, I'm no Roman senator's wife. You're no common Galilean, regardless of how well you can pretend. Perhaps God is calling us to a place where we can combine our worlds."

"Where might that be?" Titius's brushed a tendril of hair from her eyes and cupped her face in his hands. "The world is yours and you're my master."

Abigail looked into his eyes. "Why don't we board the first ship we can get from Caesarea and go where it takes us? As long as we're together, we'll learn to be who we're meant to be. The Almighty will always be with us."

Titius rested his forehead against hers. "But what about following the Messiah and sharing his message?"

Abigail hugged him. "The whole world needs to hear about the Messiah. Why can't we be the ones to tell them?"

www.ingramcontent.com/pod-product-compliance
Lightning Source LLC
Chambersburg PA
CBHW060943030726
47503CB00003B/711